INFERNAL DEVICES

"This is the real thing – a mad inventor, curious coins, murky London alleys and windblown Scottish Isles... A wild and extravagant plot that turns up new mysteries with each succeeding page."
James P Blaylock

"Jeter is an exhilarating writer who always seems to have another rabbit to pull out of his hat."
The New York Times Book Review

"Goddamn, what a book. This is like H G Wells with H P Lovecraft's descriptions of darkness run through the mind of Sherlock Holmes writer Arthur Conan Doyle. It's about as screwy as it gets, complete steampunkery, with a duo who are scamming their way across the land through an entirely different set of devices. Must read... Pure joy. I couldn't set it down."
SFBook.com

"At times Jeter can be profound, deep observation swirling into the bizarre."
Bearcave.com

"A delicious and quite insane romp through the gas-lit streets of London. Absolute must-read!"
SF Revu

K W JETER

Infernal Devices

With an Introduction by the Author
& an Afterword by Jeff VanderMeer

ANGRY ROBOT

ANGRY ROBOT
A member of the Osprey Group

Lace Market House,
54-56 High Pavement,
Nottingham
NG1 1HW, UK

www.angryrobotbooks.com
Tick. Tock.

Originally published in 1987
This Angry Robot edition 2011

Cover art by John Coulthart
Set in Meridien by THL Design

Distributed in the United States by Random House, Inc., New York.

ISBN: 978-0-85766-097-8
EBook ISBN: 978-0-85766-098-5

Printed in the United States of America

9 8 7 6 5 4 3 2 1

INTRODUCTION BY K W JETER
On Steampunk and "Steampunk"

I wish I could say that the whole steampunk thing took me my surprise. Opportunities to display a becoming modesty arrive so much less often than those calling for a well-deserved modesty, as in this case.

Of course, the creation and promotion of literary genres and subgenres, even for one the label for which has embedded itself so deeply into the hip world's current operating dictionary, is nearly always a matter of self-promotion. Writers are essentially telling readers, "Hey, look at me; I'm doing something New & Different, not like those schlubs over there at the other end of the bookstore shelf, who are just doing the Same Old Thing." For academics, of course, it's more of a tenure pitch, a ritual dance in front of their department committee, demonstrating that they are indeed keyed in to what is being texted about by the youth of today, whose parents pay the tuition bills.

Observing these endeavours, one is inevitably reminded (if one is old and recherché enough) of Seventies comedian Flip Wilson, whose television personae included the Reverend Leroy, excitedly exhorting the congregation at the Church of What's Happening Now. That's an ecclesiastical establishment where the pews are perhaps even more tightly packed these days than they were back then, since hardly anybody now wants to be called a Luddite and risk not being invited to the better party that's always down the street somewhere. (Though of course, Luddism proper is something that neither anti-Luddites or neo-Luddites, bravely contrary in their hempen shirts, get quite right as they push their own agenda-heavy carts down that same street. But that's another discussion, for another day.) If the mid-Eighties' starry-eyed, gobsmacked fascination with the siliconized future now seems more of a piece with the Kennedy-era Disneyland's Carousel of Progress exhibit than with the life we're living now, then who says mankind doesn't progress? As soon as your kids can download a smartphone app for hacking the Pentagon, we'll know the revolution is over.

So it's a tribute to tortuous human ingenuity and the blithely cheerful doublethink of pop culture (indexed under "Orwell, George; gameshow host"), that there developed a taste for brass and copper and the ticking, hissing mesh-&-grind of Victorian technology. God knows that I didn't send that particular juggernaut careening down the highway; the most I can be credited with is the vaguely modernistic nameplate under the hood ornament, as though the chrome moniker of a Chrysler Airflow had been bolted to Amédée-Ernest Bollée's 1875 L'Obeissante and sent cruising for dates at Mel's Drive-In. But as Orwell did in fact point out in his "The Principles of Newspeak" appendix to 1984, it can be pretty difficult to think about stuff for which we don't have names. My coining back in 1987 of the word steampunk originally might have been more of a humorous jab at a tendency going around those days, of labeling any two genre writers with more in common than bipedal locomotion as the "[insert word here]-punk" movement, but if it assumed some sort of life after that, or at least clawed itself up from whatever grave in which old jokes are laid to rest... well, it could've been worse, lexicographically.

And as much as the nametag is the tail to the much larger shaggy dog of the various novels and stories that have since been labeled steampunk (many of which are excellent and substantial, and would be just as enjoyable with or without the category to be stuffed into), the steampunk literature is a relatively small part of a larger enthusiasm. The concept has metastasized to the point where its cultural penetration is driven less by authors than by film studio art directors, costumers and special effects departments. (In that sense, not much different from any of the shrinking number of other concepts we have nowadays.) If saying that one is into steampunk allows young women to attend science fiction conventions while laced into visibly complicated underwear, while their weedy boyfriends are bulked up by the heavy armor of period tweeds and vests, the inspiration is likely from the movies rather than any words on paper.

While I might not have anticipated the slipping into common parlance of the word I coined, the larger steampunk enthusiasm wasn't similarly unanticipated. Yes, most of this is just a matter of people having good, clean, if somewhat gimmicky fun, but there's a genuinely worthy element to it that makes me one of those happy few who, even if we can't say we love our species, we can at least tolerate it on its better days. A fascination with Victorian tech is at its heart a salutary acceptance of the machine-ness of machines – and correspondingly an acceptance of the humanity of human beings. There's something nauseatingly pre-digested about the look of late 20th and early 21st century industrial design, all those Steve Jobs-approved rounded edges like cough lozenges sucked on for a minute or so before being spat out into your hand. Whereas Victorian machines, with their precision-cut gears and spurred mantis armatures, are unabashedly themselves rather than trying to smoothly cozen their way into your life. Thus we similarly perceive flesh-&-blood Victorians – even the fictional ones – as being more genuine than ourselves. They had lives; we have marketing. Even unto our souls; drama and ruin were possible to those who guarded their secrets and shame, as pre-digital clocks held their tightly coiled mainsprings inside themselves.

That's what makes this last fully human epoch so interesting for writers and readers alike. And why I was gratified rather than surprised that the thing to which I so offhandedly gave a name now clanks forward at its own pace. The faint tick and whir we hear across the sadly therapeutic centuries is that of our own foolishly abandoned hearts, which we'd love to wind up and set running again. Steampunk enthusiasts are engaged, however unknowingly, in nobler fun than mere mental cosplay. May God bless and increase their tribe; human beings might yearn for lost things, but never for unreal things.

K W Jeter
San Francisco
November 2010

ONE
Infernal Devices

All comfort in life is based upon a regular occurrence of external phenomena.

GOETHE

PART ONE
In Search of Saint Monkfish

1

Mr Dower Receives a Commission

On just such a morning as this, when the threat of rain hangs over London in the manner of a sentence neither stayed nor pardoned, but rather perpetually executed, Creff, my factotum, interrupted the breakfast he had brought me only a few minutes earlier and announced that a crazed Ethiope was at the door, presumably to buy a watch.

Reader, if the name George Dower, late of the London borough of Clerkenwell, is unfamiliar to you, I beg you to read no further. Perhaps a merciful fate – merciful to the genteel reader's sensibilities, even more so to the author's reputation – has spared a few souls acquaintance with the sordid history that has become attached to my name. Small chance of that, I know, as the infamy has been given the widest circulation possible. The engines of ink-stained paper and press spew forth unceasingly, while the even more pervasive swell of human voice whispers in drawing room and tenement the details that cannot be transcribed.

Still, should the reader be such a one, blessedly ignorant of recent scandal, then lay this book down unread. Perhaps the dim confines of the sick-room, or the wider horizons of tour abroad, far from English weather and the even darker and more permeating chill of English gossip, have sheltered your ear. There can be only small profit in hearing the popular rumours of that dubious scientific brotherhood known as the Royal Anti-Society, and the part I am assumed to have played in its resurrection from that shrouded past where it had lain as mythological shadow to Newton's Fiat live.

Such happy ignorance is possible. Only the sketchiest outline has been made public of Lord Bendray's investigations into the so-called Cataclysm Harmonics by which he meant to split the earth to its core. Even now, the riveted iron sphere of his Hermetic Carriage lies in the ruins of Bendray Hall, its signal flags and lights tattered and broken, a mere object of speculation to the attendants who listen patiently to the tottering grey-haired figure's inquiries about his new life on another planet.

The discretion that sterling can purchase has saved the heirs of the Bendray estate further embarrassment. Not for the purposes of spite, but to remedy the damage done to my own and my father's name, will I render a complete account of Lord Bendray's fateful musical soiree in these pages.

The rain begins, spattering on the panes of my study window. Before the heaped coal-grate, the dog sleeping on the rug whines and scratches the floor. An apprehensive tremor blots the ink from the pen in my hand, and in my waistcoat pocket a coin of no value, save as a dread keepsake, grows cold through layers of cloth against my flesh. No matter; I press onward.

Many who read this, I know, will be in search of further salacious details concerning the more disgusting accusations brought against me. I have been painted as a demon of lust. Reports of my careering through ill-lit dockside alleys in a coach-and-four, hot in pursuit of unnatural pleasures such as the "green girls" whose connection to instances of madness and physical decay among the younger peerage is so often whispered of, have been given credence far beyond that which is called for by the small bit of truth in those stories. It was through no fault of my own that the Ladies Union for the Suppression of Carnal Vice staged a torchlight march on my former shop and residence. Indeed, if the public were aware of the hidden nature of Mrs Trabble, the captain of that well-thought-of regiment, much excited talk would shift away from me.

As to the greater scandal surrounding the dual career attributed to me, that is, as a violin virtuoso equal to the great Paganini and a debaucher of women exceeding the lecherous Casanova, I

maintain that neither of these accomplishments
was mine. No Stradivarius or well-born lady ever
responded to my bow in such a way. Though my
brain was used in the production of those melodies,
so enticing on the concert stage and even more so
behind it, my hands are spotless. I can scarcely
hope that my revelations will be credited. For my
own comfort I place them here.

On other matters official judgment was rendered
in the courts. My conviction on the charge of dese-
crating a place of worship, specifically by substituting
copies of Izaak Walton's The Compleat Angler for
the hymnals of Saint Mary Alderhythe, Bankside,
and decorating the church altar with fishing tackle –
that too can be explained. Folly I may be guilty of,
but not sacrilege.

Even though my name has been connected – with
some cause, I admit – to reports from the Scottish
Highlands of the Book of Revelation's Seven-Headed
Beast flapping about and dropping flaming sheep
carcasses upon the heads of Sir Charles Wroth's
grouse-beaters while the Whore of Babylon laughed
and shouted disrespectful comments from her perch
aboard the creature, yet I still believe that an open
mind will absolve me of blame. Indeed, the fact that
the guns of Sir Charles' grouse-hunt were trained
upon me should cause a charitable nature to hear
my grievance with some sympathy.

But as I pause for a moment, lifting my pen, and
gaze through the rain-wavering glass at the thin trails

of smoke rising from the crowded rooftops' chimneys and fading towards the river's mist – a view I cannot describe in greater detail for fear of leading the gawking crowd to this, my retreat – a shiver not prompted by ague or cold reaches down my arms. The dog raises his head, ears pricking at the sound of the distant church bells that neither I nor any other Christian gentleman has heard, or should ever hope to hear. Somewhere in that city borough, the name of which is spoken only in the most muted whisper, and whose location is everywhere and nowhere in London at once, the congregation summoned by those bells – to us, mercifully silent – is sidling through narrow alleys towards a damp worship.

Restoring my name, my father's name, seems a shallow vanity now. What matter glory or ignominy, when such visions have altered the world itself in my sight? Riven in twain, as in Lord Bendray's intent towards the earth, yet still whole. For me, London's grey veil, smoke and fog, has been brushed aside. Happy are those who mistake the painted curtain for the reality behind.

The dog drops his head to his paws and resumes his slumber. Thus chastened, mindful of my own futility, I persist, scratching ink on to paper. Let the reader, thus warned, mindful of the perhaps ignoble interest he shows in these matters, do as he wishes.

Creff was visibly agitated by the stranger's appearance at our door. Memory calls to mind the

anxious wringing of his hands, resembling two fur-
less pink badgers wrestling for each other's throats,
and the perfect circularity of his widened eyes.

"Lord, Mr Dower, it's an Ethiope!" whispered
Creff. "And crazed – a murderous savage!" The
badgers throttled themselves bloodless.

I kept my own voice level, as, the shop being
downstairs from the room where I took my breakfast, the visitor was in no danger of hearing the
calumnies he had occasioned. "'Ethiope' may be
apparent on the surface," I said. "But by what
means did you discern the state of his mind?" The
grey-filled window at my back necessitated the gas
bracket's flame, despite the advancing hour of the
morning; by its yellow light I turned over a wedge
of toast, in the vain hope that the one frugal rasher
of bacon had a twin hidden there.

"Mr Dower – his eyes." Creff's own grew even
wider. "Nothing but little slits, they were. Like he
was maddened with some heathen liquor, and prepared for murder!"

Intoxication was, in fact, a possibility. With discretion sufficient to avoid offending Creff, I inhaled
deeply, endeavouring to detect the fumes signalling
a lapse in his conduct. Episodes of indulgence produced unfortunate fancies in him; only a few
months before I had been compelled to exert a good
deal of diplomacy on the wife of the shopkeeper
several doors over. Creff had been discovered in the
alleyway, on his knees before a bemused shop-cat.

Stale beer had convinced him the cat was the Recording Angel, and he had been attempting to bribe it with small confectionery lozenges, the erasure of certain regretted sins being the object of his negotiations. Mrs Draywaite had been mollified only by my hastily concocted explanation that a congenital weakness in Creff's knees produced genuflections without warning.

In similar fashion, although there was no telltale odour of strong drink on the air, the Ethiopian reported downstairs might be nothing more than an Italian of unusual swarthiness. Africans had been much on Creff's mind of late, due to the then widely celebrated performances of Prince Ko-Mo-Lo, the Abyssinian Tenor, upon a Mayfair music-hall stage, as well as the appearance of several common street-singers of similar hue. The latter, upon investigation by the constabulary, turned out to be ordinary Irish buskers underneath the lampblack they had employed to transform themselves into Africans. They had hoped that the public, now dark-minded, would reward chanted gibberish with more coins than their previous incarnations' repertoire of sentimental ballads had earned. Even after these frauds had been exposed, Creff seemed fixed on the subject, as though the anthropophagi of his childhood stories had set up kettle and knackers in every alley.

Mistaking my wary attitude, Creff leaned close over the breakfast table. "Here's what we can do,

Mr Dower. You sneak down the back steps and call
out the peelers, and I'll hold 'im at bay until they
arrive." From under his scullery apron he displayed a carving knife, the blade barely sharp
enough to threaten a cheese.

The meagreness of the breakfast, indicative of
the state of both the larder and the bank account
behind it, prompted me to other strategies. I desired no client, dark-complected or angel-fair, to
be frightened out of the shop with a knife. I took
the weapon from Creff's grasp, and bade him tell
the gentleman that I would be down to wait upon
him presently.

The spectre of losing trade, of whatever nature
Creff's "Ethiope" had brought, drew forth further
meditation as I dissected the distinctly aged egg
standing in its cup. Since my inheritance of the
shop and its business from my deceased father,
trade and my fortunes had gone through fluctua-
tions resembling a leaf in autumn, that at
moments is carried upward by the wind but always
flutters lower afterwards. Having neither my father's inborn genius at the contrivance of the
timepieces, clockwork devices, and scientific apparatus by which he established his reputation, nor
having received a compensatory education in
these matters from him, such trade as I had con-
sisted of the minor servicing and adjustment of
those creations that my father's former clientele
brought to me. That is, whatever service I was

capable of making upon my father's devices, as I could boast very little skill at this, either. The quality of my father's craftmanship warranted that simple repairs were seldom required, and the intricacy of his inventions placed the finer adjustments well beyond my scope.

Indeed, I would have been hard put to do other except sell off the collection of partially assembled machinery, cogs, flywheels, gear trains, escapements, and such in my father's workroom, and pocket whatever cash the scrap value of the brass and other metals brought as my inheritance, but for the continued tenure of my father's assistant Creff. When I had first come to the shop, mourning band from the funeral still around my sleeve and the solicitor's notification of death in my pocket, I had found the loyal Creff sweeping out the premises, the window panes and counter brightwork polished as he had done for my father. Keeping him on for these and other household tasks, I soon discovered that, while Creff's slowness of wit had prevented him from grasping the principles my father had employed in his creations, his dogged attention had by sheer rote impressed a certain pragmatic knowledge of them upon his brain. When I first managed to open the case of one of my father's simpler timepieces, a watch that a gentleman of Kent had brought me for adjustment, and I saw the dense universe of intermeshed gears and coiled springs, incomprehensible and

gleaming in a thin sheen of oil, it was only Creff's
guidance as he leaned over my shoulder that prevented my weeping openly. What his blunt,
work-calloused fingers could not do, mine could,
the minute jeweller's tools of my father's bench
guided by his instruction.

As my father's shop stood near Clerkenwell
Green, in that London district long noted for its
watchmakers, I stocked a few timepieces crafted
by my neighbours, hoping to sell one to the odd
passer-by. Creff had assumed this to be the caller's
pretext for gaining entry and murdering us.

When I at last roused myself from my thoughts,
what remained of my breakfast had passed from
unattractive to inedible. I pushed it away and stood
up. On the stairs I passed Creff, still muttering dark
worries about "savage cannon-balls", as I went to
see what manner of trade had come that morning.

My first sight of that figure, whose crossings and
recrossings through the course of my travails would
be the source of so much mystification, instilled in
me no such apprehension as had seized Creff. The
gentleman had his back to me as I reached the bottom of the stairs. He waited, hat by his elbow upon
the counter, and studying one of my father's clocks
upon the opposite wall. Of more than average
stature, yet with a narrowness through the shoulders that his greatcoat could not conceal, the man
stood stockstill, absorbed in the clock's recording of
hours, date, and position of the major planets.

"May I be of some assistance?" I announced my presence, and the man turned towards me, pivoting on his heel with a slow, fluid grace.

I saw then how Creff's fears had been triggered. At first I thought that the shop's gas bracket was turned too low, leaving the stranger's face in shadow; then the flame's glow shimmered across the high points of his countenance. The skin of his face and hands, as I then saw that his gloves were folded beside his hat, were of a deep, rich brown, reminding me of burnished mahogany or fine morocco leather, its patina grown smooth and lustrous with age. It could be no disguise, no lampblack smudged over skin pale as my own, but only the pigment of nature. Reinforcing the supposition of the stranger's African birthplace were the symmetrical lines of minute scars curving across the cheeks and forehead, such as are reported to be the self-inflicted adornment of certain tribesmen, the small wounds pricked with a thorn and rubbed with sand to make them more pronounced when healed.

His eyes were as Creff had described them, the lids drawn together to form two slits over the slightly protuberant spheres of the eyes behind them. I did not find this as disconcerting as the more excitable Creff had; indeed, the grave, unsmiling expression lent a calm dignity to the stranger's presence. Whatever savagery might have remained in his breast was well concealed under the expensive cut of his clothing.

"Mr Dower." He spoke distinctly but softly, the thin lips barely moving apart.

"I am. The son, that is." I always made this emendation to those who might have known my father only through his creations, in an effort to forestall any disappointment in my own inferior services. "The founder of the business is deceased."

"My condolences I extend." An unplaceable accent revealed itself in his speech. His slight bow allowed the gas bracket's light to graze the equally dark and polished curve of his skull.

"Two years have passed. The grief has ebbed a little, I believe." My own words mocked my true feelings, as they often did when I spoke of my father. How grieve over a man one has never known, no matter how intimate the connection? I stepped behind the shop's counter and spread my hands upon it. "Now to business, Mr – ah…" Through observation of my neighbours I had cultivated the tradesman's obsequious smile. "I have the pleasure of addressing… ?"

The gentleman ignored my forays towards his name, and produced a paper-wrapped parcel from the crook of one arm. Placing it on the counter between us, the Brown Leather Man (as I had already begun to identify him in my thoughts) undid the knotted cord and pushed aside the paper with his dark hands. "I was a client of your late father," he said. "For me he built this, upon my commission. Some element of disorder has entered its workings, and I seek to employ you in the setting right of it."

The last of the wrappings fell away. "What is it?" I asked. My eyes turned upward at the Brown Leather Man's silence, and found the narrow slits studying me with an unnerving intensity.

In relief I looked back down to what lay before me. A mahogany box a little over a foot in length, half that in its other dimensions; a pair of brass hinges faced me. With one finger I attempted to swivel the box around, but the surprising weight of it kept it motionless upon the counter. I was forced to grasp it with both hands in order to turn it about.

I unlatched the simple brass hasp and tilted the box's lid open. My heart sank within me as I looked down at the intricate anatomy of the device.

This feeling of despair was not unfamiliar to me; it often welled up at the sight of one of my father's creations. His genius had not been limited to the production of the pocket watches and larger time-pieces whose subtlety of design and intricacy of execution had established his name among admirers of the horological art. Since his death and my inadequate assumption of his place, I had become acquainted with facets of his work that are still little known, having been undertaken at the behest of a select arid discreet clientele. Scientific and astronomical apparatus of every description, ranging from simple barometers, though of a fineness of calibration rarely if ever equalled, to elaborate

astrolabes and orreries, the latter distinguished by
a set of reciprocating eccentric cams in the clockwork drive mechanism capable of showing the
true elliptical orbits of heavenly bodies rather than
the simplified circular motions employed in other
such mechanical representations of the universe –
all of these and more were my father's children.
More so than my own self, I would often think as
I gazed at some intricate intermeshing of gears and
cogs such as the one revealed inside the Brown
Leather Man's mahogany casket. The bits of finely
turned and crafted brass showed the care and attention that had been absent in the creation and
assembly of my own person into manhood.

The purpose and function of some of the devices
brought to me were unfathomable, and an odd se-
cretiveness prevailed among my father's former
clients. Amateur scientific pursuits had long been
a preoccupation with serious-minded gentlemen
of property and leisure, but the ones who came to
me were often as uncommunicative as the devices
they wished to be repaired. Sextants that divided
the sky into angles not found in the usual geome-
tries, microscopes whose hermetically sealed lenses
distorted the viewed object into shimmering rain-
bow images, other instruments whose complexity
and manifold adjustments quite overwhelmed my
powers of speculation as to their use – all of these
had in time been brought into the shop. With Creff's
assistance I had managed the simpler repairs, a

hair-thin chain slipped from its proper place or a minute cogwheel grown toothless and replaceable with a duplicate from the vast jumble of parts and half-assembled machines left in my father's work-room. The well-heeled clientele for whom I performed these services paid handsomely enough. Other devices, where the malfunction was as mysterious as the function, I was forced to return to the distraught owners with my apologies. I fear it was from the growing number of these admissions of inadequacy that my trade had fallen off, the word passing among the cognoscenti that the son was not the equal of the father. The disastrous episode of the Patented Clerical Automata, who completion and setting into motion in a London church I had undertaken while my confidence in dealing with my father's creations had not yet been sufficiently discouraged, had been suppressed from public notice, else the notoriety would have ended my trade once and for all.

Such were the well-worn reveries that weighted my thoughts as I bent over the cabinet. As needful as my personal accounts were of replenishing, I feared that this was not to be an occasion of profit. I turned the flame up on the bracket behind the counter and, while my visitor continued to regard me with his slitted stare, bent over the device with magnifying glass in hand.

My study revealed nothing of the machine's purpose, though any question of its origin was dispelled. Under the glass I discovered the floating escapement with ratcheted countervalences that my father had invented, though in this instance of a smaller size than I had ever encountered before, and linked in parallel to a train of duplicates disappearing into the brass innards. Other features were of such minuteness that the magnifying glass, no matter how I squinted through it, failed to yield the details of the device's workings. One section, brighter than the rest, appeared to be made of finely hammered gold leaf, the sheets of which were folded upon themselves in various asymmetrical patterns. Simple set-screws in the corners of the box showed where the device could be removed from its mahogany housing. A number of incomplete linkages around the sides, with signs of wear marking the collars at the ends of protruding shafts, indicated where the workings could be connected to other, larger devices.

"It appears to be some sort of regulatory mechanism," I mused aloud. I looked up to see the Brown Leather Man's eyes still fastened upon myself. I shrugged, made uneasy by his intent scrutiny. "For a clock, perhaps, with various other functions combined?" I knew that the device was far too complex for such a simple purpose.

Brown Leather nodded. "A regulator… yes. That is so. You are familiar with devices such as this?"

"I know much of my father's work," I said. "But this in particular – no. I'm sorry."

"But to repair it." His narrow gaze seemed to sharpen as he looked at me, as though the glint in his eyes were the points of needles. "You are capable of such a task?"

As with most tradesmen, avarice outweighed prudence in my nature. There was nothing to be lost in an attempt to remedy the device, however unlikely the chances of success. But the man's eyes unnerved me, arousing a taste of the fear that Creff had felt, and moved me to honesty. I closed the mahogany lid and pushed the cabinet away. "I think not," I said. "Some of my father's creations are beyond my skill. I believe I would only damage this further if I meddled with it."

My candour enabled me to look the gentleman directly in the eye. For a moment he was silent, the small points of light behind the slitted lids reading deeper past my own face. "Your warning I accept," he said at last. "Nevertheless, worthwhile will I make it to attempt what you can."

"I cannot guarantee any results."

"Please." The brown hands folded along the sides of the cabinet and slid it towards me. "Even the attempt is valuable to me."

"Very well." My fingertips briefly touched his as I drew the device back to me; a deep chill flowed from the dark skin, drawing a heartbeat's warmth from my own. "I am, ah... uncommitted to any other projects currently. If you'd care to return in a week's time? Perhaps by then. Let me write you a receipt." I took a sheet of paper from beneath the counter. "Received from... ?"

He ignored me, his gaze broken away from me and now sweeping about the shop's contents. Each clock, simple or elaborate, fell under his inspection.

"Is there something else with which I can assist you?" I asked. Free of his searching gaze, I had been able to dismiss my moment of dread as foolish. Perhaps a solider bit of business could be transacted.

Brown Leather turned back to me. "Your father's workroom," he said. "I would like to see it."

The request caught me by surprise. I blinked at him before I found my voice. "Why?" I said simply. "There's nothing—"

"Your father, Mr Dower; perhaps he left behind some articles, the use of which is puzzling to you? Mechanisms not exactly as this, but similar in part. Or even wholly different, but still of a function to you mysterious. If such are still in his workroom, I would like to examine them. They might be" – his voice arched, intimating – "valuable to me."

His surmise as to the contents of my father's workroom was completely accurate. When I had first come to London to claim my inheritance, I had been astonished at the mechanical chaos that filled the large windowless room at the back of the shop. Tottering clockwork mountains, eviscerated timepieces of every size from pocket watches with dials as small as thumbnails to the massive gearing of tower clocks with hands thicker about than a man's wrist, brass skeletons of automaton figures with the round orbs of porcelain eyes staring from the un-fleshed faces, scientific apparatus with dusty lenses peering only at darkness – a whole, universe caught midway through its moment of creation, and frozen there by the death of its Creator. My father apparently had worked on a score of projects simul-taneously, and only his fervid brain had been able to sort out the interpenetrations of each with each in the crowded space. In my brief tenure there, the dis-array had been increased by the natural decay of Time, and by my own admitted carelessness in clear-ing enough room for my own work at my father's bench. In addition, my practice of facilitating a num-ber of repairs by scavenging bits and pieces from the partially assembled devices had the unfortunate ef-fect of hastening the general disintegration.

My reluctance at allowing a stranger to see the embarrassing muddle into which my legacy had fallen was overcome by the prospect of turning a profit on some conglomeration of gears and springs on which I had never expected to receive anything other than scrap value. "By all means," I said, gesturing towards the door behind the counter. "If you'd be so kind as to step around, I'd be pleased to have your inspection."

I guided him down the hallway and the short flight of stone steps to the workroom. There being no gas bracket, I lit the lamp I kept on the bench. The flame, even adjusted to its highest, cast a light barely penetrating to the corners of the room, had they been visible behind the disordered masses of my father's abortive creations. The glow picked out highlights of brass gears and little more.

Disregarding the gloom, the Brown Leather Man was already intently peering at the jumble of devices, poking at the various mechanisms with one long brown finger and bending closer to examine the assemblages of gears. Disaster threatened as one cliff-face of brass wheels tottered at his prodding inspection, a disembodied mannikin's head looking down from above in the manner of a Red Indian stalking an explorer in the rude deserts of America.

A lensless telescope swung on its pivot away from Brown Leather as he probed deeper into the mechanical morass. "Are you finding anything of interest?" I called from my place at the bench.

The silence of his back turned to me was his only reply. A bit nettled, I lifted the lamp and carried it towards him, the yellow circle cast around my feet, more to benefit my own curiosity than to aid his search.

Holding the lamp aloft, I peered over the Brown Leather Man's shoulder, the light gleaming from the fuscous curve of his skull. Some involved meshing of gears and cogwheels, frozen in stopped Time, lay exposed before him, his extended forefinger probing like a surgeon's scalpel into a brass cadaver. So intent was he upon this post-mortem de artifice that he seemed scarcely aware of my presence behind him.

A sudden snap of thin metal breaking, and my odd client lurched backwards, knocking me over and sending the lantern flying from my hand. The light was not extinguished, coming to rest propped against the leg of the workbench, but the immediate area where the Brown Leather Man stood and I undignifiedly sat was darkened.

Enough light was reflected from the banked clutter of metal for me to look up and see what had happened. A coiled spring in the apparatus Brown Leather had been investigating now dangled crazily in air in front of him, one jagged end bobbing like a jack's head. The spring had apparently broken under his prodding and snapped sharply enough to inflict a wound on him. Indeed, I could see him with one hand clutching his opposite forearm to stanch the flow of blood from a jagged gash above his wrist.

I scrambled to my feet, moved by natural sympathy and the prospect of the damages to which I might be liable.

"My God, sir, you're hurt!" I cried, bending forward to minister to his wound. Dismayed, I saw the damp spatter of his blood upon the stone floor and the nearest brass device.

He jerked the injured limb away from me. "It is nothing," he said. "Do not worry of it." His actions belied his words; still clutching his forearm, he hastily retreated up the passage to the front of the shop, with myself close behind.

Before gathering up his hat and gloves from the counter, he clumsily fished a coin from his coat pocket and pressed it into my hand. A shiny wetness seeped between the brown fingers clamped to his forearm. "A payment on account," he said, his narrow eyes locking once more on to mine. "For your work to be done yet."

Then he was gone, the shop door slamming behind him, and the clatter of hooves on cobbles and a hansom cab's wheels fading into the street's constant murmur.

"Lord, I told you he were a mad one, didn't I? Just didn't I!"

I looked around and saw Creff watching from the stairway, one hand again clutching the dull kitchen-knife. Without looking at the coin that the Brown Leather Man had handed me – the flash of silver and its familiar weight assured me of its being a crown – I slipped it into my waistcoat pocket. "There's a bit of mess in the workroom," I said. "Some blood on the floor–"

Creff's eyes widened as though inflated by his sharp intake of breath.

"An accident," I assured him. "Nothing but a broken watch spring. Would you be so kind as to clean it up?"

A few moments later, as I stood behind the counter examining the device left behind by my morning's visitor, with an odd premonitory unease staying my hand from lifting the lid, a shout came from the workroom. Creff appeared in the passageway, wadded rag in hand.

"There's no blood here." He sounded annoyed, as if having discovered a jest played on him. "It's all wet, right enough, but there's no blood."

"You must be mistaken," I said. "In the back, by my father's old things."

"See for yourself, then,"

I followed him down the steps. In the workroom, by the brass wall of my father's creations, where I had seen the jagged edge of metal tear the brown skin, I knelt down on the stone floor. Creff held the lantern above, illuminating the spattered wetness from my client's wound.

Even before I touched it, a faint scent traced across my nostrils, evoking memories of childhood: the aunt who raised me, and our visits to the seashore at Margate. I dabbed a finger at one of the spots. The fluid on my fingertip was perfectly clear, rather than the thick scarlet I had expected. Curious, I tasted it.

Not blood, but brine. As I knelt upon a stone floor in the heart of London, memories of sand and wheeling gulls deepened, unlocked by the sharp, vivid tang of sea water.

2
Visits of Portent

I have returned from my regular morning peram-
bulation. Long acquaintance with my father's
devices, and the eliminative functions of a dog
grown old even before he became my companion in
travail and peril, have made my habits as rigidly
timed as those mechanical figures that parade in and
out of the faces of certain Bavarian clock towers.

In a smoke-darkened courtyard branching off my
route, a group of children in tattered smocks, bare
feet as black as the street grime they skipped upon,
sang and played a simple hand-clapping game. The
dog barked, as though to join in their shrill, innocent glee, but a chill settled around my own heart
as I made out the words that accompanied their
criss-crossing dirty arms and slapping palms.

Georgie's fiddle
Georgie's clock,
Georgie sets him in the dock;

With his bow
And ladies low,
Georgie's fiddle and clock!

The children ran off, laughing and shouting rude gibes at the man who gazed after them with stricken expression. Painful memories, evoked by the childish song, marched behind my creased brow as, dog at heel, I retraced my steps homeward. The game's jingling rhymes were, no doubt, a decaying echo of those street ballads – complete unto infamous detail! – that first sprang up when my affairs came under the eye of public attention. I recalled the horrid evening, when I, thinking I had at last been returned to safety and anonymity, stopped at the perimeter of a crowd assembled to listen to an itinerant singer. Within minutes, I had realised that, to the tune of "Hail, Smiling Morn," a bawdy account of my recent perils was being related to the audience. Above their heads a coloured board had swayed on the end of a pole, with an artful caricature of my own face leering at maidens swooning to my supposed violin-playing; one lady-like hand had been depicted by the artist as trembling to touch the exaggerated clock-winding key into which a private section of my anatomy had been transformed. The sight of this villainous depiction in the hands of the balladeer's accomplice had staggered me backwards; the nearest faces had turned towards me and had spotted the resemblance between me and the demon fiddler on the placard; across dizzy-heaving streets I had been forced to flee before a general hubbub could arise. Shortly after, I had decamped to my new residence and hidey-hole, in a less populous district where my alleged crimes might go unnoticed against the backdrop of the inhabitants' grey squalor.

Having returned to my desk and pen, the dog once more at his somnolent station by the coalgrate, I strive to banish the singing, mocking voices from my thoughts. To no avail: they form a constant obbligato to the actual words and tones I seek to conjure from the past.

The day on which the Brown Leather Man first made an appearance in my life would have remained memorable for that alone. That he should be followed by other visitors, who would prove to be equally significant, illustrates that principle best described as the Superfluity of Events.

My puzzlement at the morning's caller and the commission he had given me circulated through my thoughts for the balance of the day. A fit of pique had been engendered in Creff by my failure to heed his dire warnings about the "Ethiope" or, perhaps, by the same's obstinate refusal to actually murder me. The lack of his willing assistance left me unable to do more than carry the mahogany casket, weighty device inside, from the shop counter to the workroom bench. Under the lamp,

the intricate brass assemblage seemed as intimidating as before; I left it for the next day, when my
resources – and Creff – might be better marshalled.

No further custom came that day. It seemed increasingly likely that the Brown Leather Man's
device would have to be the salvation of my accounts. The coin he had deposited as partial
payment weighed heavy in my waistcoat as I
pulled the shutters against the evening's approaching darkness.

As I was about to extinguish the shop brackets,
a knock came upon the door. I lifted the shade and
peered through the glass at the barely discernible
figure beyond. The weight and fine tailoring of the
cloak revealed the person's gentlemanly status.
Before I could speak, he rapped again on the glass
with the silver head of his cane. "Come on, come
on," he called in a slightly coarse accent, unplaceable to me. "Jesus H. Christ," I heard him whisper
to another figure behind him. "Sure gotta deal
with a lot of dim bulbs around here…"

The unfamiliar inflection and incomprehensible
terms I attributed then to foreign or modish affec-
tation. My reclusive habits kept me apart from
those cant phrases "What a shocking bad hat!" and
the like – that flourish on everyone's tongue for a
season, to be replaced by something equally foolish. That this gentleman had time for such frivolity
bespoke money, and the urge to spend it; I unlocked the door and bade him enter.

He swept in with magnificent carriage, the ebony stick planted in sharp arrogance with each step. The cloak was worn with Byronic panache; the waistcoat had been embroidered with gilt thread far beyond economy or taste. His hawkish, faintly pocked countenance was surmounted by spectacles of dark blue glass, hiding his eyes, although the only illumination on the street had been the yellow, mist-shrouded glow of the corner gas lamp. He made no motion to remove the spectacles, but examined me through them as though bending forward to the lens of a microscope.

His companion draped herself on his arm, one hand resting in the crook of his elbow. I had only a moment to note her fair, somewhat sharp-nosed beauty; the gaze she levelled at me from under her dark lashes drove my own away in confusion, while the gentleman's bark turned me on my heel towards him.

"You're Dower?" He lifted his cane to point at me with its silver tip.

"I am. That is, the son–"

"Yeah, right. Sure." The lady looked up at him and squeezed his arm in some manner of signal. He fell silent, frowning and pinching his lower lip, as if gathering his thoughts. When he spoke again, his words were wrapped in a mannered formality.

"Mr Dower," he said, bowing slightly. "I have the pleasure of your acquaintance. Um, that is, let me introduce myself. Scape – Graeme Scape." He shifted the cane and extended a gloved hand, then, upon receiving another warning squeeze from the lady, withdrew it while muttering another incomprehensible word under his breath. "This is Jane – I mean, Miss McThane. May I present. Whatever."

She parted the folds of her shawl enough to reveal the white curve of her throat. I stammered some simple pleasantry, the heat of my blood blossoming across my face. The smile Miss McThane bestowed on me was of a disturbing frankness that I had encountered only once before, when, a fresh-arrived innocent in London, I had chanced to stroll through the Burlington Arcade and had been approached by a seeming lady and greeted with a such-like smile and a murmured "Are you good-natured, dear?" – an offer clear to even one as naive as myself. Then I had been able to flee that precinct of glittering jewellers'-windows and even more glittering women, and thus maintain my innocence. In the confines of my own shop, however, I felt myself cornered and stalked by the scarlet smile and discreetly lowered sable lashes.

My transfixed gaze was broken away from hers by the sharp rap of Scape's cane upon the floor. As though startled awake from a guilt-provoking dream, I looked around at him.

"Mr Dower." His smile pulled his mouth lopsided, as though we shared some conspirators' knowledge between us. "I'd like to talk some business over with you. Okay? I mean… that all right with you?"

Some aspect of his manner, an oddity in his bearing, puzzled me. He had not the polished presentation of self that marks the aristocratic gentleman born to wealth and position. Nor the assured forthrightness, blunt of word and face, that characterizes the new entrepreneurial class whose money and mercantile ideas have obscured so much of the national landscape within this generation, like the smoke from their foundries and chuffing engines of commerce. Not a foreigner; however strange his choice of phrase, it seemed clear that English of some district was his native tongue. Charlatanism or knavery of another ilk rose in my mind as the possible explanation, yet the gentleman – if gentleman he was – displayed no part of that sidling, herpetoid insinuation by which the diddler places himself inside the victim's confidence. In the space of a few seconds, my mind skittered from one hypothesis to the next, all the while pursued and confused by the ineradicable image of dark eyes and snow-white throat.

"Well? You okay?"

The impatient bark of the self-designated Scape brought me out of my muddled reverie. The blue lenses drew closer – to my face, the eyes behind endeavouring to discern my health.

"Yes... yes, of course." I stammered out the words, watching myself in the dark mirrors of his spectacles, careful to keep my gaze from straying to the gently smiling visage of his companion.

"Terribly sorry; the fatigue of a long day, I'm afraid." I stepped behind the shop counter and spread my hands along its smooth surface. "How may I assist you?"

Scape disengaged his arm from his companion's embrace and folded his hands upon the silver head of his walking stick. Miss McThane drifted with her teasing smile to examine one of the clocks on the wall, staying within hearing distance of any talk. "Maybe you've heard about me already, Dower." He lifted a hand to withdraw a card from an inside pocket, and which he then laid on the counter in front of me.

"I don't believe so." Ordinary courtesy, and a shopkeeper's self-interest, ruled out a direct disavowal. "Perhaps..." I looked down at the pasteboard square on the counter. In florid lettering, it announced

MR. G. SCAPE
IMPRESARIO
SCAPE'S CELEBRATED MUSICAL AUTOMATA
LATE OF MILAN - BUDA-PESHT - BRIGHTON

The word *Automata* triggered a wary attitude on my part. Of that segment of my father's career concerned with the production of lifelike human figures capable of motion, speech, and other appurtenances of flesh and blood, I had, from the bitter upshot of my own dabbling with the devices my father had left behind, learned to deny any knowledge. The scenes of chaos inside the church of Saint Mary Alderhythe, kept from public scandal by the good offices and influence of the parish authorities, had been sufficient warning for me. If this gentleman's interest in my wares and services were limited to clockwork jiggery that imitated corporeal habits, then there was no possibility of commerce between us. The inflections of my voice were guarded as I pushed the card with one finger back across the counter.

"No," I spoke, shaking my head, "I'm afraid not. Doubtless, if I had more time for edifying culture, I would be familiar with your contributions. Still–"

"Don't sweat it," interrupted Scape, dismissing my ignorance with a wave of his hand.

"Pardon?"

"I'll send you some tickets, next time we play London." He swayed on the pivot of his cane, watching his uplifted hand paint an imaginary scene above our heads. "Bright lights, names all lit up in neon; you bring your girlfriend around to the box office, they'll give you the best seats in the house–"

"I'm not sure I follow…" His manner had become excited and effusive, and I didn't catch the meaning, possibly lewd, of some of his words. His companion laid her hand on his arm, which had some calming effect.

"Forget it," said Scape. "No problem."

Miss McThane brought her sly smile around to me again. "We've been touring abroad a great deal. It rubs off, you know? The way they talk, and stuff." In this, the longest speech she had directed to me, the same odd accent and diction appeared, that I had noticed in the gentleman's voice.

"Yeah, right," agreed Scape. "Those crazy Italians. Hah. Wild – really wild."

"How may I help you?" I said, hoping to move the conversation to a productive vein.

"Business – yeah." He swivelled his gaze around, searching among the clock faces, then back to me. "These, uh, automata I got – I take 'em around to places. And they do their bit. You follow me?"

I could see my politely reserved expression doubled in the blue lenses trained on me. "I believe so. You refer, I take it, to musical performances–"

"You got it, jack."

"And these mechanical devices that form your troupe – are they of your own creation?" I wished to draw him out, gently as possible, to find the actual extent of his knowledge of clockwork musicians.

"No – no." Scape shook his head. "I got 'em from what's his name…"

"Jackey Droze," supplied Miss McThane.

It took a moment for the words to spark anything in my memory. "You mean Jacquet-Droz," I said. The name of the eighteenth-century Swiss watchmaker, and the two sons that followed in their father's career (with more success than I had on a similar course), was familiar to me, as it had once been to all Europe. Indeed, Creff had informed me that my father had once travelled expressly to Lisbon in order to examine the devices christened by their maker Charles the Scribe, Henri the Draughtsman, and The Musician. The senior Dower's interest in, and efforts towards perfecting, the mechanical similitude of human action, presumably dated from that Portuguese visit.

"That's the guy," said Scape.

"You are, then, the current owner of the celebrated organ-playing figure?" I knew that the mechanical woman, reputed by some to have been modelled by Pierre Jacquet-Droz after his own wife, had changed hands many times after the watchmaker and his sons had toured with their creations before the Continent's crowned heads.

"Uh, no, actually–" An echo of my own wariness entered Scape's manner. "Some other ones that he made."

"Others?"

"Yeah. A, uh, trumpet player and a couple of… what's that other thing called… with the strings? – cello. That's it – two cello players."

"Extraordinary." I rubbed my chin, feigning the depth of my musing. "I never heard tell of any such musical devices crafted by Jacquet-Droz."

Scrape gave a diffident shrug. "Well, you see, he never showed 'em to anybody. They just sorta stayed in the family, you know? And then I bought 'em off the old guy's great-grandson."

"I see." Indeed I did; whatever suspicions I'd had of this extraordinary person's less than honest intent had been all but confirmed by his exposition. Jacquet-Droz's skill in clockwork had, by all reports that have come down to the modern day, been eclipsed only by his genius for showmanship and self-promotion. The notion that he would create a veritable orchestra of musicians and not put them on display with his other mechanical children was obviously farcical. This, in combination with the muddled recall of what instruments this supposed impresario's troupe played, marked him in my eye as a person whose every word would need to be examined for fraudulency.

"And in what connection, sir," I continued, "have you come to me? I must confess I know little of music, being merely" – I smiled, lifting my hands towards the ticking wares displayed on the walls – "a simple watchmaker."

Scape returned my smile, or at least half of it; only one side of his face twitched to reveal a few yellow teeth. He leaned over the head of his cane, bringing his face closer to mine. "Well, you see… I'd like to build the act up a little. You know? I mean a trumpet-player and a couple of cellos – it's getting kinda old. People wanna hear something different. Got me? Like, maybe, something that could… *sing*…"

"That would be a marvel." It was obvious that he wished me to hand up on a platter the fish his verbal hook dangled for. From the corner of my eye I caught a change of expression in Miss McThane's face and, glancing at her, saw her dark eyes narrowed in what might have been grudging respect as they gazed at me.

Scape persisted. "Or – play... the *violin*." His words jabbed at me, in the manner of someone forcing the wrong key into an unyielding lock.

"To have such a device, I would imagine, would place one in your profession at the pinnacle of success."

He turned away from me, the better to hide the exclamation of annoyance which he muttered under his breath; I caught only what seemed to be the syllable cog (perhaps a reference to my mechanical trade) and the word succour (a prayer for divine assistance?). I smiled to myself, pleased with my fending off his pointed inquiries.

"Look," he said, mastering his emotions with visible effort. "Your old man was a very clever guy – all right? Let's just say he got... interested in musical stuff. And maybe he, like, built himself a violin player. I mean, a clockwork figure that could play the violin." Behind the blue lenses, the hidden points of his gaze probed into my visage. "What would you know about something like that?"

There; it was out; plain as simple day. Through some means, some hidden current of rumour, this

scalawag had heard of the affair at the church of
Saint Mary Alderhythe and. the Clerical Automata
that my father had left in place, but never animated
before his death. Though my attempt to set the
elaborate array of devices into operation had met
with disaster, this Scape – if that were his real
name – had evidently conceived the notion that
one or more of the automaton figures – perhaps the
priest, or the choristers – could be altered to suit
the purposes of performing in music-halls. To one
of his coarse sensibilities, there would be perhaps
no difference between a chorus'd evensong and a
collection of jigs sawed out of a fiddle; if a clockwork figure had been invested with any musical
talent, this fellow no doubt believed that it should
be as capable of one performance as the other.

"I have no knowledge of such a device." This,
in strict truth: while my father had certainly
eclipsed Jacquet-Droz, by giving his Clerical
Automata a fair approximation of human vocal
powers through ingenious assemblages of rosined
wheels rotating against a set of tuned strings, he
had not, as far as I knew then, ever envisioned a
clockwork violinist.

Scape's mouth set into a bloodless line; his
hands throttled the shaft of his walking-stick, as
through he were about to bring its length down
upon my insolent head. I took a step backwards
from the counter, fearing such violence, only to
start about in surprise when a soft hand laid itself

upon my arm.

"Mr Dower—" Scape's companion had, during our verbal jousting, stepped quietly beside me. Her gaze, half-shaded behind her sable lashes, and intimating smile held me speechless as she interposed herself between shopkeeper and *soi-disant* client. Her hand traced a feather's touch up to my shoulder. Somehow, it seemed that while she had been outside the field of my vision, the edge of her gown's bodice had crept lower, revealing an immodest aspect. My dazzled eyes could not avert themselves from her white throat or the uplifted forms below. A delicate vein swelled with her pulse from beneath a lace-fringed shadow, as though it were a stream trickling beneath fields of snow that gave off an unaccountable warmth. "You know," she said, as I watched, mesmerised, the words formed by the coral bow of her mouth, "you seem like a nice guy. A real nice guy."

(Torturing memories! I sit at the prison of my desk, gnashing my teeth and grinding my pen-nib into the mocking white expanse of the paper under my hand. The coaxing words of a very Delilah! Had I but known what lay beyond them!)

"My buddy – I mean, Mr Scape – he gets a little excited sometimes. You know?" Miss McThane's hand strayed to the top of my cravat, one slender finger teasing a loop of silk free from the knot. "Like when he's talking about something he's really hot on. Know what I mean?"

"Yes…" The word was no more than a squeaking gasp. The loosening of the constriction around my throat did nothing to aid my breath past the stone that had formed inside it. I felt my spine come up against the wall at the end of the counter; my legs, as though acting as the reservoir of all the moral steadfastness that had drained from the rest of my body, had effected my retreat from the woman's continuing onslaught.

"Like…*violins*…"

The back of my head struck the silver case of one of my father's more elaborate clocks. The force of the blow triggered the delicate mechanisms inside; dimly, I was aware of small doors opening above me, and a circle of uniformed mannikins tinkling a theme from Handel's *Jephtha* as they paraded in and out of the encircled numbers. Behind my own brow, other small doors were opening, emitting darker figures shrilling melodies more dizzying, as I watched the sinuous grace of Miss McThane's finger rise to lay its point upon my chin.

"Violins" I choked.

"Yeah There's just… something about 'em. Drives him…*wild*."

I strove to speak, but could not. A scent of lilacs, borne across the dwindling distance between us by the warmth of her bosom, enveloped my head. She seemed suddenly of greater stature, looking down at me from a height. Faintly, I realised that whatever virtue normally resident in my limbs had fled from them as well, and I was sliding slowly down the wall.

Her smile grew wider, her eyes even more shaded. "Violins…" she whispered.

(Temptress! With a start, the dog looks up from his doze by the grate, hearing the snap of the pen in my fist. I blot the spilled ink from my desk, draw forth a fresh sheet, and begin again.)

Suddenly, as though from a great distance, I heard a clatter and a hubbub of voices. The chain that held my eyes fast upon Miss McThane's was broken, as she jerked her face about towards the source of the noise. I heard my own name being shouted.

"Mr Dower!" It was Creff, in full cry, his harsh accents, echoing down the hallway behind the shop. "Thieves! Murdering thieves!"

The excitement in his voice roused me from my unwitting haze. I pulled myself upright and brushed past Miss McThane, shaking away the restraining hand she placed upon my sleeve.

At the end of the hallway the workroom door stood open. In the circle of light cast from the bench's lamp, Creff and Scape could be seen, wrestling over the mahogany cabinet held between them. Catching sight of me, Creff shouted, "It's the Ethiope's accomplices! He's sent 'em here to cosh and rob us!"

I ran towards the struggling pair, unmindful of any danger. The prospect of alteration to the odds against him spurred Scape to greater effort: he wrenched the device left behind by the Brown Leather Man away from Creff, and bulled head-downward at me. I fell from the impact of his shoulder into my chest; he charged past me, but I managed to snare his legs within my grasp, bringing us both sprawling on to the floor of the shop. Scape's hands splayed open, and the mahogany casket slid a few inches further, impelled by momentum.

Miss McThane bent down to pick up the casket, but was unable to lift it owing to its great weight. Creff, brandishing a broom handle as a truncheon, vaulted over the prostrate forms of Scape and myself, and menaced her away from the object of the pair's felonious desire. With unladylike facility, she raised the hem of her dress and forcefully placed the point of one reversed-calf boot in a sensitive portion of my servant's anatomy. Thus crippled, Creff fell in a knot upon the casket.

"Get offa me, for Christ's sake," said Scape. He struggled to his knees, breaking free of my grip. My flailing hands sought what purchase they could on him; my fingers hooked behind the blue lenses of his spectacles, and pulled them from his face. The nature of the struggle changed dramatically thereby.

"Shit!" He staggered to his feet, bent double and pressing his hands against his eye sockets. The dim glow of the shop's gas brackets, turned low for economy's sake, wrought obvious pain in him, as though he were some earth-burrowing animal rudely scooped to the surface by a rustic's hoe. Tears streamed from under his palms. "You sonuvabitch," he shouted blindly in my direction. The lenses splintered under his unguided boot. The sight unfolded Creff from his immediate personal concerns. He gaped at the stricken man as Miss McThane, abandoning her pursuit of the casket, rushed to aid her companion.

Emboldened by this turn of events, the wine of excitement drowning any remaining dregs of caution, I picked up the broom handle Creff had dropped, and laid it smartly across Scape's back. "Out you go, sir!" I cried. "Your custom's not wanted here."

"You turkey–" the agonised man spat the words in the direction of my voice.

"Come on. Later for this crap." Miss McThane dragged him to the doorway. A hansom cab waited in the dark outside; she soon had the hunched-over figure deposited inside; with no instructions given, the driver whipped the horse to speed, carrying the two away in extreme haste.

Creff, maintaining gingerly balance, peered out the window at the cab vanishing into evening mist. "The Ethiope," he said, turning towards me. "Those were his henchmen, no doubt about it." He gestured at the cabinet sitting in the middle of the floor. "Sent 'em here to steal that ruddy thing."

A tremor had replaced the strength in my arms.

I laid the broom handle on the counter before it dropped from my hands. "There would be little reason," I said, "for the gentleman to whom you refer, to hire others to steal that which he himself brought here. If he wished to have it, why would he not merely keep it in his possession to begin with?"

Creff scowled, turning this argument over in his mind, looking for its flaws.

"No," I went on. "I believe our last visitors to have some conception of this as an article of value. They apparently felt it easier to take it from our custody rather than the rightful owner's."

Unconvinced, yet unable to say why, Creff nodded. "Here," he said, looking up. "What was all that palaver about fiddles?"

"I have no idea," I said wearily. He had apparently been listening from some post upon the stairs. Fortunately so; from such a vantage point he had likely seen Scape's furtive actions.

These events had taxed me sorely. I directed Creff to carry the casket back to the workroom. I briefly considered notifying the constabulary of this foiled robbery, but thought better of it. The article over which we had struggled – and which I could identify as to neither purpose nor value – might well have been impounded for examination, and I would thus lose a valuable commission.

Some time after my first arrival at the shop, Creff had directed my attention to a secret

repository well-hidden under the floor of the
workroom. Upon examination, it had revealed
nothing but a few of my father's mechanical
sketches and a flask of antimony. In this hole, the
Brown Leather Man's property was entrusted for
safekeeping, the concealing cover placing it beyond an outsider's easy discovery.

As the reader might well imagine, my mind was
greatly preoccupied with the perplexing nature of
the day's events. From the appearance of the
Brown Leather Man in my shop, and the puzzling
spillage of sea water in the workroom – a detail
dream-like in its apparent insignificance and nagging incongruity – to the blue-lensed Scape of
jerkily animated mien and strange words, his companion of yet more frightening demeanour, and
the pitched battle that had ensued over the mahogany casket, the hours had been spanned from
one baffling occurrence to another. As though
some great unseen Clock, ticking out with regular
monotony the passage of my life, had reached a
zenith and set its bells into previously unheard
clangour and alarm – so we mistake Peace, and describe it as Eternal, when the hand is already
poised to strike the hour of dreadful change.

So deep were my musings that the pangs of
hunger reminded me of the engagement to which
I was committed for that same evening. One of
Clerkenwell's more prosperous watchmakers (that
prosperity owed more to the cheapness of his goods

than to any other quality), whose snobbishness
made him anxious to associate with one bearing
my renowned father's name, had renewed his invitation to me. The opportunity of a meal beyond
that afforded by my meagre larder and Creff's slight
culinary skill enabled me to endure the man's
stultifying company.

Leaving Creff, armed with the broom handle and
the kitchen-knife of which I had relieved him earlier,
in vigilant guard over my shop and home, I made my
way the short distance to my colleague's residence.

Nothing in the man's conversation, or that of his
wife, intruded upon the continuous hidden flow
of my thoughts. I was able to maintain a fiction of
polite society with a few appreciative comment, a
murmured "Oh?" or "Indeed" over the boiled potatoes, while all the while the spectral figures of
the day's drama trod the stage and declaimed their
lines inside the theatre of my skull.

Only when my host and I were draining a
resinous Oporto at the edge of the fire, did his
comments enter my consciousness.

"Peculiar thing – eh? – these street costers –
most *peck*uliar." He poured himself another
tumblerful. "Peddle the damnedest stuff. Never
seen the like."

"Pardon?" Perhaps I had finally grown weary of
turning the thin pack's cards over in my mind. I
emerged from my thoughts to hear his oration on
the London Street vendors.

"The other day – just yesterday, it was–" He leaned forward to impart this confidence. "I was in the Tottenham Court Road with my little daughter." (I knew the child, a wretched pug-nosed creature.) "An old Irish woman, dirty as a pig, selling dolls from a basket, approached us. 'Shure they're bhutiful dolls,' she says." He imitated the accent with mocking scorn. "'Shuted for them angels of the worruld,' meaning my daughter. With that sort of blandishments, soon enough my little Sally must have one of the wretched things." (I had often heard the child in the street outside my shop, whining for some gimcrack or lolly.) "The old witch wanted fourpence – can you credit it? – for one of the things, and eager enough she was to sell one, too, until my Sally sees a few wrapped in tissue at the bottom of the basket, and says she wants one of those. Then damned if the woman doesn't go all coy on me, refusing to bring one of the bottom ones out, saying they weren't 'shuted' for such a fine child and such-like, until my Sally was near choleric to have one. I finally had to pay sixpence to entice the woman to hand it over – and a fine show of reluctance she made, too, even then! – and when she had scuttled away with her basket, and my Sally unwrapped the doll, damned if she didn't scream and drop the thing on the street! I'm sure it's quite the ugliest creation possible, and a wicked joke to sell for the hands of a child." His broad face was red from the port and indignation, as he stood up and opened the doors of his writing cabinet. "Here the thing is – see for yourself."

I took the object he thrust towards me, and with but small curiosity examined it. It was a doll as is often sold in the streets, cheaply manufactured of *pappy-mashy*, as the costers term it, dipped in wax. The striking aspect was its extraordinary face: a crude parody, as though the maker's rude art had meant to represent some animal other than the human. Sloping forehead, goggling rounded eyes, and protruding lips over a non-existent chin; these features, in combination with the greenish cast of the wax, gave a distinctly piscine impression, as if a herring fresh off the fishmonger's slab had been dressed in a plaything's clothes. For a moment, as I turned the thing over in my hands, I again felt as if I were toiling through the rigours of a dream; it reminded me of the sea water – from where? – on the floor of my workroom.

"Extraordinary," I agreed. I reached to hand it back to my host, but he waved it away.

"Keep the damned thing," he said.

"Your little girl–"

"Faugh. She can't abide the sight of it. No, no, do us a kindness and take it away from here."

I laid it on the arm of the chair. My thoughts drifted away, to their former channels, as my host expostulated on some other subject. My hands came to rest on my stomach – stuffed to bursting against future famine – and I felt a circular shape in my waistcoat pocket. The coin the Brown Leather Man had paid me; idly, as the other's voice droned on, I took it out. A familiar shape and weight; perhaps not familiar enough of late. I looked down at it in my palm, and felt my gut hollow beneath the half-digested meal.

The face, in profile, on the coin was the twin of the hideous doll.

A sudden panic pushed me up from the depths of the chair. I made a hasty excuse to my host and, gathering up my hat and cloak, rushed from his house. Outside, I realised that the doll had found its way into my hands along with the coin. I thrust them into my pocket to remove them from my sight.

The mist had thickened, swallowing every aspect of the houses and the railings in front of them. Under the sulphurous glow of the street lamps, mere smudges of light swathed in grey, indistinct forms scurried from one dark cranny to the next. I hastened home, guided by memory rather than sight, unable to look behind me to see what blurred shadow might be entwined with my own.

3
Mr Dower Investigates

I awoke the next morning, half-believing that the preceding day's events had been but a dream, driven by its own eccentric machinery to a baffling conclusion. My sleep had been vexed with shadowy figures, dark-skinned and sombre, or with eyes hidden by blue glass and spouting incomprehensible obscenities; I would have been grateful to shake them out of my muddled head, to disappear with all the nocturnal phantoms that had gone before them. My waistcoat had been left draped over the chair by the side of my bed; reaching out my hand from under the covers, I felt the shape of the Brown Leather Man's coin in the garment's pocket. With my thumb I could trace through the wool the oddly shaped profile that had been twice revealed to me in my dinner host's parlour. If it were a dream, I had not been released from it yet.

Once dressed, I scarce touched the breakfast that Creff brought to me. I pushed aside the scant fare and set before me on the table the tangible remnants of the previous evening. The doll stood upright, its ichthyomorphic face goggling at me. A crude thing; if its ugliness could be attributed to its maker's lack of skill in capturing a human physiognomy, it would have been only a sad bit of rubbish, and no more. Its power to disturb, however, lay in what seemed the craftman's intent: however awkwardly formed, these were the features he had meant it to have.

"Here, Creff," I said. He was clearing the dishes away, maintaining an offended silence as though the untasted food were a comment on his own abilities. I picked the doll up and offered it for his inspection. "Did you ever see the like?"

Creff peered at it suspiciously, then shook his head. "Damned if I have." His taste for novelty had been exhausted by the turmoil of the day before. Perhaps he held me to account for that parade of oddities; the doll was evidently seen as another jape at his expense. "No, sir, I never have." He bore away the dishes in aggrieved dignity.

I had hoped to obtain from him some further idea of the doll's origin. He had far more experience than I with the costermongers that filled the London streets, deriving many of his simple pleasures from their wares. I had often seen him return to the shop poking among the remnants of a pennyworth's whelks wrapped in a twist of paper, or some other ambulatory delicacy. His purchases were not just of eatables: shortly after I first came to London and the shop, he began to sport a chain and timepiece. Unable to purchase one of the expensive articles offered in his employer's shop, he had bought from an itinerant vendor an example of that cheap imported article known to the watch-making trade as a *white jenny*, and festooned his stomach with its glittering links. It little mattered to him that its hands soon froze in one position, never to circulate over the face again, as he was in fact ignorant of the art of telling the hour in any manner than the sun's overhead position; he did feel somewhat swindled when the chain's sheen wore off, revealing the base metal beneath.

Regardless, he lacked either the capability or the desire to furnish enlightenment concerning the ugly doll. I laid the thing aside for future pondering, and picked up the coin from the tablecloth.

The sovereign glittered between my thumb and forefinger. As before, a comforting weight and shape to the hand, with the shield on one side, and on the obverse – the profile of, not Queen Victoria, but rather the doll's exophthalmic twin. The craft employed in the coin's depiction was finer, of a quality equal to that ever used to show a monarch of the realm. With what self-assurance as such repulsive features could muster, the figure – I assumed it to be male, from the old-fashioned short periwig shown above the sloping forehead – gazed towards the coin's margin. If the denizens of the sea had wished to acclaim themselves a ruler,

the profile might have been that of their most
noble candidate.

An inscription ran underneath. I held the coin
up to read the words. They identified the personage as one *Saint Monkfish*.

Such a figure was outside any calendar of saints
of which I was aware. Admittedly, my religious education had been sparse: the aunt who had reared
me had little interest of her own, other than maintaining the conventions of respectability, and had
received no instructions from my father on the
point. Indeed, the disastrous affair at Saint Mary
Alderhythe had been the only occasion in adult-
hood of my entry into a church for other than a
funeral service. Even now, such accumulated grim
experience produced an involuntary shudder in me
if I merely passed by any sanctified premises. Thus,
so narrow was the compass of my Christian knowledge, I could not be without doubt, as I gazed at the
coin in my hand, that there wasn't a Saint Monkfish
somewhere in the minor hagiology – perhaps the
patron of truly ugly people? A vision came to me of
those facial deformities that we pass hurriedly on
the street, dropping alms into upturned hands while
averting our eyes; perhaps those unfortunates made
their devotions at the shrine kept in some church's
darkest corner, where they and their intercessor
would be hidden from pitying gaze.

My mind was filled with conjecture and query,
raised by the two strange objects before me. I

resolved upon a course of immediate investigation; there was no work in the shop, other than the mahogany cabinet that the Brown Leather Man had left with me. Even if I had felt my cerebral powers up to the task of examining and repairing the device, my thoughts were too preoccupied with what mysterious connections there might be between the clockwork assemblage, the ugly doll, and the coin with its curious saint. Perhaps the dullness that is engendered by long periods of poverty, and the lack of sociability and amusement that it entrails, had bred in me a thirst for that which we should name Folly, but prefer to call Adventure. Things which a wiser man would dismiss as mere coincidence or oddities too trivial for notice, had claimed my attention. In a small velvet bag, ordinarily used to preserve the polished metal of a watch lying in the counter drawer, I placed my two small curios, and pulled the drawstring tight. I instructed Creff to keep the shop's window shutters down, and to inform any callers that I would resume business on the next day; then I set out to discover what I could do.

The parish church was situated closest to my shop. I made for it as my first point of inquiry, resolving thereby, if not to banish my fear of churches, to at least swallow the bitter pill of a visit to one before anticipation could make it worse.

Begrimed windows cast dim shapes of the coloured glass upon the stone floor as I peered around the arched wooden doors. A few candles

guttered and flared in the draughts whispering
around the pillars, revealing the huddled shapes of
those at prayer or in surreptitious slumber after a
cold night shuffling over the pavements that provided them their only home. A thin figure, whom I
took to be the verger, left off clearing cobwebs from
the corners of one of the larger pews, the point of
the willow branch in his gnarled hand swathed in
dusty spider silk, and shuffled towards me.

"I wish to see the parson," I informed him. I let
the church door creak shut behind me, thus com-
pleting the gloom inside its buttressed walls.

"Do ye, then?" His age and labours bent him in
such a way that his neck protruded at a right angle
from his hollow chest, giving him a tortoise-like
appearance reinforced by the snap of his near-
toothless jaws. "If ye're another scroof come round
with yer bunkum letters of reference, ye kin just
bugger off. The parson's been burned fair enough
times on that dodge to rickinize one of yer ilk be
now." His yellow eye glared at me, as if he were
about to snip my arm between his Punch-like nose
and chin.

"You mistake me," I protested. "I've no intention
of asking for money." Evidently, the clergyman
had been the victim of those professional beggars
who gain sympathy, and a sizeable gift, through
their portrayal of distressed gentility. "Only information – that's all I seek. I have a few questions of
a... *theological* nature."

"Bloody likely," muttered the verger. He did; however, lead me to the rectory attached to the church.

I was soon ushered into the parson's study, the only ornament within its severe confines being the thick volumes of sermons lining the walls. The smell of their aged morocco bindings mingled with the fumes still rising from a blackened clay pipe resting in a bowl on the desk. From behind it the aged clergyman rose, pushing himself upright with a well-worn blackthorn cane, as the verger coughed out some vague introduction before retiring behind the door.

The parson, beneath the grey tangle of his brows, glared at me with little less suspicion, as a mariner might peer through a dense sea fog to discern the friendliness of another ship spotted in pirate-filled waters. "Your name was...?" he growled with no attempt at polite formality.

"Dower, sir." I approached the desk. "George Dower. Of this parish, actually."

He lowered himself back into his chair. "I seem to have some memory of your face," he mused. "But not here in the church." He gestured brusquely at a point near me.

I sat down in the smaller chair he had indicated. "My attendance at services has been... irregular. Perhaps, on the street – my shop is nearby." In truth, his lined, scowling visage bore some reminder for me as well – but from where and what time I could not then recall.

His disordered white mane brushed his collar as
he shook his head. "I do not go out from here." He
raised his cane for explanation. "My mobility has
been impaired for some time." His blunt hands
folded across the papers on the desk as he leaned
forward. "Your business, sir – I have pastoral matters to attend to."

"I only require a moment of your time," I said.
"I'm attempting to find out whatever I can about a
certain saint. Rather an obscure one, I feel. And I'd
be grateful for whatever help you could give me."

"A saint, you say?" He nodded, frowning reflec-
tively. "Well, that is a praiseworthy endeavour –
the lives of the blessed should be an inspiration to
us. Very commendable, I'm sure. What period?"

"I beg your pardon?"

"When," said the clergyman patiently, "did this
saint of yours live?"

"I have absolutely no idea."

"Hm." He studied me, my commendable nature
apparently lowered in his eyes. "Very well – this
saint's name, then."

I gathered my breath before speaking: "Saint
Monkfish, actually. "

"Indeed." One shaggy eyebrow arched as he
pinched his lower lip between thumb and forefinger; my query had apparently plunged him deep
into thought. "Saint Monkfish, you say."

"Yes," I replied eagerly. "You know of him?"

He mused in silence, rubbing his lip.

"You see, I came across the name in rather a peculiar way." I brought out the velvet bag and undid its drawstring. "I was given this coin–"

Before I could fetch it out, the parson's voice sounded in a deep rumble. "Saint Monkfish, is it? A moment…now I think I remember you–"

I looked up and saw the penetrating stare from under his lowered brows. In the same moment, we recognised each other.

"Insolent whelp!" His cane landed across his desk with a mighty crack, scattering the papers like frightened birds. "Blaspheming wretch!"

I pushed myself backwards in the chair, away from the trembling point of the cane. The clergyman's sudden wrath made the identification complete in my mind. He had been one of the dignitaries invited to the inaugural service of my father's Clerical Automata at the church of Saint Mary Alderhythe. Indeed, my panic-unleashed memory informed me that his incapacity was a direct result of injuries suffered on that lamentable occasion.

"And now–" His eyes darted fire, his jaws working convulsively, "And now – not content with your unholy machinery's defilement – you come round here with crude japeries at the Church! Apostate!" The cane slashed through the air, whistling past my face. "Mocking – *mocking*, I say – the sacred traditions of all held holy by right-thinking men. Saint Monkfish, indeed. Very clever, that! You… you Manichean!"

The cane swung again towards me. Rising up to full height, the old clergyman seemed on the verge of lunging across the desk and driving the point through my chest, skewering me to the worn leather at my back. I scrambled to my feet, edging away with the velvet bag clutched to my chest.

"I – I meant no offence," I stammered. "Truly–"

He hobbled around the desk, waving the cane. "Monkfish!" he shouted, his lips flecked with spittle. "I'll give you monkfish, wretch!"

A stinging blow landed across my shoulders as I tugged at the latch of the door. It came open, spilling me out into the church aisle. A few rheumy-eyed faces looked up from their prayers or slumber as the sound of blackthorn against woollen serge echoed from the stone walls. The old parson was still shouting anathemas after me as I fled between the pews.

In the street, some distance from the church, I slowed my paces. The intervening throng screened me from any further pursuit by the gimp-legged clergyman. Safe once more, I assessed my injuries, working my smarting shoulder blades inside my coat as I walked. Perhaps a few bruises, and I was fortunate at that: if the old man's strength had been equal to his anger, I would fair have been beaten into the flagstones. A foul stroke of luck, to wander all innocent into the den of one bearing such a grievance – both personal and theological – against me. I had, at least, achieved some small addition to my knowledge. If ever a Saint Monk-fish had lived, his canonization had been achieved outside any Church I might know.

I briefly contemplated abandoning any further inquiries. What I had learned so far had been sorely bought. The clockwork device that the Brown Leather Man had left me still awaited my attentions; was I not shirking those duties I owed the gentleman by this chasing after small myster-ies? An ugly doll and an odd coin – what were these but mere coincidences, of no import to any except one looking for diversion? Better to tend my shop; Brown Leather had stated his intent to return in a week's time; perhaps all questions could be answered then.

Wise counsel, even if I gave it only to myself. Yet I put it out of mind, and went on with my Lon-don-bounded voyage of discovery. The sense of dream-like connections persisted, of sea water and clockwork somehow coexistent; as a dreamer dances rashly along cliff edges that would paralyse him with fright when awake, so I proceeded.

The coin with Saint Monkfish's portrait on it had caused me enough grief for the time being. I turned my steps towards the Tottenham Court Road, that costermongers' thoroughfare, where all things were bought and sold.

I soon spied such a person as I wanted. In the midst of the noise and bustle, the jostling pedestri-ans and carriages, the walking merchants who

peddle their wares from pushcarts and neck-slung
trays shouted their inducements to potential customers. I pushed my way past the common lot of
patterers, gallows littérateurs, cheap johns, and the
like; near the turn on to the Hampstead Road, a
hawker with a basket of dolls on his crooked arm
was holding aloft a pair of the mannikins for the
passing crowd's inspection.

"Yes, sir: finest wares," said the man, spotting my
interest as I approached. "Make a child happy for
fourpence – there's not many things in this world
as can do that. Have you a small one to home?"

"Actually, no," I said. "I really only require information from you."

"Mayhap you do." He poked about in his basket,
arranging the dolls to better effect. "But I doubts as
you could tell me how much trade I'd lose thereby,
there being many fine folk who'd swallow their
disappointment over not obtaining one of these
rare toys, rather than interrupt such a discussion."

I fetched out a shilling and handed it to him.

The coin disappeared into his pocket. "Very fine,
sir; very fine. For that you'll know all that Dick the
Dollman knows, though it take hours in telling. Man
and boy. I've peddled the London streets, though I
was raised to a better class of trade and am only reduced to this through harsh circumstance. My father
was a pensioner in Greenwich College–"

I interrupted a monologue that seemed, through
frequent repetition, to have taken on the mechanical

aspects of one of my father's clockwork figures. "Pardon; I only need to know the origin of the dolls you sell. Who makes them, and from where they come."

"Why, I makes them myself, sir. Very clever I am at it, too. I've made wax heads – large size, that is, big as yours or mine; I don't make these little ones – of murderers who were hung, for exhibit by a company of showmen; I did the infamous Rush, and Mr and Mrs Manning, and very convincing they were. In all aspects of dolls and wax figures and the like, I'm your man."

"You don't make the heads for these dolls?" I seized upon this one helpful fact.

"Oh, no, sir. It's cheaper to buy them, and assemble them on to the wax bodies as I make. There's no profit in fiddling with these tiny heads, as I can buy 'em seven-and-a-half-pence for a dozen, easy enough."

"Where do you buy them? Who makes them?" persisted.

"Why, they're near all made in Hamburg, but we buy them here in London. Alfred Davis', in Houndsditch – they're of a very nice quality, very fine; I prefers them to those of White's, though they be right close by. Or Joseph's – they're in Leadenhall Street; not nearly so fine, they are."

I leaned closer to the doll seller, to better separate his words from the surrounding street noise. "I take it, then, that if shown a particular doll's head, you could identify the premises of its origin?"

He preened himself a bit, smoothing his shirt-front with one hand. "As I said, in all things pertaining to dolls, Dick's your man."

From the velvet bag I drew forth the ugly doll given me by my last night's host. "If you'd be so kind, then," I said, holding it forth. "Which of the shops you mentioned sold this?"

I saw his eyes widen, startled, as he gazed at the thing; an ashen pallor drained into his face. Then he recovered a measure of his composure, and looked up at me.

"Never seen the like," said the doll-seller, shaking his head. His voice held only a fraction of its former bravado. "Never in my days. Right 'bom-inable-looking, it is." He tucked his own wares back into his basket, and moved away from me.

I clutched his coat sleeve to restrain him, "You say you have never seen one like this before?" An evident falsehood; the look in his eyes had been one of fearful recognition.

He jerked his arm out of my grasp. "No, never," he said grimly. "It's not a fit plaything for a child – best throw it away, sir, or on the fire." He began a quick walk, pushing into the shifting wall of the massed crowd.

"But surely–" I called after him.

A stern glance came over his hunched shoulder. "You've had a shilling's worth of information, sir. Believe me – you don't want to know any more." Then he was gone from my sight.

I stared after the vanished figure, long after the
intervening crowd had swallowed him up. Thus
far, my inquiries had yielded only meagre fruit:
blows in one case, and a hasty evasion in another.
I knew little more than when I had started. Indeed;
the mysteries had been compounded by the fright
that had been visible in the doll seller's face. Was
this Saint Monkfish a figure of sinister import unknown to me? I had only one other possible
informant in mind, and thus turned my steps in
that direction.

At previous times in the course of my business,
I had had some brief acquaintance with various of
the city's numismatists. When dealing with rare
and treasured articles – be they watches or whatever – an informal weave often arises, linking the
various trades that service the wealthy enthusiast's
desires. A few of my clients, being country gentlemen unfamiliar with London's commercial
intricacies, asked me for references to the most
knowledgeable dealers in various arcana, rare
coins among them. I soon acquired the knowledge
necessary to steer them aright.

Some time after my discussion with the coster-
monger on the Tottenham Court Road – my financial
condition precluded any faster mode of transportation than my own limbs – I entered the shop of the
numismatist I considered likely to be most helpful.
In the dark, museum-like atmosphere the coin dealer
looked up from a tray of ancient Roman *denarii*; long

hours of huddling over such small objects had given him the appearance of a mole with paws together, examining beetles for particular delicacy. He soon recognised my name, if not my face, and I put my query for his consideration.

I laid the coin that the Brown Leather Man had paid me on the counter for the dealer's inspection. "I'd like to know about this minting," I said. "What can you tell me about a Saint Monkfish crown?"

"Saint who?" He picked up the coin in his spatulate fingertips and held it to the light. With his other hand he brought his eyeglasses down from his high forehead. "Very curious," he pronounced after a moment. "Very curious, indeed."

"What is that?"

"There's never been such a coin minted, English or otherwise, that I know of. Not with a portrait of any such Saint Monkfish." He peered closer at the profile. "Ugly looking sort of devil, isn't he? It would have been a memorable issue on that ground alone, I would think. But here – it's not a real coin, anyway." He held it out on his palm.

I glanced from the coin to the numismatist's face. "What do you mean?"

"It's a forgery," he said simply, pushing his spectacles back up. "See; look closer – it's nothing but a lump of base metal that's been electroplated. The coiners use a galvanic battery and cyanide of silver to achieve the effect. Though this is quite a fine example of that devious art; near perfect, I'd say." He handed it back to me. "Though what the purpose would be of forging a coin that doesn't exist in the first place – I couldn't speculate."

"Indeed," I murmured, taking it between my thumb and forefinger. "Who would do such a thing?"

"Oh, who is not the problem." The numismatist gestured dismissively. "I recognize the work; I'd lay considerable odds it's a Fexton you're holding."

"Fexton?" I had never heard the name.

"Quite. There are a few collectors with an enthusiasm for forged coins, considering them as curiosities more notable than the items they imitate. And among that lot, a Fexton coin is considered the most desirable. A true artist; pity about his moral nature. Yes. I'd say that no other hand but his could have produced that."

I turned the coin round, studying it. The glittering object was even more mysterious now. "Can you direct me to this master forger?"

"Oh, I'm afraid I can't help you there." He shook his head. "I knew the man, or as well as anyone did; very secretive fellow, beyond even the requirements of his trade. Perhaps deleterious fumes, from the chemicals he used, eventually affected his reason. The last I heard of him was a few years ago; he wrote me a letter, saying that he was relocating to – what was the phrase? -ah, yes, "the borough of Wetwick," said the letter. And then I heard no more from him since."

Another mystery – I fancied myself reasonably familiar with the districts of London, but had never heard of *Wetwick* before. (Would that I were innocent of that knowledge now!) I said as much to the numismatist.

"Nor I," he agreed. "As I said, perhaps his reason was impaired. Perhaps such a place only existed in his poor knackered brain, or at the weedy bottom of the Thames. Though I confess that my knowledge of the city is not encyclopaedic – here, why not hail a cabby, and ask him?"

"Yes; yes, of course." I dropped the coin back into the velvet bag. The drivers of hansoms were noted for their knowledge of London's byways; their trade depended on it. If anyone would know of such a district, it would be one of their number. "Thank you."

My investigations, fruitless as they might have been, had nevertheless taken all day to perform. Evening was already enveloping the city as I stepped from the numismatist's shop on to the thoroughfare. Within short order, I heard the creak of wheel and clop of hoof heralding the approach of a hansom cab. I raised my hand and bade it approach; the driver, from his lofty perch, adjusted the horse's progress with rein and whip, and was soon stopped in front of me.

I looked up at the caped, top-hatted figure. He seemed a good choice; his luxuriant moustache was flecked with grey of age and experience. "Do you know the city well?" I called up to him.

"Of course; get in, sir." His pride seemed somewhat nicked by my possible lack of confidence. "There's not a part I don't know, sir."

My hand reached up to the cab's handle. "Can you take me to the borough of Wetwick?" I asked.

His look of surprised indignation stayed my hand. He drew himself upright and glared down at me. "You didn't look to be that sort of gentlemen." His voice was harsh with barely suppressed outrage at my request. "You might find some other cabby who would take you there – but not this one. A good night to you, then." He snapped the reins and sent the vehicle moving off.

My puzzlement had reached its limit; my brain could encompass no more. Every attempt to penetrate a mystery had been like a lantern's beam down an endless shaft, that reveals only receding murk. My course around London had been a pointless chase; the velvet bag with its curious contents might as well have been tied on a stick to the top of my head for all that I had laid hold of them. Wearied, I turned my steps towards home.

4
The Way to Wetwick

I returned to my shop and discovered that, in my absence, my previous evening's visitors had returned to press their own inquiries with greater persistence.

The premises were still shuttered and dark when I let myself in. No light shone down the stairway leading to the rooms above; at the end of the hallway behind the shop itself spilled a faint glow from the lamp on the workbench. The complete silence instilled in me a premonitory caution, as I stepped across to the counter. I called for Creff, but no answer came.

Perhaps, I reasoned, he had taken it upon himself to begin work upon the device left by the Brown Leather Man, and was too intent on his labours to respond to my voice. Or some other explanation accounted for the stillness; so I hoped as I made my way, with some trepidation, down the hallway.

I found in the workroom, not Creff, but utter chaos. The bench had been swept clean of all the projects and devices, in various stages of disassembly and reassembly, that had been ranged upon it. Only the burning lamp remained to cast its light over the tools and bits of intricate machinery scattered over the stone floor. As well, all of my father's materials, the great mass of gears, clock frameworks, lifeless mannikins, and other remnants of his fecund career, had been pulled away from the workroom's walls and gone through. Hands moving with burglars' haste had left the pieces in greater disorder than that into which I had let them lapse. Indeed, there was hardly a space remaining to set a foot on the wreckage-strewn floor.

Little caring to see if anything of value had been taken, I turned and ran back to the stairway, calling Creff's name once again. This time, to my ear came a muffled thumping from the floor above.

At the doorway of his small sleeping quarters, I found my assistant, trussed and gagged. He had managed to wriggle one foot from his bonds and thus give the percussive. signal that led me to him. I pulled the wadded handkerchief – a lady's, from the lace and scent on it from his mouth, as it seemed his reddened face was on the point of bursting from the attempt to vent his words.

"It was them!" Creff strained to look around at me as I loosened the knotted cords at his wrists. "Those murdering swine – they came back!"

"That fellow Scape?" I said.

"The very one, the scoundrel." He began rubbing the circulation back into his bloodless hands before turning his attention to the bonds at his ankles. "And the fine lady that was with him – she were the worse of them; vicious as a cat, she were."

I stood up, helping Creff to rise as well, with my hand at his elbow. "How did they get in?"

"No idea, sir; very clever, they were. I heard nary a thing, until a great crashing blow on my skull – I'm surprised my brains aren't scattered all over the floor, they struck me so cruel – and while things were all a swimming about me, I saw their faces looking into mine, and her laughing as she trussed me up like a goose. A fine lady, that one!"

The mystery of their entrance was soon cleared away. Leaving Creff in his room to await the restoration of strength in his wobbly legs, I made a tour of the premises. I soon found the scullery window jemmied open expertly, it seemed, from the small amount of damage to the surrounding wooden frame – and two pairs of footprints, dark with the alley's muck, across to the door.

In the wreckage of the workroom, it was difficult to ascertain if anything of value had been taken. I knew, however, what had been the likely intent of their search. Clearing away a toppled clock frame and gears strewn like brass coins, I uncovered my father's secret cache. Lifting the stone that served as its unobtrusive lid, I peered into its depths: the mahogany casket was still there. I tilted back the wooden lid: the device that my father had built, and that the Brown Leather Man had brought to me for repair, lay inside. The raid on my shop had been unsuccessful.

Kneeling on the cold floor of the workroom, gazing down at the intricate machinery in the hole as if it were some faery gold newly unearthed, yet without seeing it as my own thoughts moved in their courses, I contemplated this latest event. The proper course of action, I knew full well, would be to hail the nearest constable in the street and report the attack on my servant and the burglary attempted, if not consummated – on my shop and stock. I would thus set into motion against these malefactors all the weight of English justice. Which, I believed then in my yet-innocent state, was fully capable of bringing any miscreant to trial and well-deserved punishment. The Law, in its majesty and the power of its representatives, would take the matter out of my hands and, most important, beyond any chance of further harm coming to me or to the persons and objects within my sphere of responsibility. That was what the Law, in its constabulary and bewigged judges, was for; business such as this business had become, was their business now. Certainly not mine; the sooner the whole affair, with all its attendant apparatus of puzzling clockwork device, peculiar forged coin, and retinue of bizarre personages, was turned over to the authorities, the sooner I would be able to

return to my own proper activities. The careful
tending of my small shop through day after uneventful day, towards whatever small sufficiency
or bankruptcy awaited me at the end that was my
appointed lot.

So the thoughts marched through my head, in
proper order. I cannot excuse my later actions
with the plea that I had no idea of what course I
should have followed. All men, reaching back to
Adam in the Garden, plead Ignorance as their defence; when, if we were but honest, we would
admit that the apple was hedged with every warning imaginable. So I too fell; perhaps all sins are
not causes but effects, being the result of that first
sin, Boredom.

I gazed down into that dark hole and the glittering machinery that had been hidden there, as
though I were gazing into the secret workings of
my own heart. Some new thing had entered into
my existence; I was spellbound by it, reckless of any
consequence. That which should have set my
pulse trembling with a natural apprehension, instead hastened it with excitement. I put the
thought of constables out of my mind. The Law
would have to wait; as though already a fellow
criminal, I found it to my advantage to let the authorities' ignorance continue. I resolved to take just
a few more small steps – as all progress along a slippery path is initiated – towards penetrating these
enticing mysteries.

My blood was up; why wait further? Once restraint is loosened, the chase is afoot. I replaced the concealing stone over the Brown Leather Man's device, then supervised the revivified Creff in boarding up the scullery window. With no explanation to him, I was out to the street, the fever in my brain warming me as much as my greatcoat against the night's damp air.

As I strode along, shouldering my way past the evening's revellers, I recalled the words spoken to me before I had returned to the shop: "You might find some other cabby who would take you there – but not this one." True enough; I was evidently engaged in a dark business; matters that one person might be squeamish about, others might find to their taste.

I had, in the course of my day-to-day errands, noted the particular clientele gathered at one of the Clerkenwell public houses. A former coaching inn, it was now given over completely to the furnishing of drink, the only sleeping accommodations offered being the stone kerb outside as a pillow for the total inebriate. It still retained its yard, which provided ample space for the deposit of cab and horse while the driver was inside slaking his thirst. At no time of day or night were there ever fewer than a dozen such vehicles thus cooped about the welcoming door. No place better, I had decided, for finding the intrepid guide I desired.

Once there, I made my way past the ranked hansoms and the patient horses, their large, blinkered
heads lowered in sleep, hooves now and then paw-
ing the cobblestones as if their dreams had restored
them from the grey city to pastures greener. The
steam of their breaths mingled with the fog blurring
the public house's yellow windows. I pushed open
the door and entered, passing from the cold into the
warm stench of spilled ale and stale tobacco.

The smoke from the clay pipes present at every
table was thick enough to hide the low ceiling in a
haze of grey. As I pushed my way through the
murk, I felt pairs of eyes turn and silently watch
my progress. The cut of my clothing, though far
from the finest and unobtrusively patched where
necessary, was enough to mark my position; the
cabbies' own cloaks and high-crowned hats were
mired and darkened with long exposure to the in-
clement weather in which they were forced to
make their livings. A gentleman such as they presumed me to be was a rare sight in this, their den.

Standing between the turned backs of two cabbies pointedly maintaining their conversations
with their fellows, I laid a shilling on the raw
planks that formed the serving bar. The aproned
landlord produced a small glass of some vile-
smelling clear liquid, presumably gin. The shilling
disappeared, leaving no progeny.

Setting the glass down, I stepped back from the
counter and cleared my throat ostentatiously.

Upon repeat of this performance at a more insistent pitch, I was rewarded with the cabbies on either side breaking off their talk and turning to look at me.

"Pardon me, gentlemen," I said. "I require some small assistance, and perhaps the hire of a vehicle and driver, for which suitable recompense will be made." Their eyes brightened at the mention of payment. "I seek transportation to a certain borough of the city. I am, however, ignorant of its exact location. Therefore, I must trust to the expertise of one of your number in these matters of navigation."

One of the men nodded gravely, gathering the intended flattery more from the tone of my voice than the actual words. "Right enough," muttered a cabby beyond him, having listened along with the others nearby.

"Here," said the cabby on my right hand. "What's this borough you want to go to? Just you name it, and we're off."

"Wetwick," I said.

The man straightened up, raising his gaze from the dregs in his glass in order to train his slitted eyes at me from a greater height. On either side, and in back, I felt the others draw back a fraction of an inch. The room fell quiet, all conversations ceasing in circles around me, as the ripples from a stone dropped in water die out and are still."

For a few moments longer, the cabby stared at me, then turned away. I looked about: every face was averted from me. The noise of voices grew again, as broken conversations resumed, but subdued from their previous level.

"Pardon?" My voice fell as if against brick walls. None of them responded as if they'd heard.

I looked down to see the house's landlord snatch up my glass from in front of me and fling it, contents and all, into a slop bucket behind the counter.

"Now see here; this is very extraordinary." I felt justifiably annoyed at the general treatment I had received. "I demand–"

"Eh, bugger 'em all." Another voice broke in, from close at my elbow. "Fine lot they think 'emselves, but I warrant cheese wouldn't choke 'em, if you get my meaning."

I turned about, adjusting the level of my gaze to the height of the one who had addressed me; the brim of his tall hat, a battered piece even shabbier than the usual cabby's gear, barely came up to my shoulder. Underneath it was a face wizened with age and visibly lewd thoughts, winking and grinning at me. "What was that?" I said. "I don't quite follow–"

The brown-toothed leer grew wider. "'Follow', aye, that's good. Follow me you haven't yet, perhaps, but follow me you might – if I just happened to be going where you wanted to go. Eh?"

His words barely concealed their true intent. "To Wetwick, then?" I said. "You know the district?"

"Hold your clapper, for Christ's sake. I know this place as well, and I believe our welcome's at an end." He nodded towards the landlord, who was advancing along the length of serving bar, rolling his sleeves up over his thickly muscled arms. "I'm only in here to collect a wager; lucky for you – you'd have got no help from this tight-arsed bunch. Bozzimacoo!" The last was said to the landlord leaning threateningly over the counter. "I wouldn't touch the billy stink you push here, anyway! Come on." He tugged me away by the arm. "It'll take that thick Yorkshireman a good hour to remember his own filthy words – then he'll be hopping."

Outside, in the public house's yard, a small dog gave a welcoming yip when the cabby emerged with me in tow. "Shut up, you," growled the cabby. The dog, a mongrel resembling a ratting terrier more than anything else, nevertheless danced around the man's boots, only favouring the limp in one of its hind legs.

"Come along, then." The cabby motioned for me to follow as he weaved, somewhat unsteadily, between the hansoms. "There's a much friendlier jerry-shop down the way – my usual bin."

The cellar he led me to was scarcely better lit than the alley on to which its gap-planked door opened. A horse, its ribs showing beneath the harness of a singularly shabby cab, stood outside – the property of my guide, I assumed.

The cabby spread his black-nailed hands across a table so rickety that every touch sent the flame of the guttering candle in its middle wavering. "Arduous work, it'd be," he said, winking again, thin leather sliding over the blood-specked eye. "All the way to Wetwick – a long trip, that; very long, and parching, if you understand me."

I did indeed; an aproned figure stood next to the table. I handed over another coin, and the person shuffled away to the cellar's far side. While I awaited the bringing of drink, I gazed about the space, my eyes having adjusted to the gloom. Only a few men ringed the walls, either hunched over the half-empty jars in front of them or sprawled back in their chairs, boot heels slid into the puddles dripping off the table on to the dirt floor. One of the latter was young, a gentleman of position far above mine, as evidenced by the fineness of his coat; his youthful cheek, stretched in open-mouthed slumber, was already hollowed by the habits of dissipation into which he had fallen. In stale beer shops such as these he had hastened his destiny, pennyworth by pennyworth. A cadaverous woman in one of the room's corners slumped forward, grey-streaked hair tangling over her face; at her feet, an infant lay silent in its basket, stricken as if by laudanum or its mother's tainted milk.

Two mugs were deposited on the table, slopping over and nearly drowning the candle. My guide pulled heartily at the frothless murk, rolling his eyes

at me over the rim of the vessel. "Very tasty, that,"
he pronounced, setting it down, a quarter drained.

I left mine untouched. "Now, as to Wetwick–"

"Wetwick," he interrupted. "Yes, indeed;
Wetwick; all in good time, sir, all in good time." The
word that had raised such abhorrence in the public
house, here brought no gaze around to examine
the speaker, though the room was small enough for
all to overhear us. The sodden drinkers went on
staring into the dark spaces that held the residue of
their thoughts. "Here, you; leave off that." The
small dog had followed us into the cellar, and was
now whining and scratching at the cabby's knee.
"Leave off, I say, mange-bait; what's got into you?"
He looked around to the door and saw a figure
making its way down the damp stone steps, balancing an awkward weight across the shoulders. "So
that's it, then?" he addressed the dog. "Hungry, are
you? Well, well, a bite would not be amiss – for
beast or master." He shot another of his slyly cal-
culating glances at me.

The hawking butcher – for such a one it was that
had entered – worked his circuit around the cellar,
tilting his basket in front of each drinker to expose
his bloody merchandise. He found scant trade
among a crowd that had lost all appetite except for
drink; each inebriate shook his head in turn or
continued gazing dully before him. The cabby
whistled and signalled the man over. The dog's
whining became frenzied as the dark-stained bas-

ket approached. My own stomach clenched at the smell of the gone-high meat.

"Samuel, me lad–" the cabby and the butcher were evidently acquaintances of long standing. "What delicacies do you got tonight?" He poked through the uncut joints, sending aloft a few buzzing flies. "A tuppenny chop, then," he decided at last. "And the scraps for the hound." He watched with relish as the butcher hacked off the desired piece. Both men's faces turned towards me when the meat was held aloft on the knife's point; leaning back from the odour, I paid once more.

"Very kind of you, sir," said the cabby, dangling a raw strip down to the dog's mouth. "I do appreciate it." The chop had been carried off to a farther room; a sizzling noise of fire and grease wafted out. "This here gentleman," he said, pointing to me, "wants to be taken to Wetwick. Fancy that, eh?"

The hawking butcher, his basket up on his shoulder again, lowered the jar he had taken from its place in front of me. His wide grin was damp from the stale beer. "Does he, then? Wouldn't have thought him the type, just from looking at him. No wonder he's not hungry for this sort of meat." One blood-mottled finger tapped the side of the basket. "It's some other bit of mutton he's after." His lewd smile twisted even further as he winked at me, then turned and laboured his burden towards the door.

The cabby signalled for his jar to be refilled. "Yes, indeed," he said, leaning across the table. His creased face exuded the conspiratorial bonhomie of one who delightedly assumes that all the world is as foul-minded as he is. He fell into smirking reminiscence: "Many's the time, all these years I've worked as a long-night man – that's what we call it, mind, six of the evenings to ten the following mornings – many's the time I've had fine gentlemen such as yourself asking to be taken to the borough of Wetwick. Fine gentlemen, indeed... and roaring boys." The phrase generated some excitement in him; his eyes widened in his flushed face. "Eh? Eh? The roaring boys – out for a lark, they were, yes." He gazed at his reflection in the renewed ale, smiling as if satisfied at what he saw. "The green girls – that's what you lordly rakes want, isn't it now? Eh?"

I made no reply, stupefied into muteness by the closeness of the den and the alcoholic fumes it contained. The cabby's pallid face danced in front of me, a child's grinning puppet given over to wickedness and the relish it found therein.

"Mind you, now," he went on, unstoppable, "though it be to your heart's desire–" The last word sent him into a salivating ekstasis. "– your heart's desire, says I, a greater bargain is impossible to find. And why is that? Eh?"

I perceived that he was asking me a riddle. "I have no idea." My head had started to throb.

"Because – ho-ho! – because all it takes to get there is a single coin. Ha!" He choked and beat his fist on the table in his mirth. "A single coin! Very clever, that! Eh?"

"Yes…" I agreed feebly, attempting to mask my incomprehension. "Yes, quite amusing."

He eyed me more closely. "Of course," he said slowly, "it has to be the right coin. Don't it, sir? There's only one will do for it." He drew back, waiting for my reply.

I saw that under his smile there was an element other than jest. At the same moment, in a flash of understanding, I realised the point of his words. Keeping his gaze locked with mine, I drew the velvet bag out of my pocket, extracted the Saint Monkfish sovereign, and laid it on the table in front of him.

The cabby picked up the coin and held it glittering in the candlelight. For a moment he studied the remarkable profile on its surface; then he handed it back to me. With an exaggeratedly servile nod, he said, "Right you are, sir. Most pleased to be of service to the cognoscenti. To Wetwick, then." He looked up when a cracked plate, shiny with grease, was laid in front of him with the blackened chop upon it.

I watched as he sawed the redolent meat apart with his pocket knife, spearing the pieces with its point and conveying them to his mouth. "Shall we be off, then?" I said.

He jabbed another morsel and held it down to the dog, who adroitly licked it off the blade.

"There's no call for haste, sir." He took another
bite. "Plenty of time, as you well know." He signalled for another round.

Time within the dingy confines of the stale beer
shop seemed to congeal into an opaque substance,
similar to the speckled drops of fat on the dirty
plate. The jars in front of the cabby seemed to mul-
tiply, until there were half-a-dozen empty vessels
strewn about the table. I had even drained one, in
a vain attempt to slake the thirst imparted by the
smoky air. This further impaired the normal
progress of the hours; I felt as if I had been trapped
in the cellar with my leering companion since the
beginning of Creation.

I made an attempt to rouse myself, as though
fighting to the top of a weed-filled pond. "When,"
I said thickly, "do we leave? For Wetwick." Across
the room I could barely make out the form of the
slatternly woman, holding the baby to her flaccid
breast; its small head lolled back, the eyes two
sightless grey pockets.

The cabby looked up from his own contemplations. His grin was even looser now, slack enough
to reveal the gums at the bottom of his stained
teeth. "Why, when it's time, sir. You know that."

"Yes… of course. But–" My fuddled brain struggled to express what seemed a momentous
concept. "But how will we know when it's time?"

He shook his head, goggling at my self-evident
stupidity. "He'll tell us, then, won't he? How else?"

"He'll tell us?"

"The dog." He jerked his horn-ridged thumb at the small creature at his feet.

I leaned over the table, knocking aside the empty jars, and looked down at the small animal. It returned my stare with what seemed to be no more than average canine intelligence. I sat back heavily in my chair, perplexed as to how the indicated communication was to be made.

No sooner had I done so than an excited yapping came from the beast. The edge of its terrier yelp was sharp enough to rouse a few of the cellar's denizens from their stupor, as the dog barked at the empty doorway and back at its master in turn.

"Up you come," announced the cabby. He shoved his chair back and pulled himself on to his feet, seeming little the worse for the drinking bout as he adjusted his cloak and hat. For my part, I had need to accomplish the same in stages, balancing myself against the table to overcome the leaden deadweight that had been instilled in my legs.

The dog grew more excited, skittering around the cabby's boots on its three good legs, and still yapping at the dark open air at the head of the stone steps blundered heavily into one of the other tables as the cabby led me out; the blow destroyed the precarious equilibrium of the young gentleman who had rested his elbows there, face cupped in his palms; I heard behind me his slow pitch forward and sprawling collapse on to the damp floor.

Once outside, the night air on my sweating face
revived me somewhat. I soon found myself deposited inside the dilapidated hansom cab, its seat
of ancient cracked leather sagging beneath me, as
I listened to the driver mounting on to his perch
with the barking dog in the crook of his arm. Its
claws pattered across the roof of the cab even as
the horse was whipped into life. We had soon careered on wobbling axles out of the alley and into
the larger street beyond.

The racketing motions of the ill-sprung vehicle
sent me sprawling across the seat. My brain, still
labouring under the weight of whatever decoction
the stale beer had been doctored with in order to
increase its potency, struggled to make sense of the
vista of lamps and mist-shrouded streets reeling by
outside. The horse, perhaps through fear of further
abuse, was capable of greater speed than I would
have imagined possible; the rush of wind tore
through my hair as I gripped the window sill and
craned my neck to shout at the cabby: "Is this the
way to Wetwick, then?"

My words seemed to fuel his high humour as
much as the alcohol had. His grin grew even more
maniacal as he snapped the whip over the head of the
dog. The small creature, too, had worked itself into a
frenzy, dashing back and forth on the cab's roof,
barking louder as if to urge the horse on its exertions.
"To Wetwick!" cried the cabby. "For one of your
faith – 'tis the new Rome! All roads lead to Wetwick!"

I fell back inside, jostled by a sudden turning that tilted the cab on to one wheel for a moment. A few white faces shot past, pedestrians startled by the vehicle's clattering haste. Above my head, the barking and scrabbling of the small dog seemed to take on a perceptible pattern: when its claws pattered to one side of the roof, the yapping sounding in that direction, the cabby swung the vehicle around correspondingly at the first opportunity. Gaining the window once more, I looked out and recognised the district through which we were passing: the smell of the river was strong, wafting through a region of ramshackle docks and warehouses. We were not far from my own home in Clerkenwell, having apparently travelled about in a circle.

The dog ceased its noise simultaneously – with the hansom pulling to a halt. The cabby pulled open the small hatch in the centre of the roof and leered down at me through the opening. "Your destination, sir," he said with sly insinuation.

I stepped down from the cab and looked about. I had some vague idea of the area, if not this exact street; I at least knew I could find my way back to my shop, within a good walk's distance. Perhaps the cabby was playing me for a fool, driving about with no more idea of how to reach the perhaps-mythical Wetwick than I had. However I was glad to be free of his bone-shaker, and the area in which I had alighted was at least not deserted.

Though the street were without lamps, I could discern a considerable number of figures sidling past, close to the shuttered fronts of the buildings.

"What do I owe you?" I called up to the cabby on his perch.

"Ah! You are a card, sir!" Both he and the dog looked down at me. "You know full well I get my whack at the other end – your fare's been paid by Mollie Maud, hasn't it, then?" He whipped the horse into a trot, and had soon vanished into the river's fog.

My quest had seemed to lead me into more inconvenience than adventure thus far – home and bed now appeared to me as the most attractive notion. I stepped across the cobbled street to ask specific directions from one of the passers-by.

As I approached closer, and was able to see them better through the mist that laid its damp velvet against my face, I noted that they all, men and women alike, moved in much the same fashion, a curious hunched-over, sidling motion – as though; crab-like, they moved laterally as much as forward. For a moment I thought the cabby's dog had jumped off the hansom and had run back here, as I spotted a similar animal running ahead of one of the figures; then I saw several of the scrawny terriers, each seeming to lead its shabbily dressed master in the same direction along the pavement.

The sense of being in a dream again enveloped me. I stood a few feet away from the line of pedestrians as they scurried past me. Slowly, I reached out a hand to grab hold of a bent shoulder. The halted man lifted his head and looked round at me. I found myself gazing into the living counterpart of the face on the Saint Monkfish coin.

5

A Coiner's Fate

I have need of rest; my hand trembles even as I write these words. To retrieve the past is no great effort, when the events to be recalled are so firmly imprinted on the mind. It is existence in the present, the bleak wreckage and residue of what has gone before, that is so burdensome.

Upon completion of the previous section of these memoirs, I laid down my pen and went out of the house again, hoping to briefly expunge remembered night with the brightness of the current day. Blessedly anonymous in this district, I strolled through the crowds intent on their own business. Lost in their number, I found a moment of peace that was broken only when I thought I saw a familiar face staring at me. Turning towards it, I felt my heart leap up into my throat as I recognised the sloping, exophthalmic, and purse-jawed visage of one of the Wetwick denizens. I staggered backwards, blundering into the people nearest me, fearing that the parishioners of that region had emigrated with me from their former haunts. The appalling vision dissolved when, curious about the rising murmur behind him, a local fishmonger turned about, and I saw that the dreaded physiognomy was no more than that of an unusually large carp he was carrying on his shoulder towards his stall. With my pulse still trembling inside me, I scurried back towards the shelter of my home.

Between that sentence and this lies a good hour of lying on my bed, soothing my fright with a tumblerful of peat-smelling Scotch whisky, a comfort to which I was introduced when marooned on the Hebridean island of Groughay with the increasingly lunatical Scape. All that time, when I had but recently escaped being murdered at the hands of the Godly Army, the brown nectar had been perhaps all that had preserved my own sanity as I had watched my fellow castaway assembling his absurd flying machine from sticks and carrion.

Thus fortified, the warmth of the whisky dispelling both the chill of the air and that of memory, I returned to my labours.

On that dark London street, I saw for the first time in living flesh those features that had been represented to me before only in wax and metal. Though within the possible range of variation of general humanity, they were decidedly placed at the unnerving end of the scale. What would have been described as gross ugliness in one individual was made uncanny by the familial resemblance between the man I had stopped and the others hurrying by us – I could have found myself among no more alien-seeming tribe than if I had stepped into the court of Jenghiz Khan.

The round, protruding eyes gave the man whose shoulder I still grasped a deceptive appearance of stupidity. Certainly, he was in fuller possession of his faculties than I was at the moment. He scowled – or gave as close an approximation of that expression as his slope-browed, chinless face could provide – and twisted his shoulder free, then hurried away on his nocturnal errands.

I stepped back from the pavement to let the others pass by. Though they were all possessed of the same goggling features, the variation among them was as of a parade of human society and its constituents: I saw, in quick order, the young mechanic and tradesman, cloth-capped and with knotted neckerchief, the distinctive sidling gait marked with quick vigour; the elderly, both of rotund corpulence and skeletal wasting, assisted in their sideways progress with walking sticks; women clutching their head-shawls fast beneath their chins, of every age from grannyhood to *ingenue*, the latter blushing modestly under a stranger's gaze and hurrying close to their families' protection; and children, both well-scrubbed and ragged. These young ones, not yet instructed in their elders' ways, gaped at me

openly as their parents dragged them along, their
wide mouths falling open like latchless coin purses.
In more than one little girl's arm was clutched a
simple plaything, a doll with similar features.

One child, momentarily separated from her parents and blinded by her small fists knuckling the
tears from her protuberant eyes, blundered into
my leg. Moved to pity, I extracted the ugly doll
from my own coat pocket and placed it in the
child's hands. She gulped down her sobbing long
enough to blink in amazement at the unexpected
gift; when she looked up at her benefactor, her
mouth rounded in a startled O at my face, and she
quickly scuttled off in terror.

For a moment I had thought that the cabby's
terrier had abandoned him and returned to this
spot, as I sighted what seemed to be the exact same
creature frisking about one of the pedestrians barking with the same highpitched yap and darting a
few feet ahead and returning as though guiding its
new master in the desired direction. Then I noted
the creature's double, and yet more like it, all darting in amongst the sidling steps, barking in ragged
unison and dashing back and forth in a sheep-
herder's manner. In total there must have been
over a dozen of the small dogs along just the short
stretch of pavement that I could see, varying only
in the colours and spots of their coats.

The novelty of the situation in which I had
found myself abated after a few minutes. While

the individuals passing by were not of comely appearance, neither were they the most repulsive I
had ever seen; indeed, there was more disorienta-
tion aroused by their resemblance to each other
than any other factor, akin to the odd confusion
brought on by the sight of identical twins or
triplets, where the eye itself seems to be somehow
stuttering as it passes from one face to its exact
match. Perhaps having encountered that distinctly
ichthyoid shaping of the skull in the form of the
ugly doll and the Saint Monkfish coin had prepared me somewhat for its appearance *in vivo*. At
any rate it was with only small and easily suppressed shudders that I stepped up to one of them
again, intent on renewing my inquiries.

"I beg your pardon – but is this the borough
of Wetwick?"

The figure I addressed made his face even uglier
with a scowl, and brushed rudely by me without
returning so much as a word. I repeated the question to the next behind, and received the same
brusque silence. These seemed a very peculiar
breed of Londoner: most of the city's residents ex-
pressed their ill manners through the coarseness
of their volubility, seizing any chance to fill an unfortunate stranger's ear with their unsolicited
philosophies on any subject possible. Even if
money were required to free their tongues and
produce the information required; the transaction
was forthrightly indicated with the sign of an open

palm; the faces of the most shabbily dressed of these folk had glared at me with outright hostility and distrust.

The thought of money sparked a notion in my brain. I heard again the cabby's words: *a single coin… of course, it has to be the right coin…* I drew the Saint Monkfish sovereign from my waistcoat pocket and contemplated it. The odd coin had produced a surprising measure of service from the cabby; perhaps it was the key here as well. I could not see what I had to lose by the venture.

"My good man." I held out the coin, gripped at its edge by finger and thumb; the glint of bright metal was sufficient under the thin starlight to catch the attention of the next passer-by. "I wonder if you could give me some assistance."

The experiment met with success. At the sight of the coin, the eyes of the young man widened beyond their already extraordinary circularity. He pulled his cap off, holding it against his shirt front with his work-roughened hands as he respectfully awaited my query. The servile response seemed more suited to a village rustic than a denizen of the city.

Pleased with the talisman's efficacy, I repeated the question that had previously elicited no answer. "Is this the borough of Wetwick?"

The fellow nodded dumbly.

"I'm looking for a man named Fexton; I've been informed he lives in this district. Do you know of him?"

Another nod.

My heart lightened; at last I was making some progress in this quest. I only hoped that the silent responses did not mean I was talking to a total mute. "Then can you tell me where I can find this Fexton?"

He grasped my arm and dragged me a few yards to a narrow alley branching off the street. Jabbing his blunt finger towards the Stygian darkness, he said, "There" – or so I understood him: the sound was closer to *Nyuhair*, as if the speaker were struggling with a malformed palate.

"Mr Fexton lives down there?" I could barely discern the outlines of the building terminating the courtyard to which the alley gave entrance.

The nod was even more vigorous; the fellow had perhaps assumed that I was some person of considerable rank, engaged on official business. "Upstairs" – *uh'snyairs* – with the finger now indicating a dimly lit window some distance above.

"Many thanks." My informant, perceiving that my questions were at an end, scurried off after his fellows, manifestly grateful that the encounter was over.

I made my way down the alley, cautious against any hands that might try to lay hold of me. The night's dampness had combined with the decaying refuse on the cobblestones, resulting in a footing both precarious and odorous beneath my boot-soles. Placing a hand against the wall for balance,

I snatched it back in disgust, having felt something with the yielding pulpiness of rotten fruit; in the dark, I had the uncanny illusion of whatever it had been, crawling snail-like away. The mists had done nothing to cleanse the air of its miasma of soot and greasy cooking fires; the smells of squalid habitation pressed upon me as I stepped into the small courtyard. The end building's door swung away, unhindered by lock or bolt, when I raised my hand against the bare wood. I craned my neck to peer up a ramshackle staircase, fancying that I could see some trace of the candlelight that had been visible in the upstairs window.

"Hall–oo," I called into the darkness above. "Is there anybody there?"

No answer – at least not in words. I thought I heard a faint scraping noise, of feet or a chair-leg, on a floorboard overhead. The banister swayed in my grip as I mounted the creaking steps.

I ascended two floors and now could see the fragment of candlelight sliding from underneath a door a little way from the landing. The planks, eaten away by mould, muffled my knock. "Mr Fexton?" I bent my head close to hear my reply.

"What? What?" A startled croak from the room on the other side. To my ear came a sound as if various papers were being rapidly shuffled, perhaps to hide them from unwanted scrutiny. "Who's there?"

"I'm looking for a certain Fexton," I shouted. "I greatly desire to ask him a few questions."

"Questions? Questions?" The voice of the unseen person went up in pitch to a rasping shriek. The paper noises increased to a veritable storm flurry, punctuated by the sharp clatter of metal instruments. "What kind of questions?"

It was of course likely that one who made his living in such a fashion would be suspicious of any callers. But then, as is often the case in any walk of life, greed could be made to overpower caution. "It's in regard to, ah, a business proposition. Which would be of some profit to this Fexton, if I could locate him." No great lie there; I was prepared to pay a few shillings for whatever I could discover.

For a few seconds there was silence, which I took to signal cogitation on the other's part, broken by the scraping creak of the door's hinge. A bespectacled eye, squinting behind the curved glass, inspected me through a narrow gap. The man appeared to be extremely small in stature, the gaze being at a level quite beneath my own. A sharp-pointed nose, and a chin stubbled with grey, protruded in the manner of some sea-creature squeezing through a submerged crevice. "Business?" demanded the scowling face. "What kind of business?"

I held up the Saint Monkfish sovereign in answer.

The man's eye widened at the sight of the coin, then darted up to my face. "Where did you get that? Eh?"

Back into my pocket it went. "I wish to speak to Mr Fexton," I said with cold civility. "If you can summon him here, or direct me to where he may be found, I would greatly appreciate it."

The door opened wider to reveal the man's face in full. A few strands of greasy hair were plastered forward over an otherwise barren scalp; his face was unpleasantly rough, but not as though from youthful pustules or a later pox, which are by nature eruptions below; rather it seemed as if the skin had been corroded and etched from the outside, as cliffs carved by the ceaseless action of the ocean upon them. The impression of diminished height I had previously gained was due to the curvature of his spine, a deformity that left him hunched rabbit-like over his discoloured hands.

"I'm Fexton," he announced. (I had of course suspected as much.) He scrabbled back into his chambers to allow me entrance. "Who're you, then? What's this here business you talk about?"

I saw that there was another occupant of the room: a terrier, identical to the ones I had seen on the street, bounced from spot to spot as those breeds will, one moment laying its front paws on the window sill and the next sniffing at my trousers cuff.

"Get down, you cur!" shouted Fexton at the dog, aiming a blow at it with the stick by which he supported his misshapen frame, and nearly toppling himself with the violence of his swing. The dog cowered abjectly, just out of his reach. "Come, come–" He was addressing me again, as he tottered about the room. "I haven't time no, no, not at all – no time, y'see – what's your concern with me? Eh? Speak out, man." A deal table, rickety as its owner, trembled as he pawed through the disorder upon its surface: a zinc basin, various mottled flasks, and a series of lead moulds were the visible evidence of his occupation.

My eye was drawn involuntarily across the rest of the room's clutter. A mound of crumpled, grease-spotted wrappings in one corner indicated the site of his furtive dinners; a bed, no more than a thin pallet on the sagging floor, was covered with grey clothing and a thick coat acting as blankets. A crude shelf nailed to one wall supported a row of books: the titles I deciphered were all of the order of *Sub-Umbra; or, Sport Amongst the She Noodles* and *The Spreeish Spouter; or, Flash Cove's Slap Up Reciter*, and similar cheap lechery (not that I recognised them other than by reputation). The general impression of the man's quarters was of sad, solitary degeneration.

His rasping voice broke into my musing inspection: "Speak up! There's no time!"

"I'm searching for a maker of coins–" I began.

"Coins? Coins?" His tortoise-like neck stretched its tendons to the breaking point as he glared at me. "I don't know anything about any bloody coins – nothing, I tell you. Soldiers is what I make;

very fine, very coveted they are – in the collections
of the finest gentlemen!" His denials mounted to a
shrill peak. "No, no coins – I don't know anything!
You won't get me that easy!"

It was easy to surmise that past investigations
into his activities had resulted in unpleasant consequences for him. "I assure you," I said in as
soothing a manner as I could manage, "I make no
reference to forgeries – my interest is rather in
harmless curiosities, such as the one I just showed
you at the door."

His eyes narrowed in suspicion. He drew the
stopper from one of the flasks on the table, and
tilted it to his lips; the juniper scent of cheap gin
mixed with the sharper chemical odours tainting
the air.

I pressed on: "The coin... bearing Saint Monkfish's profile...?"

Fexton drew the back of his hand across his lips.
"Eh? What about it, then?"

"Are you the manufacturer of that item?"

"What if I am? Eh? What business is it of yours?"

His snarling manner irritated me; it was only
with some effort of self-mastery that I refrained
from sharper words. "I have made it my business,
sir; I find the article... intriguing, shall we say. I
would like to know more of its significance–"

"Huh!" Fexton's mottled skin flushed with the
effect of his liquor. "As if you didn't already know
enough of that! You and your kind – filthy bug-

gers; filthy, filthy…" His voice ebbed into a mutter, drowned at last by another swig from his flask.

As with the cabbyman, he had assumed some degree of knowledge on my part that was in fact completely lacking. "I assure you," I said, "my questions are sincerely put–"

"Oh, yah!" mocked the coiner. "Sincerely – that's good! Very droll, that is!" The gin dribbled from the point of his chin.

"And of course I'd be willing to pay…"

That brought back a measure of sobriety. His eyes grew calculatingly narrow behind his spectacles. "Pay? How much?"

I shrugged my shoulders. "It would depend; upon the value of the information–"

A furious volley of barking interrupted me. The terrier skittered to the window, placed its paws upon the sill, and yapped at some event in the night's darkness invisible to us. It turned and barked at its master, as if describing the signal that had roused it.

"Damn you! Cursed hound!" The noise drove him to a fury, saliva dappling his lip. He raised his stick and brought it with a sickening crack against the dog's spine; the wretched animal crouched beneath the blow, waiting for the next. "I'll teach you–"

I caught Fexton's wrist, holding the stick aloft. The animal's misery, compounded of pain and suffering loyalty to its cruel master, angered me. "Stop that," I ordered. "Have you no decency? Abusing a poor beast in such a manner."

"Yes, yes; of course…" He cringed disgustingly, as if expecting me to turn the stick on his bowed back. "But you don't know; you don't know–" His eyes turned towards the dog as it whined in suppressed excitement, eager attention turned back to the window.

"I came here with a few simple questions, hoping to find equally, simple answers." By now I was sick of the cramped, foul-smelling room and its noxious occupant. "If you can assist me, and wish to receive the appropriate recompense, then say so; if not–"

"But there's no time! Not now!" He scrabbled about in a corner, drawing a ragged coat over his trembling limbs. "I must go – very urgent; you don't know how much so." A partially unravelled muffler was wrapped around his scrawny throat. "Come back – yes! Come back later, and I'll tell you anything you want to know. But not now!"

He darted past me towards the door, the sadly faithful dog following at his heel. From the landing I shouted down at him as he rushed down the clattering stairs: "When?"

"After – after midnight!" The dog's renewed barking mingled with his reply. "Yes – then!"

I soon heard through the window the tap of his stick on the courtyard stones. The oppressive atmosphere of the room soon drove me out, away from the building and into the cleaner night air.

The street beyond the alley entrance was deserted now, the people of remarkable aspect having hurried along to their destination. Taking careful note of the doors I passed and the turns I made, so that I would be able to retrace my steps, I quit the district. The lights of a small public house drew me towards it; I could wait there in relative comfort until the hour of my appointment with the so-far uncommunicative Fexton. When I first looked around the public house's door, I was greatly relieved to see that this had not been the point to which the residents of Wetwick had been headed; the drinkers and layabouts inside were of no more than average ugliness, wondering with a sodden surliness about the appearance of a gentleman in their midst, but at least not staring at me with the round popping eyes I had found in the district I had just left. I must admit, that as I sat at one of the more removed tables, maintaining a careful sobriety through the judicious nursing of a small ale, my heart was beating fast and high up in my throat. The great adventure on which I had launched myself was turning out to be a capital amusement: mysterious denizens of a London previously unknown to me; the colourful squalor of poverty and vice, generally reported to people of my respectable ilk only in the columns of Mayhew's excellent reportage in the *Morning Chronicle*: a *rendez-vous* to be kept with an actual transgressor of the law and apparent prison *habitué* – at that moment it seemed as if I had completely broken the shackles of my old mundane existence and stepped into some wilder, free life.

At the designated hour I hastened back to Fexton's abode. The street was still deserted, but that was to be expected, given the lateness.

Once again I mounted the precarious steps and stood on the landing outside Fexton's door. I rapped upon it and called his name, but no answer came. But, leaning close, I could hear an anxious-sounding whine from the small dog within. Perhaps its master, returned from the secretive errand on which they had embarked, had fallen asleep.

I pushed open the door and peered within. The candle on the table had burned level with the cracked dish that held it, the flame guttering in the pool of wax. By the flickering illumination I could see, not the coiner, but only the dog scratching at what I took to be an elongated bundle of old rags upon the floor. It renewed its whining, prodding with its sharp muzzle the object so much bigger than it. As I bent closer to see, the dog's efforts succeeded in rolling part of the bundle free: the blank face of its master, one eye hidden by the shattered glass of his spectacle lens, gaped up at me. The dog let loose of the grey shirt collar and nuzzled the unresponsive visage.

I stood back aghast, seeing for the first time the shining wet surface of the floor beneath the stricken man. The front of his shirt was imbued

with the same scarlet, still oozing from the rents in
the cloth and the flesh beneath. The prints of my
boots remained in the puddled blood – as the sight
drove me stumbling backwards.

My heels caught on something soft; I only
saved myself from falling by catching the edge of
the table beside me. I looked behind me, and –
with heart racing beyond excitement to fear –
saw another form, as silent and motionless as
that of Fexton.

I knelt down, legs trembling, and found the
man's upraised shoulder. The figure turned over
on to its back, and I found myself staring into the
burnished, scar-etched features of the Brown
Leather Man. His chest was also slashed and wet,
but the fluid mingling on the floor with Fexton's
darkening blood was itself clear; the briny smell,
sharp in my memory, came to my nostrils as I
looked at my own glistening hand.

The expiring candle blew out in a sudden rush
of wind from the doorway. I scrambled upright as
the light from a small hand lantern fell upon me.
Dimly beyond its glare, I could make out the silhouettes of a pair of men.

"What's this, then?" spoke one of them. "Who's
this 'un?"

"Mother o' Gawd. I told you we should've
brought all the gear the first time." His companion
leaned forward with the lantern. "Best give him a
plumper 'n' bring 'm along."

I gathered my scattered wits, having gained the impression that these men had no good will towards me, and were possibly the authors of the carnage that filled the room. "See here—"

My argument went no further than that; the men were on either side; the larger of them stood a good head above me. Or so I thought: it suddenly seemed as if he were looking down at me from an even greater distance. "Give 'im another one," boomed a voice from miles away.

There was no need; the first blow finally breached my senses, as if it had been a cannonball shattering a castle wall that remains seemingly intact a moment before it crumbles into bits. My cheek lay against the wet floor, betwixt the Brown Leather Man's corpse and my assailant's boots. For a moment, before I lost all awareness, I fancied that I was flying, as one of the men lifted me on to his shoulder.

6
A Church Service Goes Awry

The robed sages of Arabia Felix have written:
"There are two things without limit – the stupidity
of Man and the mercy of God." (I have had time
for religious studies since my retreat from the
world's affairs.) I have not yet had proof of the latter, but the former was borne out by the fulfilment
of my own lamentable desires.

I had wished for Excitement, and an end to
Boredom; these had been given me, and in abun-
dant measure. But as I regained consciousness, my
disordered thoughts reassembling inside my throbbing skull, I would have cried out for the return of
every drab and predictable second of my previous
existence, so foolishly despised and irrevocably
lost. I would have cried thus, but for the rag
wadded in my mouth, stoppering all speech.

The precise nature of my confinement gradually
became clear to me. The back of my head – seemingly intact, though I would have otherwise

supposed that the blow to it had left fragments on
the floor of Fexton's room jostled against the
planks of a small cart, sparking a fresh throb of
pain with each cobblestone under the creaking
wheels. My hands were trussed behind me; against
each shoulder another body was pressed tight – the
cold forms of Fexton and the Brown Leather Man,
I guessed them to be. A rough cover of sacking had
been thrown across the faces of the living and the
dead, to shield us from the inquiring eyes of any
who might look out their windows upon us as we
made our progress through the night-clad city. A
few times I heard the abducting ruffians murmur
to each other from their perch behind the reins.

A softer murmur of lapping water, and a change
in the air filtering through the stiff cloth over my
face, signalled our approach to the riverside. The
cart came to a halt, shifting slightly when the two
men clambered down. From the hollow strike of
their boots I surmised that we were on a wharf
somewhere in the city's docklands.

I was fully conscious by this point, my thoughts
scurrying to find some exit from my predicament.
Whatever curiosity I had once had concerning the
affairs of either of the deceased who shared the
cart-bed with me, was now extinguished entire.
Though I had, through my amateur investigations,
discovered less than nothing, with a net result of
more mystification than that which I had commenced, I was now perfectly willing to accept

continuing ignorance of these matters' explanations as my lot. Surely these men had no malice
against me specifically; I was but an inconvenient
witness to their unsavoury transactions. I desperately attempted to indicate my willingness to blank
my mind of what I had seen, allowing them to go
about their business with no fear of scrutiny from
myself or any of the constabulary I might have otherwise alerted, but my assuring words were stifled
by the wadded rag.

"Here, you," said one of them, prodding me
through the sacking. "Stop gargling about like that."

I did not heed this admonishment, instead re-
doubling my thrashing efforts at communication.
The ensuing noises earned me a clout on the head
that left me dazed and silent, but still cognizant of
events around me.

"Where is he, then?" muttered one of the men.

"Hang on – here he comes." A third set of footsteps sounded faint against the far end of the wharf's
timbers, growing louder as they strode closer.

A servile anxiety had sounded in my captors'
twin voices. This gave rise to the hope that the
awaited figure now approaching was their master,
or in some other relationship of authority over
them. Doubtless, if I could present my case to him,
he would correct his underlings' mistake and have
me set free, not wishing to compound whatever
iniquities had been involved in the deaths of Fexton and the Brown Leather Man. The vow of a

gentleman to keep a discreet silence would surely be bond enough to warrant my safe passage out of their keeping.

The new footsteps stopped at the side of the cart. All three men drew a small distance away, their hushed tones mingling in a hurried conference. I strained at the cords around my wrists, anxious to be free again and away from the grisly freight on either side of me.

The murmuring voices lapsed into silence; I could hear the trio returning to the cart; the obscuring sack-cloth was snatched away from my face. Past the glare of a lantern held above by one of the ruffians, I could barely discern the aspect of the gang's captain. Taller and more slender than his squat and heavy-muscled minions, cloaked and top-hatted as if freshly arrived from opera or ballroom; all but his eyes were hidden behind a silk scarf that he raised with a gloved hand to prevent any possible recognition.

I returned the man's inspecting gaze, my muffled voice striving to impart to him that I had information of an urgent nature to communicate, when he drew back from the lantern's circle of light. "Yes." I heard his voice in the darkness, the one word sufficient to indicate the speaker's high degree of cultivation. "Take him out with the others," he instructed the two ruffians.

A moment passed before I realised that I was to share whatever disposition had been decided upon for the two cadavers nestled with me in the cart. I shouted, producing only a gagging cough through the rag in my mouth, and banged my heels against the wood, but to no avail: the gentleman who had so offhandedly sealed my fate could be heard striding away down the wharf. I was roughly seized and slung between the two others' hands as though I were a hundredweight of potatoes, then just as roughly deposited in the damp bottom of a small boat bobbing alongside the dock pilings. My breath was knocked from my lungs by the inert forms of the two corpses landing one after another on top of me.

The boat tilted as the two men clambered down into it. Over the top of Fexton's skull, the strands of his lank, greasy hair plastered tendril-like against my own face, I could see the edge of the wharf sliding away to reveal the stars overhead, as the self-appointed Charon used an oar to push away from the pilings.

"Leave off your be-damned snuffling and croaking." The other ruffian gave me a kick from where he sat at the prow of the tiny craft. "Save your breath; you'll be swimming soon enough." The slap of the oars against the dark water provided a dismal counterpoint to his ill-tempered growl, as his companion rowed farther into a deserted stretch of the Thames.

"This'll do," came the pronouncement. "Likely no deeper than hereabouts."

"Shouldn't we have weighted them?" The second brought the oars inside. "They'll come up again, now won't they?"

A grisly consideration: "The tide's running. If they come bobbing up, it'll be miles downriver."

As I view my hobbled actions with the grace of hindsight, I realise now I would have been better occupied with prayer and silent contemplation of eternity than with attempting to mouth words past the cloth in my mouth. I entreated the men; offered fabulous sums for my release; threatened them with legions of the constabulary – the rag reduced all to a choking mumble.

The deadweight on my chest was more than halved, as the men lifted Brown Leather's corpse from on top – "Come along, you great ugly bastard," said one, between grunts of effort – and, swinging it by the feet and under the arms, threw it clear of the tottering boat. The impact of the body on the water threw a spray across my own face.

"And you now–" The ruffians were in a quite jocular mood as they picked up Fexton's lighter weight. "Faugh! Couldn't be bothered with a bath when you was alive, from the smell of you – well, you'll have a long one, if a cold one, now, me boy. Count of three, now – one – two in you go!" Another splash followed the first.

"Mubble, mubble, mubble," mocked one of the men, as he brought his grinning face close to mine. "Wordy sod, aren't you just?"

"He can tell it all to his mates," joined the other, indicating the river's dark water with a thumb over his shoulder.

"Now, let's not be hasty." The two of them crouched at my head and feet, the first tapping my forehead with one broad finger. "Seems a very likeable sort of fellow – very likeable, indeed."

"Here, what are you on about?" Lifting my head, I could just see the other's scowl.

"Well, I just thinks a likeable sort of gentleman such as this 'un – prosperous, too, from the looks of that watch we took off him – seems a shame to just pitch him into the drink without so much as giving him a chance to express a proper sort of gratitude to us, if you know what I'm getting at."

I nodded my head vigorously, striking the still-aching back of my head against the boat's bottom, and attempted to signal with my eyes that I was in complete accord with these sentiments.

"Bugger that." The hinted proposition was rudely greeted. "Worth our flaming heads, it is – he said pitch this one in, too, so in he goes, I says."

No! I shouted – or tried to. Listen to your friend!

"Keep your braces on. I was just toying with the poor devil. See how big his eyes are! – he thought I wanted to let him go."

"Leave off – bleeding cold it is out here."

My tormentor grasped me under the arms. "Right enough. Sorry, me fine gent – it's us for the gin-shop, but we won't be seeing you there."

I felt myself raised up between them into the air, with the first swing to impart the distance necessary for clearing the side of the boat. My brain seemed to rock in identical motion inside its confines as the pin-point stars above streaked, held, then reversed their direction.

Water erupted around me, yet I oddly felt myself rising a bit higher in the chill air. I realised that the two ruffians, shouting in terror and releasing their grip on my limbs, were falling with me as the boat lifted on a sudden upwelling from beneath, tipping all of its occupants out into the river.

I struck the water, parting the thin layer of mist cloaking it, and felt the chill darkness flood upward over my face. The cloth was fortuitously dislodged from my mouth; gasping for breath, I bobbed to the surface, still bound at wrist and ankle. In the thin, spectral light I saw the overturned boat, its keel now a shattered, gaping hole.

A few feet away from me, the river murk was lashed into foam by the struggling figures of the two ruffians. Their faces were contorted with fright as a third form, a man, rose behind them. Gripping each one's shoulder, disdainful of the flailing arms, the dark shape thrust them churning under the dark water, as though they were but two stanchions by which he could thrust himself bodily clear of the river.

A moment's glimpse was all that was afforded to me. In the panic and shock that the sudden immersion had induced in me, I thought I saw the face of the Brown Leather Man, grimly terrible as the stars glinted off the wet-shining visage. his scarred grimace rigid as he drowned his murderers.

I slid under the water again. My breath burned in my lungs – briefly; then the water became yet darker, and, just before my consciousness dissolved entire, the cold drained away my own blood.

Slowly, as a dreamer recognizes the contours of his pillow, I became aware that my face was pressed against a gravelly muck. At first, I believed this to be the river bottom, and that I had come to rest upon it; my thoughts were but a last flicker before the final extinguishing, or else the beginning of that new, incorporeal nature promised to us in the teachings of the Church. I would, I hoped dimly, be shortly ascending to a higher abode.

My theological musings were interrupted by a gagging fit that disgorged a considerable amount of river water on to the damp field on which I lay. Lifting my head, I found myself shivering in the chill night air, my sodden clothes clinging about my frame; I took this to mean I was not yet dead. By some means I had been restored from what had been meant to be my watery grave, to a place of comparative safety.

Safety, if not comfort: the taste of the water was foul in my mouth; and I felt distinctly nauseated from whatever amount I had swallowed while immersed in it. Drenched to the marrow, and in the teeth of the wind that scudded the dark clouds overhead, I would soon have my trembling limbs palsied with a severe ague if I did not find some warmth soon. I pushed myself upright, and realised that my wrists were no longer bound together. My ankles were likewise free; feeling the cords dangling from me, I found them snapped in twain, rather than unknotted or cut. I quickly disentangled the pieces from me and tossed them away. I heard the bits of cord splash into water; kneeling on the wet muck, I saw now that it sloped down to the river's edge. My eyes had become adjusted to the dark, simultaneously with the sorting out of my disordered thoughts; I looked about to assess my situation.

I appeared to be quite alone; neither my captors, nor the silent forms of my fellow victims, had washed up on this strand with me. (The matter of the Brown Leather Man's murdered status was without doubt, as I had seen the stiffening corpse myself in Fexton's rooms; the apparition that had accompanied the overturning of the ruffians' boat I ascribed to the temporary collapse of my reason, my senses having been overwhelmed by the fearsome circumstances I had endured.) Dark forms, the straight edges and squared corners of unlit buildings, overlapped their silhouettes against the night sky, some distance from my dismal station. These were the warehouses, chandlers' offices, and other such furnishings to the river trade; various ships could be discerned, moored to the wharves and extending from the banks. All were seemly uninhabited at this late hour, the sailors and docksmen given over to sleep or carouse at the appointed establishments farther into the city. Whatever notion I entertained of calling out to these sources of aid and shelter was quickly dispelled by another consideration: the raising of my voice might also signal my location to either or both of the two ruffians, the tide having possibly drifted them ashore some distance beyond my immediate perception.

My solitary condition, I soon realised, applied only to the absence of other human beings. I felt the hem of my sodden coat tugged at by a smaller creature, then, when its sharp teeth let go, heard its sharp yapping. A dog, and specifically, Fexton's shabby terrier; I recognised its skipping gait as it circled excitedly around me, barking its delight at my resurrection. How had it come to this spot? The simplest explanation being that it had followed the cart bearing its dead master, faithful as the canine race is to undeserving humanity, and had undertaken a vigil at the edges of the waters where that personage had finally disappeared. It now seemed as if the dog's affections had been transferred to me; perhaps its small mind remembered my intervention against Fexton's cruelty.

The appearance of the dog suggested a remedy to my situation. I had, back in the borough of

Wetwick, noted the seeming twins of this creature,
busily engaged in leading the denizens of that area
on some common errand – just such high pitched
yapping and darting about had guided the remark-
able-looking figures. Perhaps Fexton's dog was
eager to return me to some place in that district?
Now and again, it nipped my clothing and tugged,
as if attempting to pull me to my feet. If that were
so, then from Wetwick I could find my own way
home. My own little shop and bed upstairs were
the only images of safety and rest that my fatigue-
addled brain could conjure.

"Very well," I spoke aloud; the dog barked in
reply. "See – I'm standing up." I tottered on the
muck's slippery footing. "Lead on, then." The dog
pranced away a few feet, then back to make sure
that I was following. Thus, with weary and confused steps, I made my way up from the edge of
the river, in the depths of which I had so shortly
before been immersed.

The dog led me to a flight of stone steps set into
the embankment wall. Grasping the iron mooring
rings, I pulled myself along; at the top, I was gratified to find good solid cobblestones under my feet
once again. On either side warehouses reached upward to form a narrow corridor; these were
obviously abandoned, the gaps in their doorways'
planks revealing empty, cobwebbed space beyond
and roofs sagging open to all weather. I stumbled
after my barking guide.

A murmur of voices, faint in the distance, quickened my steps. The dog pulled me around the corner of the last of the warehouses, and I saw, faintly outlined by the dim light spilling from its windows, the unmistakable form of a small church. Of classical, Wren-like proportions, with a thin spire cutting a wedge from the night's darker background; no more welcome refuge could have arisen out of the gloom. A troubling fragment of memory, as though the edifice embodied some painful recognition, passed through my thoughts, but I was too close to exhaustion to puzzle over the matter. With the dog dancing before and after my heels, I hastened towards it.

As I came closer, I saw a carriage positioned close to the church, a figure in priestly vestments beside the vehicle; I could not see his face, that being obscured by the shadow cast by the pillars of the church's portico. Here at last was succour and refuge from my assailants. Murmuring a prayer of thanks, as a combination of relief and fatigue drained the last of my strength, I stumbled the last few yards along an overgrown pathway, and collapsed into the priest's arms.

"Jesus H. Christ," I heard an oddly familiar voice say. "What the hell are you doing here?"

I opened my eyes and found myself looking up into the blue-glass spectacles of the confidence man and would-be burglar Scape.

• • • •

My old nemesis… Laying down my pen upon the desk, and massaging my brow creased with the effort of composition, I see yet that sharp-pointed visage. As, once during my rural childhood, having witnessed a ferret taking a barn rat I had been transfixed by the creature's image of low cunning, ferocious greed, and self-congratulating conceit; so I remember the man, less as *Man*, and more as *Nature* – unreasoning vivacity, no more doubting himself than does the lightning stroke that splits the tree and sparks the field into flame.

And what if Scape's self-proclaimed knowledge of the Future is correct, and some day all men will be such as he is? (And do we not see that transformation already commenced?) Men with duty but to Self, and with erratic Ambition fuelled by the combustion of their own Intelligence – they will be fearsome creatures indeed.

That day is, I fervently hope, yet a ways distant. I sit in my small, safe harbour, and unfold again a snippet extracted from an Edinburgh journal and sent to my attention by a friendly correspondent. The piece contains information from far-off communities in the Scottish Highlands; a man with blue spectacles, disfigured by both limp and burn scars (fellow veteran! – we all bear our scars, inside or out), has passed amongst them, leaving a turbulent wake…

We were startled equally. Outside the little church to which Fexton's terrier had led me, my legs failed me, and I would have dropped into the puddle of river-water that had collected around my feet, if Scape had not grasped me under the arm and held me upright.

The tone of his words made the incongruity with his clerical garb complete: "Shit – did Bendray send you here? He must have. That sonuvabitch; never tells me a goddamn thing…" The face surmounting the white collar flushed with a barely suppressed anger.

I did nothing to correct whatever supposition he cared to make concerning my presence. My travails had left me too short of breath, and scattered of thought, to summon words of explanation. Beyond this, I had no way of knowing whether Scape, already known to be guilty of the assault on my assistant Creff and the attempted burglary of my shop, might not also be in league with the murderous ruffians who had deposited me in the river. If some confusion amongst them gave me temporary safety (was this Bendray some chief over the conspirators?), I was willing to let the situation stand uncorrected. Soon enough, when my strength had returned and Scape's attention was diverted, I could make my escape unnoticed.

"Christ, look at ya." He drew back to examine me. "You're sopping wet; been swimming or something?"

"I– that is–"

"Forget it, man." Scape's hurried interruption rendered the fabrication of an excuse unnecessary.

"Don't have time for it now. Things are gonna be cracking around here pretty soon." He tugged me towards the church door. "Come on, we can find you some dry stuff inside." The dog trotted along behind us, until Scape spotted it. "Shoo – get outta here." He stamped his foot; the dog, with great reluctance, slunk back outside. "Goddamn bell-dogs." I had no idea what he meant.

Another figure in priest's garments turned towards us as we approached down the nave. To my further astonishment, I recognised the person as Scape's companion, Miss McThane. She had pulled and pinned her hair back for the masquerade, but had neglected to scrub off her face paints, thus producing a rather brazen and disturbing appearance. Her eyes widened when she saw me. "Where'd he come from?"

"Can it, will ya?" Scape, still gripping my arm, propelled me faster. "Bendray's filled him in on the whole deal." His agile mind, ever impatient with mere fact, had embroidered the erroneous assumption into a complete picture. "He sent you here to help us out on this thing, right?" He glanced at me for confirmation.

"I–"

"Right." He thrust me forward. "Come on, we gotta get going; those funny-looking fuckers'll be here any minute now. There's some more of these high-button nightgowns in the what-d'ya-call-it – yeah, the vestry – get him decked out, will ya? I'll get the rest of the stuff." He turned and strode quickly down the nave.

Smiling, Miss McThane folded her arm into mine. "Sure thing," she said. "Jeez, you're all wet. Don't worry; I'll take care of you."

I was still too weak to resist as she guided me towards a side door beyond the altar. Within moments I found myself in a dimly lit room, the air thick with that peculiar mustiness that comes with spaces too long shuttered. Miss McThane closed the door and leaned back against it, surveying my forlornly dripping figure before her.

"Here." She took a long priest's robe from a wall hook, raising a cloud of grey dust from the fabric, and draped it over the back of a sagging chair. Stepping close to me, she deftly undid the buttons of my waistcoat, then those of the sodden shirt underneath. My breath caught in my throat as she laid her pale hand upon the bare skin of my chest. "You're just about frozen," she whispered. I remembered the smile she gave me from the incident in my shop. "We better get you thawed out…"

I backed away, toppling a candle-stand and a stack of mouldy breviaries behind me. "That's… that's not necessary," I said feebly. "I assure you – I can manage quite nicely, thank you–"

My avenues of escape – were blocked by the debris cluttering the small room. Miss McThane, advancing dauntless, soon had me cornered between a small pump-organ and an upended pew bench. The eyes of my pursuer glittered with a disturbing avidity; the organ gave a despairing wheeze as I leaned back, my hand braced against its yellowed keyboard. Her voice was a lewd pianissimo counterpoint: "Come on, you sonuvabitch..."

What! I had thought was a curtained wall behind me parted, allowing me to fall back on to the floor of a small alcove. Above me, when I looked up, was a face that trembled my heart even more than had that of Miss McThane: the smooth, porcelain and wax visage of a clockwork choirboy, one blue eye staring open at me, the other sealed by a rusty spring as though· winking at my undignified circumstances.

Miss McThane loomed over her prey, but I was scarcely aware of her. With rapidly mounting horror, I realised where I was and why the small church had seemed so oddly familiar to me. Though I had been here only once before, the terror engendered on that occasion had impressed the building's aspect permanently on my memory. I had been led from the river straight to the portals of Saint Mary Alderhythe, the site of the disastrous, even blasphemous resurrection of Dower's Patented Clerical Automata. That which I had taken to be a curtain was in fact the robe of the chorister whose mock-cherubic face now leered at me; rising up on my elbow and twisting about, I could see a whole row of the mechanical creatures, lined up in the alcove like soldiers on parade;

beneath me was the brass track set into the
church's floor to guide the singing mannikins on
their appointed circuit through the church; A
mocking fate had led me to the precincts where my
meddling ignorance had unleashed those scenes of
clattering, spring-driven chaos. Not just painful to
my recollection, but the source of angry loathing
from such as the crippled pastor (his injury the direct result of that dread evening) who had chased
me from his desk only a day previously.

"Good God." I gazed up, stricken. "All I feared
has come upon me."

"For Christ's sake," Miss McThane knelt down
and grasped my shirt in her small fists. "It's not
gonna be that bad. Sheesh–"

At that moment, the the vestry's door flew open;
the church's light fell across us. "Not now;" said
Scape, seeing us. "Goddamn it; you can do that later.
We gotta get this friggin' church ready." He dumped
on the floor an awkwardly shaped bag, which immediately split, spewing its contents. "Come on," he
ordered as he strode back out the door.

Miss McThane stood up, tucking a few disordered strands of her auburn hair behind her ears.
"Next time," she assured me, straightening out her
vestments. She picked up the other garments and
tossed them to me.

When she had gone to join her larcenous companion, I quickly completed the undressing she had
commenced and scrambled into the musty-smelling

robes – the damp and chill of my own clothes had
seeped into my bones. Any escape from this ill-
favoured place would be as easily accomplished
rigged out as a peripatetic priest, as it would be for
a dripping, sneezing near-corpse traversing the
night streets.

For escape was now even more firmly centred
in my mind. As I fastened a dust-grey reversed collar about my neck, I took stock of my predicament.
That Scape was using the church of Saint Mary
Alderhythe for some criminal purpose – if not
technically sacrilegious, the building having been
hastily de-consecrated after my own ignominious
experiences there – of this I had no doubt. (I had
already perceived, at this early stage of acquain-
tanceship, that none of Scape's activities were free
of illicit intent.) They were "getting the church
ready" – for whom? What ritual was planned? It
did not seem to have anything to do with the Clerical Automata my father had built and installed
here; I investigated further into the room's various
niches, and found all the figures, some with cobwebs filling the angles of their mechanical limbs,
undisturbed since the aftermath of my own
botched attentions upon them.

I stumbled across the bag Scape had deposited
in the middle of the floor. Bending down, I saw
that the spilled contents were books, the bindings
tattered with use: they were the church's breviaries and hymnals gathered up as though by a

purloining bibliophile and cached here. I began to wonder if Scape's actions were perhaps governed more by insanity than dishonesty.

As I peered round the vestry door, hoping to see a clear path to the front of the church and the freedom of the darkness beyond, I was instead spotted by Scape, as he hurriedly lugged another bag down the nave. He signalled me over to him.

"You look sharp, man; really." He pulled the bag up against the hem of my vestment. "Start putting these out, okay?"

"Pardon?" I said. I wished him to go on believing that I had somehow been recruited into this conspiracy by another the better to lull any suspicions and thus make an unhindered exit when the opportunity came – but his rapid speech skittered past before I could comprehend it.

"The pews, man–" He shouted over his shoulder, already bolting towards the church door. "Stick 'em in the pews!"

I opened the bag and found more books inside. But not of a religious nature; instead, in such varying editions and states of wear as to indicate they had been salvaged from every penny bookstall in London, copies of Izaak Walton's *The Compleat Angler*. For a moment, I did not doubt Scape's sanity as much as my own. The dream-like nature of my adventures again impressed itself upon me; events had gone from puzzling to ludicrous, as they are wont to do when our sleeping visions course to a confusing end, all resemblance to waking nature abandoned. Surely I was about to raise my head from my pillow, blinking at the morning light, eventually (and with relief) to find no evidence of strange visitors and disastrous excursions? My thin breakfast and placid life restored to me? The notion gave comfort.

I glanced up from the dog-eared volume in my hand. From the corner of my eye I had seen where Miss McThane was arranging something upon the altar. The mock priest smiled and raised a hand signal consisting of her thumb and forefinger brought together in an O, the meaning of which eluded me. I turned away and, as instructed by Scape, began distributing the Anglers, dragging the bag between the pews and placing a copy of the Walton tome in each wooden rack or, when such were missing, on the seat itself.

This task had scarcely been completed when I heard the approaching clatter of another carriage outside the church. With the empty bag wadded in one hand, I made my way back through the pews to the nave, where I encountered a gesticulating Scape in company with another man. The latter was a gentleman considerably greyed and thinned by age, his wraith-like figure distinguished by the elegant, if somewhat antique, cut of his suit, and by the haughty bearing exhibited in his step and the angle of his head. He gave me a cursory glance as he passed by, like a lord of the manor reviewing his household staff, while absently listening to Scape's voluble description of the preparations that had been made.

"There, that's done," spoke Miss McThane at my elbow. "Hope this old bastard likes it." I looked round to where she had been busily engaged while I was setting out the books, and saw that the altar, in the manner of those rural churches that display notable examples of the parishioner's crops at harvest time, was here festooned with fishing tackle. Rods and creels, lines and barbed hooks, all formed a decorative arrangement in place of the expected cross and chalice. Dream upon dream; I felt quite giddy to see that more of the impedimenta of angling had also been strewn about the church, beneath every window and entwined about the rail.

No sooner had I perceived this bizarre transformation of the little church, than a murmur of voices came from outside. "Come on!" shouted Scape, sprinting down the nave. He grabbed my arm and Miss McThane's, and hustled us towards the vestry. "They're here – Bendray thinks it'll make a better effect if they don't see us yet."

We were soon installed in the vestry's darkness, with Scape peering out through the crack of the door. Standing behind him, I could see over his head where the elderly gentleman – the mysterious Bendray, I presumed – was waiting at the church's entrance. Miss McThane, exhibiting every

sign of boredom, had placed herself upon the
bench of the pump-organ, and was examining the
condition of her fingernails. "Here they come,"
whispered Scape at last. "Christ, they're an ugly-
looking bunch – give me the flippin' creeps."

I saw them then, peering apprehensively around
the open church doors. The elderly gentleman
raised his arms wide in a gesture of benevolent
welcome. Slowly with anxious glances around the
building's interior, the odd looking residents of that
district to which I had been delivered at the start
of this nightmare filed in, caps in hand. The people
of Wetwick had arrived.

"Just look at those bug-eyed suckers." Scape
shook his head as he peered through the narrow
aperture. "Whoops – now they're getting excited,
all right."

From my position, leaning over his bowed back,
I could see Bendray turn grandly about, his arms
spreading wider, his gesture obviously inviting the
goggling crowd to inspect the church's premises.
Indeed, some of the Wetwick residents had already
filtered through the pews, and had excitedly
picked up copies of *The Compleat Angler* from the
hymnal racks. Their extraordinary eyes grew even
larger as the books were excitedly handed around.
Others, with strangely accented cries, had discovered the fishing tackle draped at various points;
their jabbering grew louder as the barbed hooks
were brandished before each face. Soon the church

was filled with their voices as a group of them ran down the nave towards the tackle-strewn altar.

Scape pulled the door shut. "Old Bendray's not gonna need us for a while," he said, straightening up. "Looks like he's getting his point across." I greatly desired to ask what that point was, but refrained. The conspirators' proximity dictated that I continue my charade. I maintained a discreet silence as Scape paced about the vestry's confined area, rubbing the small of his back.

"Goddamn books were heavy," he muttered. "Plus all that other crap – should hit on the old goat for a hazardous-duty bonus." He gestured towards Miss McThane and myself. "Take five, guys – I think we're in here until the fish-eye brigade out there gets their fill."

Miss McThane glanced up at me, smiled before turning to silently regard her companion, then went back to the of her manicure. I backed as far away as I could in the cluttered room.

"Hey, what's this stuff?"

I looked round and saw that Scape had discovered the alcove behind the pump-organ. As I watched, he drew one of the clockwork choristers out along the brass track laid into the floor.

"No!" I shouted involuntarily. "Don't – that is… I don't think you should tamper with that."

He disregarded my warning, bending down to examine the device. "This is some of your old man's stuff, isn't it?" He looked up at me, then back to the choirboy mannikin. "Far out."

"It's – it's very delicate." I stepped across and laid
my hand on his arm. "Extremely so. I think it
would be best if you refrained–"

"Screw that." He shook me off, then knelt down
for a closer look. His hands had already found the
small panel at the back and had pried it open. "I've
been itching to get a hold of one of these."

"Please… I beg of you." Dreadful memories
urged my anxiety. "Desist–"

"Forget it," said Miss McThane to me. "There's
no stopping him when he's got a new toy." She
gazed with an expression of disgust as Scape ex-
plored further into the choristers' alcove.

"All *right*." His voice came muffled from the
depths, beyond the row of mannikins. A flaring
safety match threw his shadow back towards me.
"I think I found the master controls."

So he had; I recognised the assemblage of levers
and gears from the last time. No doubt the apparatus was still in the state of erroneous adjustment
in which I had left it; I could see that the great coil
of the central driving spring was still wound tight.

I left off wringing my hands and grasped the
back of Scape's vestments to pull him away from
the machinery. "You mustn't," I cried. "The devices
are misaligned and malfunctioning–"

He shook me off with considerable violence,
sending me sprawling upon the floor. His brow
furrowed in anger above the blue lenses. "I've

been studying your old man's gizmos for years,"
he said sharply. "There ain't anything I don't know
about them."

I made another attempt to ward off tragedy,
grasping him about his robed knees. He toppled
backwards and, flailing about for balance, grabbed
hold of the centremost lever. "Watch out!"

Scraping through a layer of rust, the lever swung
in an arc under Scape's weight. For a moment
there was silence, then a soft, unmistakable tick.
Our combat ceased, with Scape supine on the alcove's floor and I halfway above him; we both
arched our necks to see the machinery beyond us.

Another *tick*, and a groan of metal shifting from
its long-confined position. The noises began to rattle
and clatter faster, as the escapements and ratchets
of the apparatus woke into their spurious life.

"Christ Almighty–" I scrambled across my opponent's form and yanked the lever. It resisted all my
efforts; I might as well have been tugging at the
balustraded stones of the church in a Samson-like
attempt to bring the entire edifice down upon our
heads. The row of mechanical choristers shifted,
the jointed limbs beneath the robes creaking, the
porcelain faces swivelling above the ruffled collars.
In the manner of an owl, the head of the lead chorister swung all the way round, its glass eyes
beatifically regarding us. The rosined wheels that
my father had installed in the device's throat engaged; "*Glo – ri – a*," it sang in a piercing treble.

Scape got to his feet and joined me in tugging at the lever. "We gotta get this thing shut off before those creeps out in the church hear it." Our efforts were to no avail as the lever remained in its position.

A creaking noise sounded from the other alcoves around the perimeter of the vestry, as the remainder of my father's devices stirred into life from their rusting sleep. Looking behind me, I saw a white-haired priest emerge into the room's open space; the figure was entirely lifelike except for the maniacally rolling glass eyes and the hand repeating its blessing over the pump-organ. "And with thy spirit," it pronounced, or rather, the wheels inside its throat did.

"Nice going," said Miss McThane. Her sarcasm was cut short as she was forced to duck away from the benediction of the clockwork priest, now spinning about rapidly enough to lift the hem of its vestment as though it were a dervish. Light flooded into the room as the door, also connected to the machinery, flew open. A number of the Wetwick residents gaped at this sudden apparition revealed to them. The choristers rocked back and forth along the metal track, and then began filing towards the onlookers; an off-tune Latin chant sounded from the porcelain throats.

"Stop those little shits." Scape pushed past me and grabbed the robe of the last chorister in the procession. The rotten fabric tore away, showing the clicking armatures and spinning gears of the

device as it marched on. He grasped one brass
strut, but succeeded only in dislodging the cherub
head askew so that it hung sideways and groaned
in basso profundo. The priest ceased its gyrations
and followed after the choir.

The Wetwick residents were now entirely
alerted by the noise and commotion. They ceased
their round-eyed goggling at the copies of The
Compleat Angler and watched in amazement the
erratic progress of the automata into the church;
the machinery, having fallen into such a state of
decay, now jerked about with appalling violence.
The actions of the choristers were further deranged
by the fact that Scape's billowing vestments had
become entangled in the exposed workings of the
one figure with which he had attempted to interfere; flailing about, his face reddening with his
shouted curses, he was being dragged on his back
behind the choir as they made their way. The ter-
rified onlookers scrambled away, trampling each
other in their haste to avoid this apparition. Miss
McThane, her long hair in wild disarray, tugged at
her companion in a futile attempt at rescue.

From a position of relative safety at the vestry
door, I watched as Bendray, with raised hands and
quavering voice, first tried to restore order to the
panic-stricken assemblage. He soon abandoned the
effort and, wisely fearing for his own skin, slipped
out the church door, moments before the great
mass of the Wetwick residents jammed the egress,

tearing at one another's backs and limbs in desperate flight, the crazed energy of their numbers resulting in virtually none of them winning through to the darkness outside.

Inside the stone walls, echoing with cries of terror and grating mechanical noises, the carnage had become even more nightmarish than on that long past occasion when I had first attempted to put my father's devices into their appointed motions. With the furiously struggling Scape in tow, the choir had reached their positions, but had split into various factions, as if arguing amongst themselves on the proper course of their further ritual. One group of the mannikins seemed bent on another procession, and to that end had turned about, battering against the others as the deranged machinery drove them along the metal rails. Scape's imprecations mingled with the cacophony of hymns sung simultaneously, the artificial voices shrilling ever higher as the rosined wheels wore down to the bare metal beneath. Two of the porcelain heads butted together as though in the combat of rams, cracking and spraying throughout the church bits of the smiling cherub faces and the springs and gears beneath. The headless choristers went on battering into each other's robed chests as one of the church windows dissolved into glittering fragments from the impact of one such missile.

Simultaneously, the priest, in carrying out the cycle of duties that my father had built into its workings, had become entangled in the fishing gear that had been draped across the altar. Dragging the lines and barbed hooks along, it seized upon one poor creature who had been frozen in his steps from sheer fright. The ugly Wetwick face was even more contorted as the mechanical priest dragged him to the baptismal font and immersed him therein. A great surge of water splashed upward from the struggling man's arms and into the gently smiling countenance of the clockwork priest, as it recited an appeal for donations to the bell rehanging fund.

These sights assured the Wetwick residents that they had been lured into the church as the objects of mayhem. They redoubled their efforts at forcing their way past their fellows, and out the door. Their gargling cries grew louder as well, as though they were already being murdered en masse.

No one's attention was directed towards me. The wisdom of leaving such a site was even more apparent now. I sidled past the empty pews to the window shattered by the fragment of porcelain cherub's-head. The voluminous folds of my clerical costume protected my hands as I scrambled up on to the thick stone sill and vaulted out, landing on the thickly overgrown grass outside. I quickly gathered up the skirt of the vestment and plunged into the darkness, away from the church's clattering and shrieking chaos.

Running with no thought but to put distance between myself and the awful scene, I soon collided with the iron fence around the churchyard. I found a side gate that creaked partly open when I pushed against it; the freedom and concealing safety of the dark streets was just beyond; I squeezed through the narrow gap and was grasped by strong pairs of hands on either of my arms.

"Here, what's this?" The lamp was lifted above me, and by its glow I saw two constables· sternly examining my face. "You're a rum-looking sort of priest."

I realised I very likely did look suspicious, flushed and out of breath, and my clothing torn and disordered. I gasped out a few syllables without managing to link them into any words of explanation.

"What's going on up there, anyways?" the one constable lifted his lamp to indicate the church. Over my shoulder I could see its windows lit up. "Come along, you – let's just have us a look."

"No!" I shouted. I vainly tried to pull free from my captors. "Don't go up there–"

"Oh, don't, is it? Something going on there you'd like us not to see, eh? Hop it, then; let's go see what you and your mates have been up to." The two of them lifted my feet nearly clear of the ground as they dragged me back towards the church.

The building was silent as the constables pulled me up to the door. Neither carriage was positioned outside. The constables pushed open the door, and we gazed upon an empty space inside.

Empty, that is, of human habitation. Scape, Miss McThane, and the denizens of Wetwick had all departed, having made their various escapes into the night at last. All that was left, to my own appalled eyes, and to the amazement of the constables, was the wreckage of my father's Clerical Automata. In the midst of the fishing tackle strewn about, and the copies of Izaak Walton that had been flung from the hands of the panicking Wetwick residents, the choristers lay tangled as though in the aftermath of some juvenile battlefield. Their shrill piping voices were silent now; the porcelain faces, those that were still intact gazed with rosy-cheeked serenity at the ceiling.

The mechanical priest creaked about in its position by the altar; enough force was left in the master driving spring to force through a last few fragments of its liturgy. One stiff hand raised, knocking its white hair to the side of its benignly smiling face. "*Pax vobiscum*," it wheezed. "Jumble sale." It then toppled over.

I looked up at the constables as they slowly turned their gaze on me. They were silent, awestruck by the enormity of my blasphemous crimes.

7

Mr Dower Leaves the Capital

Of the details of my incarceration I have scant memory. Perhaps the ignominious shock of being placed in the charge of the constabulary had combined with the cumulative fatigue wrought in my constitution, to temporarily overthrow the balance of my reason. I recall a voice faintly like my own answering the various questions. put to me, though at a distance, as if overhearing some street conversation of only mild interest. The censorious, scowling faces of the Law's guardians passed in front of me, yet they too were far removed; from an angle somehow slightly above, I listened to them reciting the impressively long list of misdeeds attributed to my person – desecration of a holy place and criminal blasphemy chief among them – and heard their gruff comments on my vacant inattention, as though they were Smithfield porters describing a particularly unattractive carcass of beef. Only when I was at last placed in a cell, entirely alone upon a cold stone shelf jutting from a damp wall, did some realization sink upon me that the dream-like nature of my experiences had eroded through to reveal a grim reality. The dark cell was actual, my presence therein equally so; something with bright eyes and soft pattering feet regarded me from a drain-hole in the centre of the floor before scurrying away. I could hear someone close by singing with drunken, inarticulate glee, the voice echoing from the walls until the thump of a wooden truncheon upon flesh produced a cry of pain and subsequent silence. By various follies I had reached this nadir; I wrapped my arms about myself to ward off the chill of the gaol's foetid air, and, with chin heavy upon my breast, contemplated my misery.

At some point, though I knew not how many hours of imprisonment had passed, the heavy door creaked open and a gaoler with keys jangling upon a ring entered; he tossed a bundle upon the bench beside me and withdrew without speaking. I roused myself to investigate, and found it to be a set of my clothing. The explanation of its arrival hither was provided by the appearance of the faithful Creff's face at the small barred grille set into the door; he strained to look inside the cell, as if forced to stand on tip-toe in the corridor outside. "Mr Dower, sir," he called. "They told me–" The comfort of his familiar visage disappeared,

and I heard the gaoler ordering him to move
away. "Here, you–" His voice faded as further
prodding was applied. "Watch what you're doing
with that stick – ruddy blackguard..."

I exchanged the tattered vestment for my own
garments, the accustomed attire of my second-
best suit restoring my appearance, if not my
spirits. There was some comfort in the thought
that I could at least await whatever fate was in
store for me garbed as a gentleman, and no
longer masquerading as a bogus cleric.

I had not long to wait. The door presently
opened again, sending a wash of light across the
dank confines of the cell. I looked round and saw
not the gaoler's stolid figure, but rather that of
Scape. His clerical costume had likewise been discarded; I saw him restored to the over-rich finery
in which I had first seen him at my shop. In the
cell's gloom his blue-glass spectacles seemed two
dark, unreflecting holes in his pallid face.

"Rise up, Dower, old fellow. " He smiled and
made a grand gesture with his cane, as if he were
about to commence the conducting of an orchestra
in some opera *seria* overture. "Come on, up and at
'em – the hour of your deliverance is at hand."

The appearance of this figure, now fixed in my
mind as the bellwether of the troubles that had
come upon me, further oppressed my spirits.
"Please go away," I said, shrinking back upon the
bench. "Haven't you brought me enough grief?"

"Grief? Hey, lighten up–"

I ignored his protest. "Your reasons for coming here are of no interest to me. I would prefer to remain undisturbed while I await whatever judgment will be deemed appropriate by the bench." Stoic, with the little dignity I had left to me, I turned my face away from the door.

My words brought a derisive snort from Scape. "Yeah, well, you can just forget that crap. It's been taken care of already – old Bendray's gone for your bail, so to speak. He's got more strings to pull than the average Lord. You're being released in his custody – that's why I came down here to get you."

So the apparent architect of my travails – or at least a good part of them – was Lord Bendray, then. The title sparked as little recognition as had the name. I could envision no reason why a member of the nobility would be engaged in the absurd vandalism of a church, of which I was now falsely accused; no reason other than sheer insanity, that is. Perhaps this Lord Bendray was of those much-gossiped-about bloodlines, where generations of inbreeding and later bibulous riot had gone to produce a congenital weakness of mind? At any rate, I had no wish to have further involvement with him, even though my own freedom was used as bait. I was about to reiterate this point to Scape when I saw that the bright-eyed creature that had looked at me from the cell's drain-hole had now become bold enough to investigate the toe of my boot with its small naked paws. It scurried away when I leapt with an involuntary shudder from the bench.

"That's right," said Scape, linking his arm with mine. "You can trust us – really." He pulled me towards the brightly lit corridor.

"But–" My protests collapsed; the cell's darkness drove me into the hands of my enemies. The gaoler, markedly more respectful now, placed a twine-bound bundle in my arms. As he led us away, I recognised it as my clothes, still damp from the river, retrieved from the church of Saint Mary Alderhythe. Beneath my prodding finger I felt the circular outline of the Saint Monkfish coin inside my wadded-up waistcoat.

Outside the grim walls, I stood blinking in the morning sunshine that, at various points in my nocturnal quest, I had despaired of ever seeing again. Scape opened the door of a brougham – the same I had seen outside Saint Mary Alderhythe – and guided me up into it. No sooner had I sat down than I became aware of the vehicle's other occupants. Seated across from me were the enigmatic Lord Bendray and, restored to her feminine finery, Miss McThane. I endeavoured to ignore the signal of her lowered lashes and slight smile as Scape found his place next to me and the brougham jolted into motion.

I gazed out the carriage's window at the London

streets passing by. A one-legged crossing-sweeper hobbled out of our path and tugged respectfully at his cap; perambulating costers and stall-keepers alike were arranging their merchandise for their customers' inspection; the city buildings and population had regained that apparent reality of which the vertiginous night had robbed them. This bright diurnal world had seemed a phantasm, existing only in deluded memory, when the dark waters had been swirling over my head or I had been running from the church where piscine physiognomies gaped in horror at a clanking priest and choir; now those night events slid together in confusion as I tried to recall them. I was too exhausted to sort the real from the false; sanity often consists of knowing what not to think about.

I looked up from my fatigued musings as, with his brown-spotted hands folded over the head of his cane, Lord Bendray leaned his cadaverous face towards me. "I wanted to express my deep appreciation to you," he said in a septuagenarian quaver. "For taking upon yourself the blame ensuing from our little, ah... church social. Hehheh-heh." His amusement at his own witticism evoked a spasm of coughing that lasted nearly a minute. He dabbed at his phlegm-spotted lips with a handkerchief before speaking again. "I had always received excellent service from the senior Dower, but had never expected such loyalty from the son as well."

I had not the slightest idea to what he referred; I had never seen the name Bendray in any of my late father's account books. As to the night's events at Saint Mary Alderhythe, it now seemed the path of wisdom to dissociate myself from them by proclaiming my ignorance about what intent, if any, lay behind them. "I'm sorry, your Lordship," I said coldly. "I don't–"

Scape's elbow had dug sharply into my ribs, expelling my breath and thus silencing me; his blow had been concealed beneath the fold of his greatcoat. I looked around into his face and saw beneath the blue lenses the threat of further violence.

He turned towards Lord Bendray. "Mr Dower told me back at the gaol – when I went to get him – that he was feeling kinda exhausted. Been a long night, you know? So he doesn't really feel like discussing things right now." Scape brought his ingratiating smile around to me, where it hardened in place. I kept my tongue still.

Lord Bendray had taken no notice of any of this byplay. "A pity," he said, leaning back into the brougham's leather plush. "I do hope, then, that he'll accept my invitation out to my country estate. You'll find it most restful there, Dower. And, of course, there is so much business we would be able to discuss at our leisure – propositions I'm sure will be... most interesting."

I received a hidden nudge from Scape. "Ah...

yes. Yes, of course," I said quickly. "Very gracious of your Lordship, I'm sure. However – I'm not sure I could get away right now." I could in fact envision no more dreadful prospect than being spirited away to some remote mansion, there to be further mauled by this man's lunacies, without even the benefit of the constabulary's timely intervention. "Pressures of business, you know. Yes; very busy time for me. The watch trade always picks up this time of year–" I caught, from the corner of my eye, Scape's frowning glare, and bit off my rattling elaboration.

Lord Bendray's chin wrinkled below his child-like pout, as though he were enduring the refusal of a playfellow to come to a birthday fete. "Well," he said, gazing stoically out the window, "I do hope you'll be able to see your way clear."

"I'm sure," said Scape heavily, "that Mr Dower will give it every consideration." He leaned closer to me, displaying my pallid reflection in his dark spectacles.

There was no further conversation; I was let off with my bundle of clothing in front of my shop, and the brougham clattered hastily away. Before I could turn my key in the lock, I heard a sharp yapping from behind. I turned and saw Fexton's terrier, somewhat dust-covered from running behind the brougham, looking up from the pavement. Its tongue lolled panting from the side of its mouth as its bright, expectant gaze held on me.

"Poor wretch," I murmured as I bent to scratch behind its up-pricked ear; the animal wriggled in pleasure. I was not alone in having had a tortuous odyssey through the night. The dog had been clever enough to transfer its innate loyalties to me once it had perceived that its master Fexton had been murdered; then that faithfulness had drawn it along to every station to which I had been forced. No doubt it had been waiting outside the gaol when I had been released.

"Well, then; come on." I pushed the shop door open and bade the animal enter. "Fellow campaigners owe some civility to each other, I suppose."

Creff hurried downstairs to greet me. "Thank the heavens you're back, sir! Most worried, I was... when they came and told me – what's that?" He peered down at my companion, busily engaged in scratching himself with a hind leg.

"That, I have been informed, is a bell-dog. Find him something to eat, will you? I'm sure the poor creature is famished." I shuffled past him and laid my hand on the railing of the stairs. "And leave the shutters down; we shan't be opening today. I'll be retiring to my bed for some time." I shifted the bundle under my arm and wearily pulled myself up the first step.

"Your pardon, sir – but there's someone here as wants to see you."

I halted and looked back at him. "Here? Surely

you turned any callers away–"

"Oh, no, sir; I tried, but I couldn't; she was very *form-a-double*, you might say."

A formidable woman, here, to see me; my gaze travelled up the stairs to my parlour door. For a moment I quailed, thinking that perhaps Miss McThane had somehow managed to be transported from Lord Bendray's brougham where I had last seen her. "Did she give a name?" I asked.

"A Mrs Trabble, sir. She wouldn't state her business. Said it was a matter of some… ahem…" His voice sank to a whisper. "… delicacy."

I could well imagine. I could feel the blood draining out of my face as I contemplated the prospect of confronting such a visitor. Mrs Augustina Trabble, in her role as founder and leader of the Ladies Union for the Suppression of Carnal Vice, had made considerable impact of late, both in London society and in the popular press. Rumours of her assaults upon the titled habitués of London's demi-monde – the result of her moral outrage and complete fearlessness – were rife; had she not in fact confronted the Prince of Wales himself in his box at the El Dorado music-hall in Leicester Square, and upbraided him for the poor example he had made of himself to the lower classes? (Other stories went so far as to attribute the fire that made smouldering ashes of the establishment to her doing.) There was likely not a cigar divan in the

whole city where her name was not cursed by
swells impatient with her interference in the pursuit of their sordid pleasures.

But what did such a daunting figure have to do
with me? I had no idea. Perhaps – the best that
my poor tired brain could imagine – merely a
request for a donation to her organization's good
works? The installation of a gaslight in the alley
behind the shop, the better to discourage its use
as a *rendez-vous* both romantic and mercantile in
nature? There was, unfortunately, but one way to
find out; with faltering tread, I mounted the
stairs.

"Mrs Trabble." I closed the door behind me.
"I'm honoured–"

"Sit down, young man," she said sternly, indicating the chair across from her.

Her intimidating gaze skewered me to the
faded horsehair upholstery. A large woman, in
unornamented black bombazine; there seemed to
be enough of her great bosomed presence to
make two or three such as myself; a fierce square
jaw, as though a block of granite had been interposed between the brim of her feathered hat and
her high lace collar, and a grim visage chiselled
therefrom – in all, a person of some reckoning,
even beyond her reputation. I sat, unable to do
otherwise.

"Reports have come to my attention." Her large
hands folded themselves on the reticule in her

lap. "Disturbing reports; most disgusting reports, if I may say so."

"Reports? Of – of what?"

"Of your behaviour, Mr Dower." Her chin thrust itself towards me, like the sharp prow of a warship. "Your little… *adventures*. For far too long, your kind has believed that the night affords you the anonymity to pursue and indulge in the filthiest of practices; well, you may disabuse yourself of that notion as of this moment, Mr Dower. There is no security for the sybarite in the darkness; the Ladies Union has vigilant agents in all corners of the city, and all share my abhorrence at the mischief of your bestial tribe. You may rest assured of that."

I stared at her in astonishment. "I have no idea what you're speaking about," I protested.

"I think you know very well, Mr Dower." Her eyes narrowed to pinpricks of loathing. "Will you attempt to deny that you have been heard seeking directions to certain establishments of ill repute, kept by a certain Mollie Maud? Establishments of a nature even more sinister than the usual sinks of vice – were you not intent on seeking dalliance with the infamous green girls?"

For a moment I couldn't remember where I had heard the name she had spat at me; then the voice echoed in my memory, of the cabby who had first agreed to take me to Wetwick.

"No," I said after the moment's confusion.

"That's entirely untrue…"

"You know nothing of this villainous woman's enterprise?"

I shook my head in mute denial.

"And the green girls – I suppose you maintain ignorance on that distasteful subject as well?"

The phrase had also been spoken by the cabby. "I've heard the name, but–"

Mrs Trabble snorted in disgust. "That admission alone bespeaks your guilt. If you had kept to the paths of virtue as diligence and a proper upbringing should have dictated, such a topic would be completely beyond your ken." She stood up, the stiff bombazine of her dress rustling like distant storm clouds. "I take it that you are not prepared to confess your intimate knowledge of these matters; that you intend to mask your shame with a brazen charade of innocence. You'll derive scant comfort from it. The members of the Ladies Union for the Suppression of Carnal Vice have striven to our utmost to stamp out these heinous practices of which you're so fond, and I can assure you that your own transgressions will not escape notice."

I rose to follow her. "Really – you must be mistaken."

She turned to glare at me from the head of the stairs. "Good day, Mr Dower," she said frostily. "You shan't have long to wait."

The veiled threat, delivered with such authority, left me rooted to the spot. Distantly, I heard her curt bark to Creff downstairs, the shop door opening, and her sweeping exit.

This last encounter, on top of all else that had happened, surfeited me to exhaustion. I found my bed and toppled into it, sinking into a blackness more comforting than the moiling thoughts that filled my battered skull.

I was roused into that desolate condition, familiar to anyone who has ever fallen asleep in daylight and woken in darkness; that bleak, entombed feeling somehow tinged with both guilt and self-pity. A stifling dream of falling under black water ebbed away as I sat up and watched the familiar contours of my bedchamber take shape in the gloom. Voices had been shouting in the dream; I could hear them still. As my brain cleared, I realised that the heated words were coming from the shop downstairs. I quickly pulled on my clothes and hastened towards the clamour.

In the shop, I discovered Creff in furious remonstrance with the villainous Scape. Both had grasp of the kitchen broom between them; Scape resisted my assistant's efforts to push him, and his companion Miss McThane, back out of the door.

"Call this sonuvabitch off," cried Scape, catching sight of me at the doorway behind the counter. He wrested the broom away from his opponent and threw it into a corner.

Creff assumed a pugilist's stance, with first circling in front of his face. "They forced their way in,
sir," he shouted to me. "Knocked, they did, and
before I could recognize the brigands, they was
in." He took an easily dodged poke at Scape.

"I'll handle this," I said, interposing myself
between them. I drew myself up to full height and
directed a stern expression at the other's blue
spectacles. "Quit these premises," I ordered.
"Immediately; you have nothing of interest to
relate to me."

Scape finished straightening his greatcoat, disarrayed by the exertions of his brief combat. A
thin smile broke in his angular visage. "Think so,
huh? Well, maybe you better think again, fella.
Ol' Bendray asked us to come round and… *renew*
his invitation to you. He wanted to make sure
you knew just how much he'd like you to come
on out to his place."

My voice went colder: "You may tell your
employer that I have no desire to accept his hos-
pitality. Not at this time, nor, I doubt, at any point
in the future. Convey my regrets however you
wish; I would rather return to gaol than set eyes
on any of you lot again."

"Really?" Scape's tongue distorted his cheek as
he gazed at me. "Maybe we could make the invitation seem more interesting to you… you never
know…"

A hand lightly touched my shoulder; I turned

and saw Miss McThane, eyes half-lidded, smiling at me. "It'd be really nice if you came," she said. "There's a lot just you and I could talk about—"

I pulled away. "Please remove yourselves; both of you. My mind is completely resolute on the matter. You are wasting your time – nothing will alter my decision."

"Maybe; maybe not." Scape stepped over to the window and flung the shutter open. "How about this for starters?"

Massed torch-flames at the end of the street cast a lurid, flickering glow over my face, as I stepped close to the glass and gaped out at the scene. A mob of people were shouting encouragement to the speaker who addressed them from atop an overturned crate. To my horror, I saw an effigy stuffed with straw, swaying over their heads. It was no Guy Fawkes at the end of the rope; a crudely lettered sign around the figure's neck spelled out *DOWER THE JACK*.

I staggered back from the window, but not before recognising the upraised speaker as Mrs Trabble. "My God," I said hoarsely. "She's... she's gone and—" I broke off, unable to contemplate with what infamies she could be regaling the riotous assemblage.

Scape surveyed the mob with a calmly critical eye. "Lot more of 'em now," he noted. "Look like a fun-loving bunch, too." He turned towards me. "It's probably nothing against you personally – just an excuse to drink a bit… and bash somebody up a bit… and stuff like that, you know…"

The distant torches waved higher; I could hear some sort of chant beginning. "I've got to flee from here–"

Scape's arms spread wide. "Hey – that's what I was just saying, man. A country vacation; what could be nicer than that? Especially when you got a whole bunch of people who want to kick your ass right outside your front door. You can just cool out at Bendray's place, you know, wait for things to die down back here… this bunch'll forget about you after a while. And if you and Bendray find something, um… interesting to talk about while you're there – hey, that's a bonus." His smile returned as he stroked the point of his chin with one long finger. "So what do you say? Hm?"

The formidable Mrs Trabble, having been the latest terror to appear in my life, perhaps out-weighed all other considerations. My resolutions regarding Scape and Bendray, and the entire insane carnival they represented, were washed away in the sudden flood of panic engendered by the sight of the mob being whipped up outside. I turned and shouted towards the rear of the shop: "Creff! Quickly – my trunk…"

"Screw your luggage, man." Scape shook his head in disgust as he addressed his companion. "Can you believe this turkey's just about to get stomped into the pavement, and he's worried about having enough clean socks."

"Pardon, sir... I took the liberty..." A travelling case, with the sleeves of several of my shirts dangling from under its lid, came bumping down the stairs after Creff. Evidently, his encounter with Mrs Trabble had likewise impressed him, and spurred him to appropriate action. I saw that he had put on his much-patched coat, his cap crammed into its pocket.

"Of course, my assistant comes with us," I said to Scape. "We couldn't leave him here – to their mercies–"

"Yeah, yeah, sure." Scape was growing visibly agitated, perhaps by the increasingly louder shouts of the mob. "Bendray's rich, he's got a big place, no problem. Just come on, will ya?"

"And Abel!" cried Creff. "Him too!"

"Who?" This sudden interjection baffled me.

"Abel, sir! The dog! Who'll look after him?"

I looked down at my feet and saw the liquid, trusting eyes of the animal that had once been the wretched Fexton's, and was now apparently mine. It gazed up at me, waiting patiently for its fate to be pronounced. The realisation struck me – of course! – that Creff had taken my introductory explanation of the dog's nature – a bell-dog – as its name: Abel Dog. As good as any, I supposed.

"For Christ's sake!" shouted Scape. "Are you going to just stand there, looking at that stupid mutt? Bring the friggin' dog along – what do I care? But let's get this show on the road, okay?"

Miss McThane gave me a forceful shove in the small of my back. "Out the other way – the carriage is in the alley. Move it, move it."

"One more thing–" Scape grabbed my arm. "You got something ol' Bendray's real interested in. And we know it's here. Get it," he ordered. "Quick."

The commotion from the crowd had grown both louder and higher-pitched. I shook off the befuddlement with which the rapid course of events had seized my thoughts. The device that the Brown Leather Man had lodged with me – that was the item of which he spoke; no doubt it had been Lord Bendray who had commissioned their unsuccessful attempt to steal it from these premises. So he desired it still and the promise of sanctuary was dependent upon my furnishing it to him. Without hesitation, I ran down the hallway to the workroom and came staggering back with the weighty mahogany cabinet in my arms.

In a matter of moments, my trunk was lodged on top of the carriage with Creff and the driver – one of Bendray's men, I assumed – and the balance of the party was safely installed inside. My father's creation, the source of so much skulduggery, lay on the carriage's floor between us.

Abel, as he was newly christened, scrambled up into my lap as the carriage, its brace of horses whipped into flight, shot from the alley. He barked furiously out the side window at the sight of Mrs Trabble's mob moving from its point of assembly towards my now-empty shop, their torches waving in gleeful anticipation. The shrill whistles of the constabulary, summoning others of their number to the scene, echoed through the surrounding lanes.

Such was to be my last sight and memory of that small haven, once so peaceful and undisturbed, for many a day to come. The carriage clattered on towards the dark boundaries of the city, and beyond.

PART TWO
An Evening's Entertainment

8

The Complete Destruction of the Earth

Long periods of travel induce a somnolence that neither refreshes the body nor soothes the mind. Whether one is enduring the nauseating roll of a ship caught between the crests and troughs of the ocean, or having one's spine jerked by the lurching crash of a carriage's wheels in the ruts and holes of England's roads, the effect is the same. One cannot sleep; dismal vistas pass by one's gaze, in day or night; one swallows over and over again the sour, nagging protest of one's digestion, rising constantly into the throat; comfort there is none, nor peace sufficient to order and reconnect the thoughts shaken against each other like the fragments of a crumbled mosaic.

I have little patience with the Oriental maxim *It is better to travel hopefully than to arrive*. (Who has not savoured the delicious pleasure of stepping once more on to motionless ground and feeling one's muscles and bones sweetly unlock themselves?) Rather I believe that, if a dull and cramped Hell were to be one's final punishment, it would be best achieved in a perpetually rolling carriage.

Such was the nature of my reflections, once the initial excitement of my flight from the hands of the street mob had ebbed. We passed the greater portion of the journey in an uncomfortable silence. From time to time I would open my eyes and look about the vehicle's dim interior, lit only by the moon and starlight slanting through the side windows. Across from me, Miss McThane had managed to fall asleep, her mouth open to emit a soft, ladylike snore. Beside her, Scape sat with folded arms and chin heavy on his chest; his blue spectacles made it impossible to determine if he was unconscious or merely sunk in the contemplation of further villainy. When we had first left the precincts of the city, the carriage entering the deep quiet of the Kent-ward road, he had spent some time bending down to inspect the mahogany cabinet on the floor; he had at last given up the attempt to fathom the mysteries of the device owing to a lack of sufficient light. Abel – the only creature inside the carriage worthy of my trust, Creff being stationed atop with the driver – rested his chin oil my leg, only closing his eyes in an ecstatic swoon whenever my hand strayed to scratch behind his ears.

My own thoughts – or fragments thereof – chased and battered themselves against my brow. I knew not where we were bound, nor what my reception would be when we arrived. Perhaps I had been inveigled thus to my own murder; one attempt towards this end had already been encountered by me; of the circumstances that had delivered me from the cold embrace of the Thames, I still awaited explanation. Certain it was that ruthless forces had arrayed themselves in the London night: the corpses of Fexton and the Brown Leather Man attested to that. (The vision of the latter overturning the ruffians' boat I was even more certain of being a delusion; the sight of the poor man's fatal wounds remained sharp in my memory.) If Scape and his employer Bendray were not in league with these desperate men, there was still little else to recommend them to my confidence. Surely, I asked myself as the back of my head jolted against the carriage's thinly padded leather, surely these people were insane? How else account for the lunatic blasphemy of their attentions upon the church of Saint Mary Alderhythe? (A blasphemy, and lunacy, that I bitterly knew was now attributed to me.) I had yet to wake from the dream that my life had. become; my sleep had been rewarded not with the dawn's returning of my old dull life, but with the continuation of awful night and chaos.

These and similarly cheerless ruminations were interrupted by the dog Abel. His ears pricked up, and he started from his doze; in a trice he had scrambled into my lap the better to unleash a volley of furious barking against the window, his front paws pattering on the glass.

"Jesus H. Christ." Scape had been apparently asleep behind his dark spectacles; they rose for a moment up on to his forehead as he rubbed his stiff face. "What the hell's all the racket about?"

Beside him, Miss McThane burrowed her shoulder deeper into the corner of the seat, in a futile attempt to escape the sudden noise. "Shut your goddamn dog up, Dower," she muttered unladylike.

"Abel... I say–" I grasped the thin collar that his former master had bestowed on him and tried to pull him back from the window. "Calm down, old boy."

A small gap at the top of the window had been left open for ventilation during the journey. With renewed determination, Abel wedged his sharp muzzle in the space and howled even more vigorously.

"You know – I think he's seen something." I positioned the side of my face against the window, the better to view behind the carriage. "Something out there."

This pronouncement brought Scape sitting bolt upright, his irritable fatigue forgotten. Miss McThane lifted her head as well, her eyes widening.

Scape leaned forward, balancing himself with one hand against the opposite seat, and joined me in my scrutiny of the night unrolling behind the carriage's progress. We had been travelling out from London for such a time that dawn was no more than one or two hours away; already the darkness had thinned sufficiently to bring a thin grey outline to the black tracery of country hedge and tree.

The shapes of cloaked riders moved against those, keeping pace with us.

"Shit," muttered Scape. He had lifted his spectacles in order to discern the silhouettes following us; the slight radiance of the stars produced a slow tear from the corner of his overly sensitive eyes. "It's that friggin' Godly bunch."

"Them again?" Miss McThane sounded peeved. "How'd they find out about us coming here?"

He adjusted his spectacles to their original position. "Beats me – must have an inside line somewhere. Maybe ol' Bendray's butler or somebody is working a double."

"Godly bunch?" I echoed. "Who are they?"

"Never you mind." Scrape lowered the window and shouted to the driver: "You wanna pick it up a bit?" The whip snapped in response and the carriage jolted harder in the ruts as Scape began rummaging through the pockets of his coat. "This'll take care of those suckers."

I saw that he had extracted a bulky cap-and-ball pistol of considerable antiquity. "Watch it with that thing, will ya?" said Miss McThane. "The last time–"

"Yeah, yeah," said Scape irritably. Part of the gun's mechanism had fallen off, and he screwed it back into place with his thumbnail. "Don't worry." To me: "Slide over."

Restraining the still-agitated dog, I moved aside. Scape took his position, bracing his arm against the sill and squinting over the top of the pistol. A dull click of metal against metal sounded when he drew the trigger.

"Shit. All this friggin' rain." He banged the pistol against the inside wall of the carriage as both Miss McThane and I cringed in the opposite corners. As soon as he pointed the pistol out the window again, it went off with a deafening report and burst of flame.

"*Chinga tu madre.*" Scape nursed his singed hand with his mouth. The several pieces of the gun had flown out of his grip. "Son-of-a-bitch."

The shot had seemed to cause no damage, the bullet having gone slanting into the muddy road. Its noise, however, had managed to inspire our horses to greater effort. Peering out the window, I saw that our ghostly escort had wisely fallen back as well.

Scape nodded with satisfaction when I pointed this out to him. "Chicken-shit bastards," he said as he prodded the small burn on his palm.

"Jee-zuss," said Miss McThane. "You idiot." She gave Scape a final glower before adjusting her wrap about her shoulders and resuming her interrupted slumber.

When the morning light broke over the horizon some time later, there was no longer any sign of our pursuers; they had vanished as though they had been but animate fragments of the ebbing darkness. From the carriage's window I looked out on to a passing landscape of remarkable cheerlessness and foetidity. The rising sun glinted red across weed-choked marshland. At irregular spacing though these fens, the rounded hillocks of high ground supported a few stunted, crook-branched trees and decaying hovels. Thin-shanked pigs rooted though mud distinguishable from the surrounding countryside only by intervening walls of rough stone, shaggy with ancient moss. A figure in the distance, blurred by the mists drifting up from the stagnant waters, toiled with stick along one of the muddy paths winding through the mires.

The thick, musky odour of rotting vegetation prompted me to draw my head back into the carriage. Scape looked at my appalled expression with some amusement. "Great place, ain't it?" he said with a thin smile.

I made no reply. The carriage slowed down, and I saw that we had entered a small village. Low buildings, some appearing to have subsided so far into the muck that their thatched eaves nearly touched the ground, squatted around an open space. At its centre, marked by a well that was little more than a circle of stones outlining a crumbling hole and a slanting cross-beam with bucket and rope attached, a ragged cluster of the locals stood about.

"Where is this?" My spirits, already drained by the rigours of the long journey, were further oppressed by this picture of rural squalor.

"The scenic village of Dampford," said Scape. "These poor slobs are all Bendray's tenants. His Hall is just a little further on."

As I gazed out, the carriage's wheels spattered mud across the backs of the clustered villagers. Some of them turned, tugging at their caps in respectful deference. I saw their faces and fell back against the seat, horrified. "God in Heaven!" I faintly heard Scape's and Miss McThane's mocking laughter.

The faces of the Dampford villagers were the same exophthalmic, slope-browed visages as those of the residents of that London borough called Wetwick.

The piscine physiognomies swam in my vision, those from out of the memory of that nocturnal ordeal in the city's depths merging with their apparent brethren gaping after the carriage. There could be little doubt that I had been transported to the native soil – or marsh – from which this enigmatic and ugly race had sprung. And what of Bendray, their landlord? He was not of their blood, yet he maintained some manner of proprietary concern over their cousins in distant London – I had noted the paternal expansiveness in his welcoming of them to the church of Saint Mary Alderhythe. A shiver descended the vertebral ladder between my shoulder blades as I mulled over these affairs – the faces of the Wetwick and Dampford broods had become inextricable fixtures of my nightmares, and here I had found myself amongst them yet again.

The squalid village fell behind as the road began to ascend. I pressed myself into the corner of the seat, my thoughts obscuring the sodden view as I grimly contemplated the possible explanations for my journey hither.

"Dower – how good of you to come. Yes; yes, most welcome. There's so much we have to discuss. Much, much... indeed."

Lord Bendray himself had come down the wide stone steps to the carriage in order to greet us. He clasped my hand in both of his and held it with the tender, if trembling, regard due to a long-lost relation. His rheumy eyes peered at me without benefit of the lenses of the complicated magnifying spectacles pushed up on to his brow; he had evidently been engaged in some scientific endeavour when his manservant had brought the news of our arrival. A similar pair of spectacles had been found by me in my shop's workroom; I could recognize my father's craftsmanship in these adorning Bendray as well.

"How was your journey? Uneventful, I trust?" He took my arm, supporting his own age-feebled steps as he drew me towards the Hall. Its vine-encrusted walls loomed above; the crowning turret of one wing had been amputated at some time in the past, to accommodate a brass sphere, now discoloured with verdigris. An articulated opening in the metal curve revealed the polished barrels of various astronomical apparatus.

I looked behind me to see Creff officiously su-
pervising the unloading of my trunk from atop the
carriage, while Scape assisted Miss McThane in
alighting. Beyond them, the approach to the Hall
slanted down through elaborately terraced gardens, or to be precise, the remains of such. The
sculpted ponds were filled with stagnant green, the
silent fountains in their midst choked with dead
leaves. On either side of the formally laid paths,
the topiary hedges had grown vague, their previous shapes lost beneath the unrestrained new
growth. The state of decay seemed due more to
inattention than to that discreet poverty into
which the landed gentry so often decline; Lord
Bendray appeared to have no lack of household
staff. A pair of grooms were leading the unhar-
nessed carriage-horses to the stables; at the Hall's
entrance I could spy a rank of butlers and other
servants awaiting us.

I turned my attention back to my host. "There
were some men, your Lordship. Riders–"

His other brown-spotted hand made a gesture of
dismissal. "Yes, yes; the Godly Army. Tiresome lot.
Think nothing of it."

"Here, you – where do you think you're getting
off to with that? Personal property of Mr Dower,
it is."

We turned about at the sound of my assistant's
raised voice. Creff had arrested Scape in mid-stride,
grasping him by the lapel of his coat. Under one of

Scape's arms was the weighty cabinet that held my father's device.

"Capital!" shouted Lord Bendray. His smile deepened the wrinkles in his face. "Is that it? You've brought the Regulator? Well done!" He beamed at me and Scape in turn; a wave of his hand sent one of his liveried staff over to relieve the other of the burden. "Take that to the laboratory; there's a good man." As he was instructing his servant, he did not observe the silent glare that Scape trained upon Creff. The desire that he had manifested for a closer examination of the device had been frustrated once more. For his part, Creff returned the angry look, seconded by the dog Abel held against his chest.

Lord Bendray's arm linked with mine pulled me up the stone steps. "Great things will be accomplished now, my boy. Your father's creation – the Aetheric Regulator – marvellous thing!" He lapsed into an excited muttering, his eyes brightening with the contemplation of some interior vision. "Yes, yes; your father was a genius, no doubt of that... great things, great... yes; and with the Regulator – and your assistance – the culmination of my researches! You'll see!" His claw-like grip tightened on my arm, his withered face peering eagerly into mine. "Great things!"

We had arrived by this time in the foyer of Bendray Hall, with the train of attendants, Creff, Scape, and Miss McThane following after. Underneath the domed ceiling, I halted, having come to a decision. My various pretences at knowledge, and of membership in the conspiracies surrounding me, had not served to enhance my safety. Indeed, the masquerade had only embroiled me further into hazard and, as evidenced by my hasty flight from London, disrepute. I thus resolved to make a clean breast of my ignorance; I could not envision how it could possibly place me in difficulties greater than those which I had already endured.

I withdrew my arm from Lord Bendray's, and placed myself directly in front of him. "Your Lordship – I must confess – I have absolutely no idea of the matters whereof you speak. I fear I have been introduced into your confidence under false pretences–"

Scape had overheard me; he quickly came up behind me, grabbing my arm to pull me away. "Sorry; guy's a little over-exhausted from the trip, I think." He gave Bendray a strained smile. "Nervous type, you know…" He brought his mouth close to my ear and whispered: "What the hell do you think you're doing?"

I shook him off and renewed my address to Lord Bendray. "It's true; I am in complete ignorance of these things–"

"Don't pay any attention to him! He's flipped out!"

The vast interior of Bendray Hall, with its colonnaded, marble staircases, seemed to wheel about me as I spun about on my heel with hands up-raised. "I don't know for what purpose you've brought me here; what you expect me to be able to assist you with – and this thing you call a Reg-ulator... Granted, my father may have constructed it, but what it is, and what it does, are subjects be-yond my comprehension!"

"Indeed?" Lord Bendray greeted this revelation, not with the outrage that Scape had apparently ex-pected, but with a quizzical smile. "My dear boy – why didn't you tell me this sooner?" He took my arm again, solicitously patting it with one veiny hand. "There should be no secrets in matters of Science. My word, no; I forgot that you had not the opportunity to spend time with your late fa-ther as I had. A brilliant man, he was – yes; yes, indeed; brilliant." He drew me on, his tottering steps leading into one of the Hall's wings. "You shall know all; that I promise you–"

I looked over my shoulder and saw Scape, palms upward, shrugging mutely at Miss McThane.

"Ah, here's the port. That will be all." Lord Ben-dray dismissed his servant, but retained the bottle from the silver tray. I took the offered glass and fol-lowed after him. He had guided me down several flights of stairs, the walls mouldering with damp and age, to reach his laboratory beneath the Hall.

He swallowed the contents of his glass in a single go, head thrown back and the cords of his thin neck tightening around the wobbling bob of his Adam's apple. The dark port brought a diluted spot of its colour into his grey cheeks. He sauntered beneath low stone arches, the bottle angling in his hand, appearing the model of a London *roué* entering some haunt of dissipation.

I looked about the space as I sipped from my own glass. It stretched as far as I could readily see; from the aspect of the walls and ceiling, it appeared as if the various chambers beneath the Hall had been knocked into one, leaving only the great stone pillars to support the weight of the house towering above. Rows of gas jets provided illumination; several of these had lens and reflector contrivances to magnify and focus their light upon the various workbenches and racks of equipment strewn through the area. Everywhere the glitter of polished brass reflected into my eye. Again, my father's craftsmanship; more of it than I had ever seen before in one place, including the workroom of his that I had inherited with the shop. Some of the items I recognised as duplicates, albeit in better preserved condition, of those in my possession. Others were unrecognised by me, and of unguessable function, in form as varied as what seemed an articulated spider taller than a man, or a simple pocket watch with dial calibrated into unknown hours. The latter I picked up as I passed the bench it lay upon; the motion of my hand triggered some internal mechanism; a soft, bell-like chime sounded. The note stopped only when I realised it was counting out the measure of my pulse, and I dropped the device with a sudden unreasoning panic. I hurried after Lord Bendray as he progressed through this clockwork Aladdin's Cave.

"Great things…" Lord Bendray's wavering voice echoed from the limits of the subterranean space. The level in the bottle had gone down by several measures; his spirits were correspondingly elevated. "The man was a genius…"

"Your Lordship – perhaps you had better rest a bit." We had come far from the stairs by which we had descended; looking about, I could not even see in which direction they lay, so confusing were the interlacing arches and pillars. Alone as we were, I was concerned if the elderly gentleman should meet with some accident due to excitement and inebriation. "You said… explanations – careful, your Lordship– "you shall know all" were the words, I believe… Oh! Are you all right?"

In his increasingly unsteady progress, he had stumbled over the edge of one of the flooring stones. I rushed to his assistance, but he sat up unaided and held the intact bottle triumphantly aloft. "Sit down, my boy." He patted a raised section beside himself. "Sit; and let us talk… about…" He swayed gently from side to side as he stared in front of himself, "… great things…"

I did as he instructed. "Are you all right?" I asked again.

"Never better," he said brightly, snapping a wide-eyed gaze around to me. "My dear boy – we are on the verge…"

"Of great things?" I suggested.

He nodded, raising a skeletal finger for emphasis. "New worlds," he spoke in a quavering whisper. "We… are not alone."

I looked around the cavernous laboratory, but saw no one else. "Beg pardon?"

His finger jabbed towards the ceiling. "Up there… no, not in the Hall, you doll… Beyond! In the skies! The stars! Intelligences – not like us, you understand, different; and much more advanced… marvellous stuff. Makes us look like children in the nursery. Whizzing about…"

"Whizzing about in the nursery?" I grew even more concerned about the effect of the alcohol on his enfeebled constitution. Perhaps this was the explanation for some of the other lunacies generated by him.

"No, no; in the skies! Between the planets – and the stars! I've seen them," he concluded with decisive finality.

"I'm not sure I understand…"

Lord Bendray sighed and poured himself another drink. "Evidently not. Your father did, however; what insights that man had! The Cosmos was an open book to him. Mind you, I had long suspected their existence. But your father proved it! Showed them to me!"

"Showed who?" A display of interest on my part seemed to have a calming effect on the old gentleman. To myself, I was debating whether it would be better to drag him along in search of the stairs leading out, or abandon him and seek some helpful member of his household staff.

"Them! Who else? Creatures of worlds not our own, intelligences far greater than ours." He leaned closer to me, his voice dropping to a secretive pitch. "Mark you, my boy – the earth is the subject of scrutiny by beings from other planets." He straightened up, maintaining a wobbling dignity. "I – myself – have seen them," he announced.

"You have?" It was worse than I had thought.

He nodded. "Not here – though I've tried; bloody fortune in telescopes and what-not up on the roof. They seem," he mused, "to prefer isolated locales for their occasional forays into our atmosphere. On Groughay that's where I saw them. In one of their great celestial vehicles."

"Where's that?" Perhaps if he talked out his mania, a measure of sanity would be restored, and we could return to the Hall proper.

A bony hand waved towards some vague distance. "A little island – Outer Hebrides. Ancestral seat of the Bendrays. Godforsaken place; nothing but rock and seaweed. Nothing wrong with seaweed, mind you. A lot of money to be made from seaweed. That was the first commission I ever gave your father… seaweed."

He appeared to have drifted off into some recess of memory. Oblivious to my presence, he gazed abstractedly in front of himself.

I prodded him: "Seaweed, you say…"

"Seaweed?" He turned his fierce glare one me. "Bugger seaweed; filthy stuff. Keep your mind on the important matters. *We can contact beings from another world* – think of it! The things they could tell us: Science; the Secrets of the Universe… and more, perhaps! We have but to signal them. And they'll come to us."

"Who will?"

He rolled his eyes at my obtuseness. "I've told you: those beings from other worlds. Who already have observed our puny, earthbound comings and goings, in the lenses of their powerful observatories and close at hand. I tell you again: they are but waiting for our sign."

I at last perceived the general outline of his obsession. "Yes… well, your Lordship… that's really quite interesting. A sign from us, you say? Hm. I don't suppose a rather large banner would do?"

"Certainly not." He got to his feet, the dregs of port sloshing in the bottle. "Come with me, my boy. You shall see… all."

Lord Bendray led me further into the laboratory's reaches. "Steady on, there," he cautioned after a few minute's wavering progress.

"Pardon? Christ in Heaven!" I leapt back from the edge of a circular chasm; another step would have precipitated me into its inky depths. A fragment of stone fell from the stone lip; no sound came back of it reaching bottom.

Lord Bendray stationed himself before the hole. It curved round in either direction for some distance, appearing large enough to have swallowed a small village such as the loathsome Dampford beyond the Hall's gates. The far edge was hidden from view by rough stone pillars that descended into the pit, their lower ends lost to sight in the darkness. Above them, an intricate arrangement of cross-beams, great geared wheels taller than a man, chains thick enough to suspend houses by, and other machinery looped and dipped to make connection with the pillars.

My host gazed raptly at the stone. "They go down," he pronounced solemnly, "straight to bedrock. And beyond – hundreds of feet." He looked back at me. "Your father's last creation. Such a tragedy that he died before this – his masterpiece – could be set into operation."

I held myself well away from the chasm's edge. My eyes travelled across the massive beams and chains. "What is it?"

"Soldiers, my boy..." Lord Bendray's vision went straight through me and on to his private contemplations. He took a swallow directly from the mouth of the bottle. "Marching soldiers..."

Behind me, I could see the glitter of the brass devices on the distant workbenches; the supportive

arches intertwined confusingly. The prospects of
my finding my own way out appeared dismal.

Lord Bendray's eyes focussed on me again. "Soldiers marching across a bridge – ever see that?" I
shrugged. "I suppose so, your Lordship. A military
parade, or some such."

"Good." He waggled a finger at me in school-
master fashion. "Now, this is fairly common
knowledge – I suspect you've heard of it – but very
often, when a troop of soldiers is crossing a bridge,
the men are ordered to break step. Not left-right,
left-right, all together; but every man going along,
out of step with those next to him. Until they're
all safely on the other side; then it's off they mer-
rily go again, left-right, left-right in unison. Now,
then; why is that? Eh?"

"Well…" I searched my brain for some half-forgotten explanation. "It's the vibrations, isn't it?
Um. Reverberations, or something. If all the men
went marching across in step, the bridge might
start to vibrate along to the rhythm of their pace.
And – let's see – if they kept on marching over it,
the bridge's vibration would be reinforced, and
would grow stronger, and – possibly – the bridge
would eventually shake itself to pieces beneath
their feet."

"Oh, not just possibly, my boy – it's happened
many times in actuality. Miliary practice is not de-
rived from mere intellectual speculation, you
know; destroying something is really the best way

to learn. No, the best method of crossing a bridge is something that has been proven on the field, as it were."

Seaweed; beings from other worlds; now correct marching drill. I felt sadly perplexed by this evidence of incipient senility. "Yes, well... fascinating, I'm sure. Um... perhaps we should be getting back... rejoin the others... tea, perhaps–"

He shook his head impatiently. "You will admit, then, that through this principle, an item of considerable mass – say, a bridge – can be destroyed by the precise action of a smaller mass – such as a troop of marching soldiers?"

"Yes; I suppose so..."

"And can you conceive of any reason why that destructive principle should not hold true, regardless of the relative disparity between the larger and smaller mass?"

"Well... I've never really thought about it–"

Lord Bendray pressed on, his wrinkled face tightening with excitement: "Provided – of course! – that you can determine the exact rhythm of pulsations to apply to the larger mass... Eh? What say you to that?" he concluded triumphantly.

I shrugged. "Sounds reasonable to me." Best to go on humouring him, I supposed.

He whirled about at the edge of the precipice, raising his arms in adoration of the stone pillars. "That, my boy, is the purpose of this, your father's magnum opus!"

The hairs at the back of my neck began to stand up, as I sensed a madness even greater than I had at first suspected.

Glancing over his shoulder, Lord Bendray read the awful surmise visible in my face. "Yes – you've got it – you've got it, my boy! Exactly so! The senior Dower was a master of that Science properly known as Cataclysm Harmonics. Just as the marching soldiers transmit the vibrations that bring the bridge tumbling into bits, so this grand construction–" He gestured towards the stone pillars stretching down into the pit. "Your father's greatest creation – so it is designed to transmit equally destructive pulsations into the core of the earth itself. Pulsations that build, and reinforce themselves – marching soldiers! Hah! Yes – until this world is throbbing with them, and shakes itself to its component atoms!" The vision set him all a-tremble. "The bridge collapses; the world disintegrates... Just so, just so." He nodded happily.

I stared up at the construction, appalled by the old gentleman's fervour. Could it be? I was struck with a dread certainty that he had spoken the truth. My father's creation... Surely there could be no doubting it. If such a thing were the product of his genius, then, for good or ill, it very likely was as potent as all else that had come from his hand and mind.

"But–" I looked to him, baffled. "What would be the purpose of such a destruction?" A terrible vision centred itself in my thoughts, of mountains splitting in twain, deserts shivering as the oceans welled up in their midst, the grinding of splintered stone and the shrieking of women. "What cause would it serve?"

He gazed at me with patient benevolence. "Why, that of which we were just speaking," he said. "That of contacting those wise, advanced beings on the other worlds. What possible signal could be better? Surely, creatures that are capable of shattering the world on which they live, would be perceived by those intelligences as beings worthy of respect and attention. It stands to reason."

His calm voice, speaking in measured tones of annihilation, echoed inside my skull. "But – but if what you say is true… there won't be any contacting these beings – or anything else! We'll all be dead!"

"Pooh! You worry yourself needlessly. Come over here." Lord Bendray strode away from the chasm's edge, towards another section of the laboratory. I followed behind him, glancing over my shoulder at the awesome machinery containing the earth's demise in its gears.

"Here we are." He slapped a curved wall of brass, that rang hollow beneath his hand. "The Hermetic Carriage I'm proud to say that this, at least, is all my own design."

I followed the direction of his gesture, and found myself gazing at a great riveted sphere, looming up to the stone ceiling. Various excrescences – round windows, lanterns, and incongruously, a large

Union Jack on an articulated metal arm-studded the polished brass.

"Quite a thing, eh?" Lord Bendray beamed at me. "Come up here – this way."

Our boots clattered on a flight of metal steps that led to a platform halfway up the sphere's circumference. Lord Bendray tapped one of the small windows. "Observe," he said. I pressed my face close to the thick glass and saw a reduced version of a gentleman's sitting room: a thickly upholstered chair and ottoman, a wall of books close by, a humidor and small rack of bottles. The curved walls were clad in tooled morocco, the floor covered with an antique Tabriz. The only inappropriate notes, in this picture of comfort were various metal flasks linked to each other by coils of tubing.

"See – those are for the breathing supply." Lord Bendray pushed his face close to mine, the better to point out the details inside the sphere. "Food and other essentials in those cabinets over there. The controls for the signalling lanterns and other external armatures... Rather well thought out, don't you agree?"

I drew away from him. "I'm not sure I understand the purpose of this device."

"Well, it's really all very simple. When the earth shatters apart, something like that can't fail to come to the attention of beings from those other worlds. They'll surely come to investigate the debris. And when they do, I'll be able to signal to them, as though from a lifeboat bobbing about over a sunken ship. Once they've ascertained my peerage and citizenship, I imagine they'll take me back to the place whence they came for long discussions and consultation." He rubbed his chin meditatively. "I would think... Mars. Yes; very likely to Mars."

The platform's handrail grew damp in my grasp. "But what of the earth? And all the people on it?"

"Tut, tut. We can't let mere sentiment intrude. This is *Science*."

"But all of Mankind destroyed? In one final cataclysm?"

"None of that," scoffed Lord Bendray. "Look at those camp beds in there. I'll have you know I've made extensive provision for several of my household staff to come along with me. A gentleman couldn't very well travel without them, could he?"

I swayed backwards, dizzied by this calm discussion of death and horror. "This is madness, and you know it! Yes!" I seized the front of the old man's coat. "No one could actually contemplate such a deed – that's why you've never set this hideous machinery into operation!"

He brushed my trembling hands from his lapels. "Hardly," he said with lofty disdain. "The fact of the matter is that the device was left incomplete at your father's death. The great structure is there, set to hammer its destructive rhythm into the earth's core; but what has been lacking is the subtle regulatory device necessary to determine those pulsations and set the machinery into the appropriate motion. Lacking until now, that is."

Retreating from his words – for my heart had already plummeted, knowing what they would be – I came close to falling down the metal steps, retaining my balance only by my grip upon the rail.

"Yes," said Lord Bendray, smiling at me. "Now the great work can be completed. You have brought the Regulator to me."

I turned and fled, headlong down the metal steps, away from his quavering soft voice and benign smile, and into the maze of stone arches before me.

9

An Interrupted Recital

"The man's insane – we have to stop him! Before he destroys the world!"

Even through the blue lenses, Scape's pitying glance was clearly readable. He tilted a bottle of port, identical to that private stock from which Lord Bendray had served me, then wiped his mouth with the back of his hand. "Did he lay that tired old wheeze on you? What a jerk." He shook his head in disgust.

I was still out of breath owing to my panicked flight from Lord Bendray's subterranean laboratory, my hands bruised from collision with the stone arches. Guided only by desperation, I had blundered my way up into the Hall itself, and had at last found Scape in one of the upstairs rooms, sitting in his shirtsleeves on the corner of a bed. My brain was still awhirl with the quavering voice and its words. "Don't you understand?" I cried. "The cataclysm – everything, bits and pieces – like marching soldiers–"

Miss McThane wandered in from an adjoining bathroom, her arms bare as she rubbed her damp hair with a towel. "What's all the shouting about?"

Scape pointed his thumb at me. "Ol' Bendray just told Dower that he's planning on blowing up the world."

"Oh, that." She drifted back out of the room.

I grasped him by the shoulder. "But, we have to do something–"

He shook me off. "Simmer down, for Christ's sake. I can't believe you just now flashed on the fact that Bendray's crazy."

"But – the machine – underneath the Hall–"

"'Cause he is nuts, you know. Completely round the bend. I could tell that the first time I ever laid eyes on the sucker. That's where all that stuff about blowing up the world comes from – right out of his little loose-screw skull."

I took a step backwards. "You mean… it's not true?"

"Shee-it." The bottle lifted to his mouth again. "He couldn't crack an egg with that pile of junk. Your old man was running a fraud on Bendray – one of several, actually. Did he give you that line about people from other planets zipping around in the sky? Yeah, well, I got my suspicions about where he got that one from, too. Him and the rest of his buddies in that dingbat Royal Anti-Society of theirs; if one of 'em wanted anything from a perpetual motion machine to a – whatever; pogo stick that worked on the ceiling, or some damn thing – your father would throw one together for 'em. Most of these old boys are so senile they wouldn't notice if any of it worked or not."

"Really…" I stood amazed. This was an aspect – or the imputation of it – to my father's character that I had never encountered before. "I can scarcely believe it."

"Come on, Dower. Two minutes ago, you were running around here, quacking that the whole world was gonna go bang. You gotta get hold of yourself, man."

My thoughts, that had been so agitated, began to settle into some form of order. 'Then the Regulator – the device that you had me bring with us from London…'

"No sweat," said Scape. "Granted, the old boy's been looking for it, but he's not gonna be able to turn on that giant cuckoo clock in the basement with it. I mean, after all; one of the reasons tried to swipe that gizmo out of your shop was because I knew Bendray wanted it. You really think I would've sold it to him if I thought he was gonna be able to blow up the world with it?"

"I suppose not," I mused. "Just a moment – how did you know that I had the device?"

"Jesus, Dower – what kind of business do you think I'm in? I'm supposed to find out about stuff like that. I got ways."

I nodded, undisturbed by this frank admission of criminality of his part. A great sense of relief had

come over me; whatever mysteries still surrounded me, they were at least not compounded
by the imminent annihilation of the earth.

"Maybe you better go lie down or something,"
advised Scape. "You look wiped." He stood up
and guided me by the elbow to the doorway,
from where he pointed out the room farther
along the hallway that had been designated as
mine. "Get some rest, man – Bendray's head butler told me there's a dinner party tonight; some
of the old boy's Royal Anti-Society bunch are
coming over."

"Who are they?" I had been mystified by the term
when I had heard it before from Lord Bendray.

"Nobody." Scape gave me a push towards my
room. "Just a buncha old geezers. Crackpots.
Nothing to worry about." The door closed in my
face before I could ask any more questions.

I found Creff laying out my clothes upon the
bed. The dog Abel was curled asleep upon the pillow; his ears pricked up on my entrance, but he
made no other motion. "Rum lot round here,"
grumbled Creff as he pulled more items from the
trunk. "Never seen such queer coves, have I."

Weary, I sat down in a convenient chair. "You
little know," I said, "how true you speak." I tilted
my head back and closed my eyes.

I awoke some hours later, with the gas-mantles lit
to dispel the evening gloom. Creff was prodding

my shoulder. "There's people arriving soon, sir. For some sort of to-do."

"Um… yes. Quite." I tasted my sour, dry mouth, and pushed myself up in the chair.

A vigorous application of soap and water brought me back to full consciousness. As I dressed, I felt an oddly familiar weight in the waist-coat pocket of the suit Creff had laid out. I drew out the Saint Monkfish crown and stood gazing at it for a moment.

How far had this mere bit of metal brought me, and yet no closer to answering the riddles it posed! That day on which the Brown Leather Man had given me the coin in payment seemed ever more from another time, another life. I had set out in blithe curiosity to ascertain this mysterious saint's identity, and to what end? The coin had bought me only the witnessing of two deaths – poor Fex-ton, and that dark-skinned progenitor of so many enigmas – and the threat of my own in the chill waters of the Thames. Those who promised to an-swer my queries, such as Lord Bendray, did so only by interjecting fresh conundrums.

There had to be an end to this. I re-pocketed the coin, resolving that if my demands for clarifi-cation were not met in the course of the evening, then I would strike out on my own for London, and have nothing more to do with these "queer coves", as Creff so aptly called them. An honest confession of my folly would be my shield against whatever spurious charges were being laid against me.

"Jesus H. Christ!" An out-of-breath Scape collided with me when I stepped out of my room. "Quick!" he said, and pulled me back into the doorway. "Now listen to me–"

I drew back from his flushed and panting face. "Whatever's the matter?"

He clutched my arm tighter. "I'm trying to tell ya, all right? Just listen, okay? I didn't know these people were gonna show up here tonight. So you gotta–"

"Who?" My resolve extended to refusing to be chivvied about by this excitable character. "What people?"

Scape brought himself under control, lowering his voice. "A guy named Wrath. Okay? Sir Charles Wrath, and his wife. They're the ones. I got told that Bendray had invited some of his Royal Anti-Society bunch over tonight, but nobody told me it was gonna be friggin' Wroth. So what you have to do–"

I peeled his hand fram my sleeve and dropped it. "I don't have to do anything," I said testily. "Unless I'm given a bloody good reason. What's so significant about this – Wroth, or whoever it is?"

"That's what I'm trying to tell ya, Dower." Scape's voice constricted to a hoarse whisper. "He's kind of… another client of mine. So to speak. You get what I mean?"

"You mean," I said coldly, "you engage in some sort of criminal activity on behalf of this gentleman."

"Well… yeah! Jeez!!" His words went up in pitch. "Give me the firing squad for trying to make a buck, you smug sonuvabitch!" He mastered himself again. "Look do me a favour, will ya? When you talk to the guy, just act natural. Okay? But don't–"

"Dower! There you are – come and meet my guests."

Scape was interrupted by Lord Bendray. The old man, returned to an apparent state of sobriety, came down the hallway and fastened on to my arm, by which he pulled me towards the stairs. "I'm sure you'll find them most interesting," he said. "Sir Charles has a keen interest in all things Scientific."

Beside me as we walked, Scape leaned close to my ear and whispered: "Just be cool, okay?"

As was often the case, I remained baffled by his puzzling syntax. I took it to be some sort of warning, but of what I had no idea.

I shortly found myself in a chandeliered banqueting room, under the inspection of a figure whose grey-haired age was belied by his upright military bearing. "I hope you'll excuse me," said Lord Bendray. "Small matters to attend to." He then scurried away.

Sir Charles leaned forward, peering at me even more intently. "Marvellous," he murmured to himself. "Really quite extraordinary." Surprisingly, he prodded at my chest with one finger. "Most life-like. Do you speak?" he suddenly addressed me.

I was somewhat taken aback by this odd query. "Well, yes. Of course." Behind him, I saw Scape making a variety of surreptitious hand gestures to me; they puzzled me enough to keep me from saying anything more. Beyond this, I was disturbed by an odd familiarity to Sir Charles' voice; it seemed to me I had heard him speak some time before, but I could not imagine where.

"'Of course,'" repeated Sir Charles with a smile. "Very droll, that." He turned round to Scape, who hastily ceased his signalling. "My congratulations – you've produced it here in remarkably fine operating order."

Scape shrugged modestly. "Yeah, well... we try our best." Miss McThane, her hair in an upswept coif, had entered the room, and stood beside him, smiling graciously.

A woman, younger than Sir Charles, and of considerable beauty and startling *décolletage*, stepped from beside him for a closer look. "Yes," Mrs Wroth said huskily, reaching up to run a silk-gloved hand down the side of my face. "Very... lifelike." Her hand trembled as it smoothed the curve of my shoulder; her eyes, limpid cerulean, narrowed in the manner I had observed before in Miss McThane. J could not speak for the sudden congestion of my pulse in my throat; Sir Charles seemed oblivious to the evident nature of her interest in me.

"I congratulate your maker – or I would, if he were still alive." Sir Charles served himself and his wife from a tray of claret brought around by one of Bendray's staff. "Superb workmanship – simply superb. I look forward to tonight's performance."

Mrs Wroth took a sip of wine; the tip of her tongue caught a red drop at the corner of her mouth. Her elegant hands toyed with the stem of her glass as she gazed at me. "Yes," she said. "It should be... very moving." She looked round at Miss McThane; the two women exchanged venomous glances.

Scape strode over to me and grabbed me by the arm. "Needs some minor adjustments, however, folks." He smiled and gave a small wave with his free hand, as he tugged me away from the others. "Drink up... you know, kick back... we'll see you in a little bit." He forced his smile even wider. "Show time, right?" To me he whispered under his breath: "Come on. Don't blow it now."

"What is the meaning of all this nonsense?" I demanded as soon as Scape had pulled shut a door between us and those in the banqueting room. "What was he talking about – "superb workmanship" and all that–"

"Hey! I can explain." Scape made a pacifying gesture with the palms of his hands outward. "It's nothing to get worked up over – Sir Charles just happens to believe that you're... um... made out of clockwork. That's all."

I stared at him. "What?"

"Clockwork. You know – like machines. Like your father built. Sir Charles thinks you're a machine. Simple, huh?"

The absurdity of the explanation nettled me. "That may well be; however, I see no point in letting him go on suffering this misapprehension."

"Well…" Scape sucked his breath in through his teeth. "Actually, there is."

"If you expect me to help perpetrate some fraud upon this gentleman, for the benefit of your criminal enterprise–"

"Hey." He spread his hands farther apart. "It ain't just my ass on the line here, sucker. Sir Charles is a heavy dude in the Royal Anti-Society. They don't all take as kindly to somebody sailing in under false pretences as ol' Bendray did. I mean, they're a kick-ass bunch. They haven't lasted for a couple of hundred years by being all sweetness and light. They've had people snuffed for less."

"Snuffed…" I had a mental image of a candle flame being extinguished between a thumb and forefinger. "You mean, killed?"

"Way to go – you get the cigar."

"You told me they were a harmless bunch of old men!" Scape shrugged. "Harmless, shmarmless; you don't screw with them and you won't get harmed. All right? And if you do what I tell you to do, you'll be okay."

I glanced nervously over my shoulder, concerned

that the others might have heard our rising voices through the door. "What do I have to do?" I whispered. The threat of violence had dissipated my earlier resolve.

"Piece of cake." Scape took an elongated leather case from a sideboard and laid it on the table in front of me. He snapped it open and withdrew a violin and bow, which he then held out to me. "All you gotta do is... play a little."

"Pardon?" I looked at the instrument in his hands. "You mean – play the violin?"

"What's it look like, a friggin' trumpet? Yeah, the violin. Go on, take it." He thrust it towards me.

I shrank back from it. "But why?"

He sighed with exaggerated patience. "Look. Sir Charles thinks... that you... are a device... created by your father. Called the Paganinicon–"

"*The what–*"

"Listen up, will ya? The Paganinicon. A clockwork violinist. Modelled after the big wha-hah virtuoso. You follow? You are a clockwork – what's it – automaton, right; and you can play the violin as good as the real Paganini. Or at least that's what we want Sir Charles to go on thinking. See? I told you it was simple."

"But–" I looked in bewilderment from his face to the instrument. "I've never heard Paganini play; I've never even held a violin in my life!"

"So? How hard can it be?" Scape thrust it into my hands. "Go on, take it."

I held it awkwardly, the bow somehow having got tangled with the strings. "This is impossible–"

"Not like that; the other way around. Don't drop it, for Christ's sake – that's a genuine Guarnerius, that Sir Charles sent over. Worth a lotta money someday; already is, probably."

"No; no, I can't do it." The violin felt incredibly light in my hands, as though it could float off into the air if I released it. The glowing wood trembled with my pulse. "They'll never believe it–"

My protests were interrupted by the door being pulled open by one of Lord Bendray's servants. I could see beyond him that the banqueting room was now empty, as he informed us that the other guests were awaiting us in the music room. "Is your boss there?" asked Scape.

"No, sir; he is in his laboratory, with orders not to be disturbed."

Scape breathed a sigh of relief, and I realised a further extent of his duplicity; neither Lord Bendray nor Sir Charles was aware of how he had represented me to the other. Thus his panicky state when he had discovered that Sir Charles was here at Bendray Hall; his intrigues depended upon the two men being kept apart, at least as long as their attentions were centred upon me.

"It won't work," I whispered to him as the servant led us down another of the Hall's great high-ceilinged corridors. "This is madness!"

His words came from the corner of his mouth,

as the blue lenses of his spectacles stayed fixed
ahead: "Just give it your best shot. What've you
got to lose?"

From a small curtained alcove, I could see Sir
Charles and Mrs Wroth seated some distance from
a grand piano. The same butler as before served
them from a tray held between them. When they
had their sherry glasses in hand, the butler turned
to Miss McThane, just behind them; his eyes
widened a bit when she took the bottle off the tray
and kept it. Her sullen, narrow-eyed gaze bored
into the back of Mrs Wroth's neck as she drained
her first glassful.

Scape prodded me forward. "Go on. Break a leg."

"What?" The neck of the violin slid in my sweating grip.

"Never mind – just get out there." He placed
both hands in the small of my back and pushed
with some violence. I found myself next to the
grand piano, blinking at my audience, with the violin in one hand and its bow in the other.

Sir Charles frowned as he gazed at me. He leaned
forward, cupping his chin in the angle between
thumb and forefinger as he studied the actions of
what he assumed to be a mechanical automaton. As
before, he took no notice of the disturbing interest –
of an entirely different sort that his wife signalled
with her small half-smile and unnerving gaze.

Unseen by their intimidating eyes, my mind
was spinning through ever-faster revolutions. The

violin Paganini – what did I know about either? As a trickle of salt ran from my upper lip into the corner of my mouth, I racked my brain for some fragment of memory, some overheard and half-forgotten scrap of information cursed myself for having paid no attention to the breathless accounts of the virtuoso's performances that had appeared in various journals; how was I to have known that the topic would ever have any importance to me?

I could recall nothing, not a word of anything that anyone had said about this musical conqueror astride the world of concert stages and salons; a vague impression, gleaned more from occasional comment and witty allusion by those more *au courant* with the refined realms of culture – that was all my frantic scurrying through the cupboards of memory produced. Had one of my titled clientele, pleased with the restoration of his timepiece to working order, called me "a veritable Paganini of watch menders"? And had I not smiled at the compliment, as thought I had known exactly what had been meant, the two of us being such well-informed men of discernment and taste? A common failing, this; we pretend to knowledge, and never find out; until at some final assize, our ignorance becomes both accusation and confession.

Sir Charles continued to stare disconcertingly at me how soon would he guess the truth? My life had already been threatened at short notice; it was easy enough to imagine that this grey-haired, erect gentleman would also be capable of issuing such an order on behalf of the mysterious Royal Anti-Society. My fingers squeaked on the taut strings as I gripped the violin's neck tighter.

A steel engraving – where had I seen that? The image of a sharp-faced man, of skeletal physique, his long fingers bending with the flying pressure exerted on the instrument, the sweep of dark hair tangling over his piercing mad eyes – it must have been some journal's illustration of the virtuoso. Mad; surely he was mad; in every picture of him I had ever seen, he had certainly looked mad. And satanic – yes, that sounded right. A hint of sulphur and brimstone clinging to him; hadn't there been some silly story of him having sold his soul to the devil in return for his proficiency? Moody; temperamental; towering rages – but then weren't all virtuosi supposed to be like that?

Either they started out that way, or ended up so. Very likely a good number of the audience would be disappointed if there were no flash of temper, having come more to see that than to hear the music.

I seized on this notion with the desperation of a man being dragged to his execution. "The–" I made a hopefully dramatic gesture with the bow. "The light is too bright in here. It – it's entirely unsuitable."

Sir Charles leaned forward with evident interest. Beside him, Mrs Wroth opened her eyes a bit wider.

Thus encouraged, I pressed forward. "How can I be expected to perform under these conditions?" For a moment, I wondered if I was merely sounding peevish. Stronger stuff was called for. "It is an outrage," I cried, my voice rising to what I imagined was a madman's pitch. "And for – for an audience the size of this? An insult! I play for hundreds, thousands – the whole world! Not for any mere gaping handful! The crowned heads of Europe take their humble places with the rest – I am no children's conjuror hired for a birthday fete."

I heard Scape hissing at me from the alcove, and saw from the corner of my eye his frantic gestures to capture my attention. I ignored him; he had got me into this predicament; obviously it was up to myself to achieve extrication.

Perhaps it was the repeated contact with so many obviously unhinged people, that gave my own enactment an edge of veracity. I strode back and forth in front of the onlookers, waving the violin above my head in a transport of emotion. "An outrage, I tell you. Such ignorant peasants do not deserve my genius!"

Sir Charles and Mrs Wroth seemed more entranced as my display of anger mounted.

I felt quite dizzy, as if all my breath had been exhausted through my shouting. Delirious, no longer mindful of any division between a placid shopkeeper and the insane virtuoso I had conjured up, I swung the violin aloft as if threatening violence.

"The light! You, you fools! Great art cannot be born in these circumstances! Those hideous draperies! And–" I halted, gazing at the grand piano as if seeing it for the first time. "Where is my accompanist?"

A red haze drifted over the faces watching me.

"Where is my accompanist?" I thundered. My towering rage elevated me above the piano. I heard a crash of wood and a discordant echo; I looked down at my hand and saw my fist grasping only the neck of the violin, its strings curling loose around my wrist. The lid of the piano was scarred from the impact; splinters rained down upon me.

"Magnificent!" I heard someone shout. Dazed, my mock virtuoso evaporated in the aftermath of the violin's destruction, I saw Sir Charles leap from his seat and dash towards me. He went past and pulled Scape from the alcove.

"Simply marvellous," said Sir Charles, pumping Scape's hand in his. "A magnificent achievement – the exact duplicate the real Paganini's temperament in every detail! You are to be congratulated."

Scape regained his composure after a moment's confusion.

"Yeah, well… It's no big thing, really." He smiled modestly.

As I watched them, I felt the uncomfortable sensation of another's gaze fastened upon me. I turned with the remains of the shattered violin in my hand, and saw Mrs Wroth, head tilted to one side, eyeing me with an even more disturbing interest.

Before another word could be spoken by any of us, we were frozen by the sound of a window shivering into bits. A heavy curtain at the side of the room flapped with the impact of some missile. Sir Charles let go of Scape's hand and rushed to the spot. The shards of glass crunched under his boots as he flung aside the curtain, revealing the evening's fading light outside. "They're here!" he shouted. "The Godly Army!" He turned and rushed from the room, his face contorted with anger.

There were shouts and more noises from without. I joined Scape at the window. "Shit," he muttered under his breath. "Why'd these turkeys have to show up now?"

It required a few moments to perceive the shapes moving in the advancing darkness. A torch flared, revealing the cloaked riders I had seen pursuing the carriage that had brought us to Bendray Hall; now there were several score of them. A glitter of light on steel showed the weapons in their hands.

"To arms!" sounded from the corridor. I heard feet running in the Hall's corridors, and excited shouting close at hand. Scape had disappeared from my side, taking Miss McThane with him; I crossed to the music room's doors and threw them open.

From the head of the great staircase, I could see Lord Bendray with an antique musket under his arm. He was still in his shirtsleeves, with his magnifying spectacles perched upon his forehead, having been apparently summoned from his laboratory by this emergency. The household staff, butlers and footmen, milled about him. Swords and pikestaffs had been stripped from the various suits of armour that stood beside the doorways, and Lord Bendray was intent upon distributing these and organising the defence of the Hall. Some little distance away, Sir Charles concentrated upon the loading of a brace of pistols. As I watched, the front door boomed with the impact of a battering ram against it.

"Come with me," said a voice at my ear. I turned round and saw Mrs Wroth. She pulled me away from the banister. "Quickly – there's not much time."

I had no desire to be pressed into the martial preparations on the ground floor; as she led me down the corridor, I glanced nervously over. my shoulder as the shouts and clanging weapons sounded. "What is happening? Who is it outside?"

Mrs Wroth pushed me up one of the house's rear staircases. "The Godly Army," she answered me. "Best to stay out of their path."

"But Scape told me they were nothing to worry about."

Behind me on the stairs, she laughed scornfully. "My husband may trust that fellow, and Lord Bendray may think equally highly of him; but I know that he is an unmitigated rascal. I would advise you to regard all of his assertions with the greatest scepticism."

I was out of breath, having come up two flights

at a quick pace. Panting, I halted at the next land-ing's rail. "Who – who are these people, then?"

She stood beside me, her roseate bosom rising with her deep inhalation. "The Godly Army?" She reached up and solicitously brushed a strand of hair from my sweating brow. "Ah, they go a long way back – a very long way, Nearly as far as the Royal Anti-Society itself."

I would have asked her about the latter organi-zation as well, but I was distracted by straining to listen for the noises of attack and repulse filtering up the stairwell.

"Some of the more Puritanical elements of Cromwell's forces," said Mrs Wroth as she play-fully wound a lock of my hair around her forefinger. "They heard about what sorts of things the noblemen in the Royal Anti-Society were get-ting up to – all sorts of…mmm… deviltry, they probably thought it was."

Her last few words were whispered in my ear, as she leaned close to me. I drew away, seeing in her intent gaze the same disturbing expression I had spotted there before.

Voices, shouting but incomprehensible, came from downstairs. "Perhaps… we'd better–"

She brought her hand down, caressing my neck. "So you've got one secret organization," she went on, "and another secret organization combating it. They've both rather declined in number over the years – I'm afraid those… old passions… die out after a while. Like old families – the blood gets thin." She levelled her disconcerting stare straight into my eyes.

I slid away against the bannister. "Are – are we safe here?"

Taking my hand, she drew me to the next flight of steps. "We don't want to be disturbed," she said, smiling.

A musty odour of long-shut-off rooms greeted us on the next storey. In the dark, Mrs Wroth pulled me along. "Quickly – they won't find us in here." Enough moonlight filtered in through an uncurtained window for me to discern her fumbling about at a small table. A safety match flared, then the warmer glow of a candle cast about us. A cloud of dust blossomed as she sat down on the side of a bed. "Now let's see." Her smile grew as she grabbed me by the wrist.

"God in Heaven! What? Mrs Wroth–" Clasped to her bosom, I tumbled back with her full-length on the bed. Her arms, as slender and delicate as the rest of her, were imbued with the fierce strength of her desire. I struggled vainly, scarcely able to breathe, by the force of her embrace. "Please – what are you doing–?"

She rolled over, pinning me against the bare mattress. I looked up into eyes glittering with a lust bordering on madness; her gown had become disarrayed in the sudden assault, revealing an expanse of pearl-like flesh shining with perspiration.

"Tick-tock," she said, and giggled as she bent low to bring the sharp points of her teeth into my chin.

"What?" I managed to wriggle one arm free, but only for a moment until she had bound it with hers again.

"You clockwork confection, you." Her bite, going lower, brought a yelp from me. "Tick-tock, mmm." Her hands busied themselves at my clothing. "Let's just see if we can find the key to wind you up."

"Madam – good God–" I gasped for air. Somewhere far off, voices were shouting. "Don't... most improper–"

"Just a moment – what–" She suddenly reared back, pushing herself away from me. She gazed down at me, her eyes wide. "What's the meaning of this? You're not clockwork at all!"

I caught enough breath to speak. "No... no, I'm not..."

"You're flesh and blood!" she shouted angrily. "You're no Paganinicon!"

I pulled my shirt. together. "I'm afraid not, madam." The back of my head bumped against the wall as I pushed myself away on my elbows. "I'm sorry..."

"That bastard." Mrs Wroth's face darkened, her eyes narrowing to slits. "He told me..."

"Pardon?" I was relieved that her attention had turned elsewhere. "Who's that?"

"Sir Charles," she muttered. "My husband. I'll pay him out for this. He informed me that there would be a clockwork replica of Paganini here tonight. An exact duplicate, in every detail." She gnawed furiously at one of her fingernails.

"Well… I'm afraid I can't play the violin." I looked past her to the door; the shouting sounded louder.

"To hell with the bloody violin. It was the other thing I was interested in. That blackguard…"

"'Other thing?'" I inquired.

She glared at me, as if I were the general representative of the gender that included her perfidious husband. "You know very well what I'm talking about. The great Paganini… he has a reputation for virtuosity in more areas than just music. He's cut a swath through the rich. and titled ladies of every country in Europe. Some of them – my friends, ha! Bitches – have told me what it was like. Those eyes… those piercing eyes…" Her own drifted away in contemplation of this romantic vision, then swung viciously back. "And what do I find here? You!"

I shrank back from her fury. "There… has been a misunderstanding," I allowed.

She snorted in disgust and stood up from the bed. Straightening her bodice, she marched out of the room.

After I had managed what repairs I could to my own clothing, I went to the door and looked out. There was no sign of her in the hallway, but the sounds of pitched battles were frighteningly closer. The Godly Army had apparently managed to penetrate Lord Bendray's defences, and the struggle had climbed relentlessly up through the Hall's storeys.

Crossing to the head of the stairs, I looked down-over the rail. A mistake on my part; no sooner had I done this, than one of the combatants, face sweating, spotted me above. "There it is!" he cried, pointing me out to his cohort. "The devilish machine itself! Blasphemous parody of God's creation!" Thus inspired, they renewed their attack. They mounted the stairs, flailing about with fist and stick, only slightly impeded by Lord Bendray's rapidly flagging household staff. "Destroy the mocking puppet!" cried their leader.

I stood frozen in horror for a moment, then darted back to the room. There was no bolt on the inside of the door; if there had been, it would not have provided security for long against the furious tide rising towards me. I ran to the window.

In the darkness, the horses milled about, their riders engaged in the battle inside the Hall. I crawled up on to the sill and grasped the ancient vine growing up the stones. The shouts rang in the corridor as I clambered out into the chill air.

No sooner had I descended but a few feet, scraping my knuckles and shins against the wall, than my weight began to pull the vine loose from its moorings. With a sound of ripping cloth, the vine dangled me as though I were a fish on a line. Desperately, I scrambled to get my bootsoles a purchase on the rough wall, but to no avail. The vine pulled free along its entire length, dropping me stone-like to the ground.

My fall was impeded sufficiently by the foliage to save my spine from shattering when I landed on my back. The stars whirled overhead as I struggled to regain the breath that had been knocked from my chest. Still gasping, I managed to wobble upright.

The shouts came from above me now. I looked up and saw faces in the window from which I had made my exit; they scanned the grounds for any sign of me.

Panic overcame any further thought of strategy. Trailing the vines that had become wrapped about my limbs, I ran towards the darkest limits of the Hall's gardens, the castellated walls and the sheltering marshes beyond. I tumbled headlong when the vine reached its full length, the other end of it still being rooted to the ground at the foot of the building. Tearing myself free, I picked myself up and renewed my flight.

10

Mr Dower is Pursued

Years of neglect had taken their toll on the wall circling Lord Bendray's estate. I easily found footholds where stones and mortar had crumbled away, and had soon gained the top. Breathless from running through the dark gardens, I looked back towards the Hall, and was gladdened to see that Lord Bendray's household staff had summoned their strength for a counter-attack against the forces of the Godly Army. Across the wide porticoes of the house, the battle raged anew, torchlight gleaming on the clashing weapons. The shouting voices and clang of metal against metal drifted through the night air to me; for the moment at least, my pursuers had their hands full with more pressing business.

All was dark on the other side of the wall; I could not even discern the ground at its base. At some distance, across the marshy fields that I had observed from the carriage, a few yellow lights glinted feebly through the intervening mist. That must be the village of Dampford, I decided. It was just as well that I could not make out the narrow ribbon of the road leading from the gates of Bendray Hall to the village; doubtless I would be less subject to detection, as I sought the villagers' aid, if I struck out across the countryside.

I leapt down from the top of the wall and, in an instant, regretted it. A pool of water, choked with reeds, had collected against the stones; the mud splashed up to my chest before I found any solid footing underneath: Chilled to the marrow, I struggled forward through the ooze sucking at my boots, grasping handfuls of the rank foliage for leverage. I at last crawled shivering up on to ground that, if still soggy and yielding to my hands and knees, at least afforded some security against drowning.

Spitting out a mouthful of the thick water, I stood up to reconnoitre my position. Several yards away, the black expanse of the wall hid the battle raging in and around Bendray Hall. Looking about, I feared for a moment that I had lost the direction in which the village lay. Then I spotted a plume of smoke blotting out a thin wedge of stars, and at its base a faint glow of lantern-light through a crossed window frame. I set out for this promise of safety.

By the time I reached the village, I was even more thoroughly drenched, having blundered into a good half dozen of the rivulets and stagnant ponds that had lain in my path. One such had been a stream of current sufficient to pull me off my feet and send me thrashing for several yards until I managed to grab the bankside weeds for anchor; a family of water rats, bright eyes glittering, had stared at me before retreating into their nest. Thus, dripping mud and oozy vegetation from every limb, I at last staggered into the central open space of Dampford.

The plume of smoke I had spied earlier arose from the largest of the squatty buildings. I assumed it to be the village inn, or what passed for one; through its open doorway I could hear voices in mingled conversation – a dialect so thick, combining the mangled syllables I had heard in Wetwick, with the heavy guttural "r" of the countryside, that I could not make out the words from only a few feet away – and barking laughter, all to the clink of tankards against wooden tables.

I was correct; a good portion of the village's population, both male and female, appeared to be inside. Beneath a sagging beamed ceiling obscured by a haze of tobacco smoke, their goggling eyes turned towards me as I presented myself in the doorway. Talk ceased; pipes were laid down; and at the tables in the far corners, heads were raised from pools of spilled ale. Even the lumpish village women, grey hair straggling across their sloping brows, ceased the gossip and knitting in which they had been engaged around the smouldering hearth.

Doubtless I seemed an appalling spectacle as I grasped the edge of the doorway for support. A brownish puddle began to form around my feet.

"Good people–" I managed to speak before halting to gather my swirling thoughts. The piscine faces continued to stare at me with no discernible emotion. "There's been frightful events–" I raised my arm to point into the night, sending a cold rivulet trickling down my sleeve. "At Bendray Hall – men attacking… some sort of ghastly army – you've got to help…"

The villagers looked amongst themselves back to me, then resumed their conversations as before, though perhaps at a slightly lower pitch. One or two of them cast a further inquisitive eye in my direction before raising a tankard; but none of them made any expression of interest in my plight, or any motion towards assistance. I staggered forward into the room, looking amazedly around at the indifferent villagers, ostentatiously ignoring my pleadings. "Don't you comprehend? Lord Bendray… up at the Hall… your duty as his tenants–"

One of the ugly women stared at me before sniffing haughtily and returning to the low whispering directed at her neighbour's ear.

"Simple Christian charity, for God's sake–" I grabbed the arm of one of the men, interrupting his guzzling pull at his ale. "You've got to hide me – before they find me here–" The man swore something ill-tempered and incomprehensible and roughly shoved me away.

It struck me where I had encountered an incivility similar to this before, from people who were the urban counterparts of these unsightly rustics. In that London borough of Wetwick; there had been a remedy as well, for their bad manner towards a stranger. A token commanding respect; one that I still had upon me, in my waistcoat pocket. My fingers dug into the sodden garment, and drew out the Saint Monkfish crown.

"Your attention, please!" I held the coin triumphantly aloft; anger at my shabby reception sent my voice ringing to the far walls. "Do you see what I have here? Eh?"

The voices fell silent again; the protuberant eyes were fastened on the glittering object.

I thrust the coin under the nose of the nearest man, who a moment before had pushed me away with the flat of his beefy hand. His trembling fingers took the bit of metal; his companions at the table crowded about his shoulders to gaze down at it. Throughout the room, a general hubbub broke out. Men and women swarmed around the table, gesticulating and jabbering. The coin was the focus of their excitement.

Smiling to myself with satisfaction, I stood apart from the noisy pack. The token had worked its still-inexplicable magic, shattering the villagers' sullen indifference. The rising clamour, as the coin was passed from hand to hand, was more to my liking; I awaited the deference it had wrought before, and the speedy offering of the assistance I had requested.

The Dampford villagers looked up at me. One of the women shouted an angry curse; a thrown tankard struck me on the forehead. En masse, they churned up from the table, scattering chairs and benches behind· them, and were upon me. Dazed from the blow, I was lifted backwards as though by a wave. Arms pinioned, I was borne out the door, above the heads of the shouting crowd.

My head was still ringing when my vision cleared well enough to see that the population of Dampford had formed a surging ring about me. I discovered that my hands had been bound behind me; a rough hempen rope had been tied around my neck and looped over the branch of a gnarled tree in the village's centre. One old crone marched up to me, thrust the Saint Monkfish sovereign into my shirt, and spat in my face. A debate had broken out amongst the men holding the other end of the rope; from their violent gestures I quickly discerned that one party advocated dragging me up into the air forthwith, the other group maintaining that I should be placed on a wooden bench that could be pulled out from under me.

"Wait!" I cried. The rope burned across my throat as I twisted about. "There's some mistake! I haven't–" My protests only fuelled the villagers' anger; their shouts and imprecations grew louder; torches and lanterns were thrust higher, the yellow glare serving to make the contorted faces uglier still.

One viewpoint had prevailed among the men. I felt the knot tighten at the back of my neck as they pulled the rope.

For a moment, I was lifted up on tip-toe, the abusive crowd swimming in my sight; my tongue seemed suddenly too big in my mouth, stifling me from any further call for mercy. Then, through the blood roaring in my ears, I heard a distant volley of explosions. Another woman's scream cut through the clamour, as the rope went slack and I pitched forward on to my hands and knees.

Gasping for breath, I stared at my fingers clawing into the trampled ground. Above my head, the villagers' excited jabbering mounted into frenzy. The noise came again; I could recognize it as pistol shots now. I looked up and saw the villagers scattering towards the inn and the other low buildings, leaving me in the middle of the deserted space.

"Here you go, mate – how's your windpipe, then?" inquired a jovial voice. I was lifted up on to my feet by hands underneath my arms. Two men supported me on either side; they were such as I, even if unshaven and considerably more muscular in build, and not of the repellent physiognomy of the Dampford villagers. A third man facing me was the one who had spoken; all three of them were dressed in rather stained and greasy velvet jackets over dirty frilled shirts. Though still of imposing physique, with the coarsened features and calloused ears of former pugilists, the buttons of their vests were now strained with the swelling gut that heavy drinking puts on such men.

My interrogator prodded me with the muzzle of his pistol. "Did them bloody fish-faces bang you about much, then?"

I coughed to clear my throat, and shook my head. "I'm – I'm all right."

The two others withdrew their grip on my arms, leaving me wobbling but still upright. They stuck their own pistols inside their waistbands.

"We'd best be away from here," said the leader of the small band. "Afore them pop-eyed coves get their knobs up and see as there's more of them than there is of us. Steady on; this way, right smartly now." He turned me by the shoulder towards a path leading out of the village; in a close bunch we struck off for the countryside.

"Fresh up from London, then, are you?" In the darkness, the leader bent close to peer at my face as we marched along the boggy road.

I took my hand away from massaging my chafed neck. "That's right," I said. Though they had come as angels of deliverance, the men were of an appearance sufficiently rough that I refrained from volunteering any more information about myself until I was sure in whose agency they were employed. An innate trust was an element of my nature that had been dissolved through harsh experience.

He nodded sagely. "I thought as I didn't mark you from the bunch Mollie Maud brought out with herself. But seeing as she set out a general call for every brothel bully from Whitechapel to Marylebone, I'm not surprised there are a few new faces in the crew."

Discreetly, I cast a glance at the other two bringing up the rear of our party. My initial impressions were confirmed upon this less hurried examination: the three of them had that brutalised aspect, smirking dull and sly at the same time, of those guardians seen slouching in the doorways of houses of ill repute, charged with the profitable intimidation of those unfortunate women whose erring footsteps on the pathways of shame had brought them under the exploitation of a brothel-keeper, and the maintenance of a riotous order among the inebriated hedonists who sought their carnal pleasures in such dives. Bully was the name such men earned by their bulk and careless violence; and here I was surrounded by a party that had assumed me to be one of their squalid number. Outraged decency would have occasioned an outcry against such an insulting presumption, if caution had not dictated a more circumspect quietude.

"New at this here dodge, are you?" The leader was in a talkative mood, his face flushed with drink and the military triumph over the villagers. "Not been out on one of these recruiting drives, I takes it."

Recruiting? Another mystery to be added to the mounting list. "Ah... yes. Quite." I drew myself up and attempted to ape their rolling swagger, to add conviction to my performance. "Rather jolly fun; I think it."

"'Jolly'?" spoke up one of the others. "I can't bear it until we're back in the city, meself. This muck they call country – trees and bogs and shite–" He spat at the side of the road to express his opinion. "If the toffs want their mackerel-mugged green girls so bad, they should bloody well come out here and get 'em themselves, says I."

"Green girls" – my memory shifted itself, casting up the voice of the London cabby who had taken me to Wetwick; he had mocked me with those words in the low alehouse.

"Aye, and where would us lot be then?" The leader sneered over his shoulder at his compatriot. "They pays for their pleasures, them fine gentlemen do. And it's jingling coin in Mollie Maud's purse, and a bit of it into our pockets, because they do. What do I care if them swells are so jaded they prefer these fishy delights – green girls and suchlike – to a good, honest round-heeled lass? As long as they puts their rhino up front, then Lor' bless their wicked hearts, says I."

"Unnatural blighters," muttered the other, wrinkling his nose in a show of distaste.

A tentative hypothesis began to form in my mind: perhaps the "green girls" were the young daughters of the Dampford villagers, that these employees of Mollie Maud – evidently a brothel-keeper of some import in the city had come to this rural district in order to enlist as prostitutes. Such practices as this, the seduction of the countryside's innocents into London's sordid netherworld, were common, by all informed reports. As to what qualities the Dampford girls could possess, that would make them particularly attractive to rakes no longer excited by normal female charms, I shuddered to hazard a guess.

"I expected you was fresh at this game, when Nigel–" The leader pointed his thumb at the third in the band, "he said he'd seen you through the window of them lot's scabby inn, a-trying to pass off a rum couter on 'em."

"Pardon?" I said, puzzled.

He stared at me as we continued walking. "You know a couter, a crown, that is. He saw you flashing one of them dicey coins, with the phiz of the fish-face pope on it."

"Fish-face… You mean, Saint Monkfish."

"Who else, indeed? It's no wonder they mobbed you like that. Hadn't ol' Mollie given you the skilamalink on that, then?"

I hazarded a small confession of ignorance: "No…"

"Well, then, me lad." He brought his beefy face, smiling with lubricious secrets, close to mine. "You see, we gives these silly country lasses, as what doesn't know any better, one of them bright shiny coins to come with us to London town., where they'll soon see a fair parcel more of 'em. It reassures 'em, like, to get such a precious bit with the bust of someone who looks just like 'em stamped on it. And a saint, too! Makes 'em think London must be a respectable sort of place – we tells 'em as much – where they'll come to no harm. What we don't let on is that all they'll see of this Saint Monkfish when they're working on their backs in Mollie Maud's cribs, is if some spiff gentleman drops the coin he uses to show that he's a member of the discerning clientele what appreciates a spot of green." The bully smirked, obviously self-satisfied with his inside knowledge. "Clever, eh?"

I nodded, feeling a general distaste welling in my throat. If not all, a few mysteries – such as the cabby's jocular remarks – were illuminated.

My informant pursed his thick lips in a pantomime of thoughtfulness. "It's grown a bit shiny with use, I personally think. Harder and harder to find one of these goggling bints who hasn't tumbled to it; and sure all their parents know what the Saint Monkfish coin means!" He laughed and slapped me on the back. "They'd got their clammy hands on a seducer of their fair virgins all right, when you waved that silver bit around – if Nigel there hadn't seen it, and come and fetched us, you'd have been in a deal of trouble. Mollie should've warned you to keep it on the hush."

"Yes…" I managed an abashed smile. "I rather suppose so."

"More 'n likely, she'll say it's your own bloody fault, for being such a gawp. But you can make your own complaint to her, if you care to. Here we be."

The path had slanted upward from the surrounding marshland to a rise of relatively dry ground. A team of horses grazed the coarse vegetation at the limit of their tether; the carriage to which they had been harnessed stood at one side, sheltering a simple fire. Near a dozen more brothel bullies roistered in a semi-circle around the blaze, passing bottles back and forth, laughing as they drank until the red liquor trickled from the corners of their mouths. They formed a sycophantic court around a woman of large stature, seated with her back towards me. A garish red wig was piled on top of her head, and laced with strands of pearls; more of them swaddled her thick neck. A bottle for her private enjoyment was grasped in a be-ringed, pudgy hand; the fluid sloshed and bubbled as she swung it about, joining in the rough badinage of her attendants.

I halted in my tracks; certainly I had no desire to meet the queen of this distasteful band. "Perhaps... I should just... go back to the village, and look around a bit. Attend to business, as it were – now that I've got a better idea of how to go about it."

"Naaw – there'll be no more ugly girls sent on their way to London this hour of the night." A slab-like hand was clapped on my shoulder, propelling me forward. "'S time for a piss-up – Mollie would be right offended if you got all this way to the fire and didn't have a drop with her."

The circle of ruffians brayed at our approach, slapping each other and holding their bottles aloft in invitation. the large woman wiped her mouth with the back of her hand and looked up at us.

"Here you go, Mollie." The leader of my rescuers gave me a push between my shoulder blades, nearly throwing me off balance. I stumbled directly in front of the woman. "Your lad here's a bit on the raw side – maybe you should've seasoned him up a bit before you sent him out here." The two others choked around the bottles from which they were already swigging, and sputteringly began to explain this witticism to the rest of the party.

"Who's this, then?" The woman blinked at me, focussing through the haze of her own inebriation. "I don't bloody remember any–" She fell into amazed silence, her jaw dropping open as she recognised me.

I was equally stunned. The bullies lapsed into quiet, as they regarded the two of us staring at each other. Though I had seen this woman only once before, the occasion had been seared into my memory.

"You!" cried Mollie Maud. The bottled dropped from her hand, and shattered upon the rock she sat upon.

"Good Lord," I muttered. I felt quite dizzy; beneath the florid rouge of the brothel-mistress I could clearly see the stern, commanding features of Mrs Trabble, the leader of the Ladies Union for the Suppression of Carnal Vice.

Perhaps the strains of my recent existence had at last overpowered my reason; perhaps, in place of mere confusion and bewilderment, my mind had begun to produce its own visions and phantasms. My skull filled with this airy notion; I seemed to drift skyward as I mused, leaving the fire and yapping crowd below. The thought of the arch-respectable Mrs Trabble, the doyenne of all London's moral crusaders, rounding up women for the servicing of some unspeakable vice, struck me as most amusing.

"Get him!" A screeching cry plummeted me to earth. I blinked, and found myself looking into the rage-contorted face of Mollie Maud – or Mrs Trabble; one and the same as she pointed a trembling finger at me.

The bullies, befuddled with drink, gaped stupidly at me. Before the nearest could lumber his great bulk up from where he sat, I plunged through a gap in the circle. A hand nipped at my leg, too late to catch me, but sending me tumbling down the slope and splashing into the marshy darkness below.

"What's the matter?" I heard one of the bullies say, his sodden puzzlement complete. "Who is he, then?"

The woman's howl pierced the night. "Dolts! Just get him! He knows who I am!"

Crouching in the muddy stream, I parted a screen of reeds and spied her frenziedly belabouring the backs of her henchmen with her meaty fists. A few of them fumbled out their pistols from their waistbands and began clumsily working their way down the slope towards my hiding spot.

My masquerade with these ruffians was effectively at an end; there was nothing for it now but simple flight. The surrounding countryside was too boggy to make any progress through; panicky wallowing in and out of the maze of streams and fens would bring the brothel bullies on top of me. If I could make it to one of the roads crossing the landscape, I would have at least a small chance of putting some distance between myself and my pursuers. As quietly as possible, with the oozy muck up to my chest, I waded towards a dark ridge blotting the bottom of the night sky. Behind me, I could hear the splashing and angry shouts of the bullies as they blundered into one another in their search. I made it to the gravelly bank and crawled up from the tangled weeds at its base. When I reached the edge of the rutted highway, I cautiously lifted my head to see if any of Mollie Maud's crew had anticipated my intention and circled around to intercept me here. Seeing no one, I climbed up on to the road.

No sooner had I done so, than I heard the splatter of horses' hooves in the mud, distant but rapidly approaching. Silhouetted against the night were the cloaked riders of the Godly Army, heading straight for me. At their head, a sword was waved aloft, and a triumphant cry sounded: I had been spotted.

For a moment, I was frozen as though I were a rabbit startled by hunting hounds; then I dived from the edge of the road, sliding through gravel and mud to the marshy stream below. There was no time for quiet now, as the Godly Army reined their mounts to a halt at the point I had just vacated. In desperation, I plunged through the water, tearing aside roots and tangled weeds impeding my way. Behind me, I heard this fresh band of pursuers abandoning their horses – useless in the fens – and scrambling after me.

In my unthinking haste, I nearly slogged into the arms of Mollie Maud's gang. I spotted their torches in time the bullies, waist-deep in the marsh, were poking through the vegetation with the muzzles of their pistols – and, stifling a cry of alarm and despair, clawed my way through the reeds in another direction. Shouting arose behind me as the two groups collided; I was given a little respite as muddled fighting broke out amongst them. Pistol shots and shouted curses rang over the landscape; only when they realised that their common quarry was getting away, did they disengage battle and resume their increasingly chaotic, splashing and wallowing searches, exchanging blows whenever their paths crossed.

The confusion among my pursuers had enabled me to put some distance behind me, though I could easily glance over my shoulder and see their various torches weaving through the choked streams. I was nearing exhaustion, praying silently that I could make it to another of the roads before either the bullies or the Godly Army fell upon me. That was the only hope I could devise for myself; my dazed brain could conjure no other strategy than that.

Suddenly I heard more voices raise in angry tones, this time from in front of me. I crouched down behind a clump of reeds and peered ahead. A moan of anguish escaped my lips when I saw that it was the villagers of Dampford, brandishing pitchforks and other brutal implements as they waded through the marsh. Their piscine faces were made even more repellent by the ferocity displayed there; they had apparently regained their courage and had come seething after the sacrifice that had been snatched from them just a short time ago.

The three factions – Mollie Maud's bullies, the Godly Army, and now the villagers – were on all sides of me save one. I plunged in that direction, heedless that it led nowhere except farther into the weedy streams and stagnant pools of the marshland. There was no longer a conscious thought in my head, only blind panic impelling me into flight.

Something in the water tangled about my feet, and I went headlong into a muddy bank. Raising

my head from the muck, I heard the overlapping
shouts grow louder: some yards away, the villagers
had collided with the others. Cries of Fish-face bastards! from the bullies mingled with the Godly
Army's Heathens! Devilish spawn! overlaid with
the villagers' indecipherable curses. More shots, the
clash of sword against scythe, the splash when one
body was thrown back from another, torches hissing as they were extinguished by the dark water –
thus the renewed battle raged. No alliances were
possible among such disparate elements; each man
fought against the members of the other parties,
and occasionally, in the confusion, his own.

I spat out the mud that had filled my mouth,
and panted for breath. It would only be a matter
of time before one of the factions prevailed against
the others and, with as many of them as might be
left standing, resumed their search for me. Or, seeing the futility of their combat, some sort of truce
might yet be achieved, and all three parties would
spread out for that purpose. Wet, cold, and miserable, I huddled behind the weeds, stifling the fear
that would otherwise have sent me wallowing
noisily in any direction.

Before I could assemble my scattered wits, a
surge of muddy water slapped against my chest. A
figure rose up before me, blotting out the night sky
as I fell backwards. My only thought was that one
of the combatants had separated from the others
and silently tracked me down. His hand reached

out and gripped me by the shoulder before I could make any attempt to escape.

I had been caught. I squeezed my eyes shut, awaiting the inevitable pistol shot, sword, or pitch-fork into my vitals. Instead, I heard a voice, familiar from far back in my memory: "Dower – heed me." The hand shook me. "Little time is there."

An obscuring cloud slid from the moon as my eyes shot open. By the thin light, I saw the dark face ornamented with its lines of scars. The Brown Leather Man gazed down at me.

11
A Great Career is Launched

"But – you're dead…"

The Brown Leather Man pulled me close to the shelter of the stream's bank, and laid a finger on my mouth, silencing any further cry of astonishment. I could see that, above the water to our waists, the upper half of his body was stripped bare. Clouds parted before the moon, the thin light glinting from his powerful chest and arms as the rivulets coursed over lines of scars such – as those that decorated his face. "Be quiet, Dower," he whispered close to my ear. "Great danger you are in."

Cowering beneath an outcropping of tangled roots, I could hear the shouts and mingled violence of the searchers, surging first in one direction, then another, like a storm-driven sea. "Yes–" My own voice was close to breaking into a sob. "The villagers… and that Mollie Maud woman–"

The dark head nodded impatiently. "She is a person of evil, the mask of good using to better hide."

"I don't understand…"

The Brown Leather Man shook me roughly, breaking off the trembling small voice of my confusion. "Now that is not important." The slitted eyes bored into mine. "Many explanations will be later. First you must escape her, and the other."

"Yes… yes, of course!" I seized his arm, the veil of my exhaustion having been pierced. "But how–"

He signalled again for quiet. "Arrangements I have made. I have been following you – hidden – until you I could help. But now all will be safe. The crossroads there." He drew me away from the bank and pointed, his dark arm shining in the darkness. "Do you see?"

A pair of the region's gnarled trees stood sentinel over a raised bank a few hundred yards away. After a moment I could discern the flat surfaces of the two roads that met by them. "Yes," I whispered.

"Go there. This water–" He jabbed a finger at the murky ooze around us. "It goes there. Curves, yes? But if in it you stay, the others will see you not. At the crossroads, wait. Down below until a carriage you hear coming. Then go up. Away it will take you, to safety." His gaze searched my face. "Is all clear?"

"I understand. But – you'll be there? With the carriage?" I desperately hoped so; his was the first voice in a long while that, despite its odd accents, seemed untinged with either hostility or dementia.

"No." He drew away from me, into the deeper part of the stream, lowering himself into it so that the water lapped up to his chest. "Later – again you will see me." Only his head was visible; then one hand broke the surface and pointed. "The crossroads – go." He disappeared entire, leaving only a circular ripple in the moonlight.

I was alone again, as if the apparent resurrection of the Brown Leather Man had been but a phantasm born of a despairing mind driven beyond the limits of its endurance. In the distance, I could hear my pursuers – Mollie Maud's bullies, the villagers, and the Godly Army all muddled into one baying pack – as they combed the sodden landscape; they were undoubtedly real enough. I eased my way along the side of the stream, striking out for the appointed rendez-vous.

Though my breath was a rock in my throat the entire time, my progress was uneventful, save for when a torch was thrust directly above my head. I cowered into the edge, crouching below a tangle of reeds while a silhouetted figure – of which party I could not tell – viewed the stream's surface. "He's not here!" was shouted back to the others. "He must've gone round the other way." I waited until the splashing of footsteps receded some distance before cautiously resuming my course.

When I was but a few yards away from the crossroads, the gnarled trees outlined against the night sky, my anxiety had mounted to such a pitch that I pushed forward through the water, heedless of the noise I made. I mastered myself sufficiently to hesitate at the base of the sloping bank going up to the roadway; I was overjoyed to hear the pounding of the horses' hooves. Clawing at the muddy turf, I scrambled up to the top..

My elation plummeted as I stood in the centre of the crossroads, water sluicing from my limbs, and surveyed all four directions. No vehicle was approaching. Just as I realised that I had been betrayed by the pounding of my own heart, hammering in the cage of my chest, I also spotted a line of torches freeze in position some distance away. A shout rang out over the fens: "There he is!"

Standing thus exposed on the high ground, I had been spotted by my pursuers. I whirled about again, and saw the silhouetted figures in the dark quadrants between the crossroads' arms, surrounding me; the alerting cry was echoed by the others; the torches were raised higher as their bearers forded across stream and bog in their eagerness to lay hands on me.

I could not escape them by plunging back down the bank and into the fens; they would soon fold in on me from either side, trapping me between them. The quicker footing of the road was beneath me, however; I shook myself free of the paralysis that had gripped me, and started to run, my boots splashing in the ruts.

I had gone but a few yards, however, when a sight ahead pulled me up short. Some of the more clever among the factions had not come straight across the marshy turf towards me, but had cut across to the nearest of the roads. I saw them now scrambling up the banks; I looked behind and saw that the same tactic had occurred to others. I was completely encircled, every avenue barred by my pursuers.

In the distance ahead, they reached the road's surface, and raised themselves from their scrambling crouch. I could see them catching their breath and gloating at my predicament; in a moment they would sprint towards me, to claim my blood as their honour.

Then, as I watched, they were scattered to either side as though they were tenpins. A brace of horses surged through at a dead gallop, trampling one of my pursuers beneath their hooves. The driver atop the carriage behind whipped them to even greater speed.

Shouting broke out from behind me; I looked over my shoulder and saw a combined party of villagers and bullies no more than twenty yards away, and racing towards me. I turned and ran, waving my arms at the carriage as a pistol shot rang over my head.

The driver spotted me; he laid on the whip again; the carriage was almost on top of me when he reined the team in to a violent, skidding stop, nearly toppling the vehicle over. I took a hurried glance behind and saw the maddened face of the fastest runner, his outstretched hands straining for me. Someone threw open the carriage's door; the unseen person grasped my elbow and helped me scramble up inside. I collapsed on the floor as the horses were whipped into motion again; the pursuer cried out as his grip was torn loose from the door and he fell beneath the rear wheel.

I raised my head at the sound of more shouting and pistol shots; through the small window I could see the flare of torches as the carriage careered through the party that had been closest at my heels. Their furious voices faded behind as the carriage picked up speed, jolting over the rutted highway.

"He looks all right," a woman's voice said coolly. I saw that my hands, braced against the carriage's floor, were next to her white kid boots. I looked up and, by the soft glow of a travel lantern swinging on a hook, recognised Mrs Wroth smiling at me.

"Seems to have come through rather well," a man's voice agreed.

I looked around to the opposite seat. For a moment I thought I was gazing into a mirror; I saw my own face gazing back at me. Then the image's lips moved, forming words as my own mouth went slack in amazement.

"I'm glad you could be with us." The elegantly dressed figure folded his gloved hands together in his lap. He smiled, exhibiting a mocking self-assurance in the features I had thought were my own.

"You're... very important to me."

His laughter, joined by Mrs Wroth's, rang inside the carriage as I gazed dumbfounded upon
this apparition.

"You look a sight, Dower." My double's amusement
was evident. "You're sopping wet. Fortunately, we
thought to bring along a few of my things – I'm
sure you'll find them a suitable fit." He reached up
and drew open the small hatch to communicate
with the driver; the carriage slowed and came to a
stop in accordance with his instructions.

We had left the scene of my flight across the
fens – and the combined forces of Mollie Maud's,
the villagers, and the Godly Army that had occasioned it – sufficiently far behind us. The carriage
driver, whom I recognised as the same employee
of Lord Bendray that had brought me out from
London, lifted down a small trunk from atop the
vehicle. By the light of the travel lantern, a selec-
tion of clothing – fitting me as my double had
promised, but smelling remarkably musty, as
though stored for a considerable length of time –
was exchanged for mine. I dressed by moonlight,
standing on the edge of the open deserted road;
the comfort of dry garments outweighed any possible bemusement at the situation. From my fouled
shirt, a glittering object fell to the road. It was the
Saint Monkfish sovereign – so many travails had
it brought me! For a moment, I was poised to

throw it into the ditch; then I altered my decision and placed it in the pocket of the coat I wore. I tossed the mud-befouled garments into the ditch alongside, and climbed back into the carriage.

Mrs Wroth had joined my double on one of the seats; I sat facing them as the carriage rocked into motion again. Her arm rested along the top of the leather, one hand toying languidly with the fringe of hair at the enigmatic figure's collar. She gazed at him, then smiled at me as though in possession of some great and satisfying secret.

"I imagine you feel better now." My double rolled his head back against the woman's caress. "I'm sorry you had an anxious moment – we tried to get there as soon as we could."

I leaned across the space between us, searching the face that I had only seen before in a looking glass. "Who are you?" I said after a moment's wondering silence.

Mrs Wroth's laughter chimed again.

"Didn't Scape tell you?" he said softly. "About me?"

The realisation began to grow in my mind. "You're the…"

"That's right. You should have known me, anyway; after all, we have the same father. So to speak."

I fell back against the leather seat. "The Paganinicon," I whispered.

He made a mock bow, bending forward at the waist and flourishing his hand. "Indeed. At last we have this… mutual pleasure, I hope?"

"But – you're not clockwork... are you?"

His hands deftly undid the centre buttons of his shirt, and drew it apart. By the wavering glow of the travel lantern, I saw, not flesh, but a skin of moulded shiny metal. He reached beneath where his bottom ribs would have curved, and lifted upward.

I stared in utter amazement. No heart, no bone, no human ligament or vein. Inside a metal cage, gears whirred and meshed. Wound springs intertwined with each other, and ticked off the slow measuring of his artificial life.

Looking up, I saw him savouring my astonishment: "Yes," he said, smiling. His hands restored the metal covering, and buttoned the shirt over it. "The man who made me – the man who made you – he was a genius, wasn't he?"

"It's–" Words failed me. "It's impossible–"

His eyes seemed to flash, as though in anger. "Oh? Is it?" The voice took on a sharper edge, cutting through the affected humour. "And if I were to open you up – would you see anything less remarkable? Less intricately dazzling, in its squelching, spongy way? Lungs and heart and spleen, and all the rest – ticking away, as it were? Yet you walk down the boulevard, and pass any number of such wonderful devices, all ticking away as they walk, and think it no great marvel."

The vigour of his outburst caught me off guard. "But but human beings–" I stammered. "They're not made; except, perhaps, by God." No sooner had I spoken it, than I regretted the mawkish-sounding religious sentiment.

The Paganinicon seized on it: "Ahh! You find it possible to believe in an invisible Creator; but one that you could have seen, and talked to, while he was alive – that's beyond you, is it?" He smiled triumphantly, pleased with his rhetoric.

A little while ago, I had been running for my life through the marshland, and now I was debating theology with a clockwork violinist; my brain was not so much whirling with events, as it was drifting free of all moorings to reality. I struggled through my exhaustion to assemble a riposte. "The operations of an invisible Creator are meant to be beyond our comprehension; such are Mysteries. But clockwork – gears and wheels and springs – that is another matter."

He gave a scornful laugh. "Don't try to split that sort of hair with me, Dower; I know as well as you do that the simplest watch is as much a befuddlement to you as the workings of the heart that beats inside your chest. It's all a mystery to you, isn't it?"

I felt a sting of resentment at his insinuations. "I can't imagine," I said stiffly, "on what grounds you make that assertion. I run my father's business, as he did–"

"If you please." The Paganinicon winked at me. "We know the truth about that one, don't we, now? "Run my father's business," indeed – run it into the ground, more like. You don't know the first thing about those gimcracks that the old boy left behind."

"How – how would you know that?"

He leaned close towards me. "Because, Dower, my somewhat brother – we share the same brain. Don't we?"

The carriage's interior seemed much closer around me; the smug, knowing gaze of two pairs of eyes weighed heavy against me, as we continued to rattle towards an unknown destination in the inky night. "I... don't know what you mean..."

"Oh, tell him," cooed Mrs Wroth at the Paganinicon's ear. "Stop toying with him; you're so cruel." Her eyes narrowed in a species of rapture as she spoke the last word.

"Very well." Though he bore my face, its outlines were filled with a sly knowledge, rather than my continuing bafflement. "Now listen very closely, Dower; do try to make elastic these petty definitions of possible and impossible that you entertain." He settled back and regarded me. "Thus: I am a thing of clockwork. Your scepticism does not outweigh what is. You have seen my jewelled heart. Yet, admittedly, I am no clanking mannikin, pivoting a fixed smile and glass eye on the world. Behold." He held his hand palm upward and flexed it through a sweeping gesture similar to a magician's. "I have subtlety of movement, rather better than yours, in fact; I could play the violin, if one were here. No, my future audiences will not be disappointed in my skill. Everything that human beings of flesh and blood are capable of, is within my power."

"Everything," said Mrs Wroth. She gazed raptly at him.

"Yes; yes, that's true." The Paganinicon nodded. "There will be no disappointments in that aspect, either..."

"I've already made sure of that," she said smugly.

"... for, of course, that is where the, ah, fire springs from, is it not? The passion that goes into the music? And how, I ask you, could I perform like the great virtuoso Paganini, if I were not... equipped in all ways like the original?"

"I couldn't imagine," I said frostily. Even in my fatigued state, and under these strange circumstances, my companions' sordid references were clear to me.

The Paganinicon raised his finger towards the carriage's roof. "Yet surely it must puzzle even such a stolid nature as your own, my dear Dower, how this is possible. Those crude forerunners that your father – our father – devised, those Clerical Automata back in London... you know yourself what an intricate assemblage of gears and springs is in those devices, all to propel them through the simplest, repetitive gestures and squawkings. How much more must then be necessary, eh? – for a masterwork such as this!" He slapped his chest with a bravura flourish; it gave a dull metal thud. "What possible mechanism could govern a range of motion, speech… everything, exactly human in every respect? Eh, Dower? What could it be?"

His voice had mounted from enthusiasm to mania. "I have no idea," I said carefully, drawing back.

"What else but a human brain! Of course! It's obvious!"

I studied him for a moment. "Are you saying… that you have a human brain inside you?" It seemed a grisly notion; I had an involuntary vision of one sloshing about in a zinc-lined tank behind his eyes.

He reached across and tapped me on the brow. "No… but you have one inside you." His smile grew wider, revelling in the perplexity he generated.

I admitted defeat: "I'm sure I don't have the slightest idea what you're talking about."

He folded his long hands – the duplicates of my own beneath his chin. "Let us examine," he said in scholarly parody, "the principle of sympathetic vibrations. You are familiar with the concept? Good. Let us say… a violin string is plucked; across the room, a violin string tuned to the exact same note – not the least shade higher or lower vibrates with the first, though no hand has touched it. A commonly observed phenomenon. It is most often seen with musical instruments, as the nature of their construction makes them especially resonant; yet all things are resonant to some degree; it is merely a matter of finding the particular vibration that would make, say, a stone vibrate in tune to it. These vibrations with which we are commonly familiar are vibrations in air; yet other media exist which are capable of transmitting vibrations even more subtle than the sounds a plucked violin makes. Some vibrations are so rarefied – yet real – that they are beyond our modes of perception; that is to say, perceptions of which we are aware. These vibrations, and the media in which they travel, surround us, penetrate us, even shape our very thoughts and existence – yet we know them not, much as a fish would be unaware of the water in which it swims. Do you follow me?"

"I suppose so," I said, shrugging. "Though I can't see the point in conjecturing about things that can't be perceived. You might as well assume they don't exist at all, and be done with them."

"Well, well – this from the man who was invoking God a moment ago; I admire the flexibility of your logic, Dower. But no matter. This medium of which I speak, and the subtle vibrations that pass through it – it can be rendered perceptible, and useful for those with the necessary skill. You see, it is the medium in which the fine vibrations of the human brain radiate from inside every human skull. Each brain is tuned, we may say, to a particular note in this medium, just as an infinite number of violin strings may be tuned to an infinite range of pitches sounding in the medium of the air. All that is lacking is a means of sensing those vibrations, and tuning another object to their pitch, for a resonance to ensue, exactly similar to a violin string sounding along to another string's note." The Paganinicon's voice dropped, the hush of secrets being imparted. "That, my dear Dower, is what your father accomplished."

"Indeed." I was baffled as to what point this explanation was leading.

"Don't look so befuddled," said the other. "It's simple enough. Dower, Senior created a device sensitive enough to pick up the vibrations of a particular human brain. There is an incredible amount of untapped cerebral capacity inside even the most prodigious genius – your father saw that that capacity could be the means for controlling and modifying the actions and responses to external stimuli of a complex automaton such as myself.

"The brain to whose vibrations the governing mechanism is tuned thus serves to regulate two creatures, one of flesh and blood, the other made of clockwork. Now, then who do you suppose it is, whose brain is being used in this manner?" His eyebrows arched in counterpoint to his smile.

A grotesque suspicion formed in my thoughts. "Do you mean… me? My brain?"

"Very good! You're quick, Dower! And it's quite a personal history you have, if I may say so. Your father, having discovered this principle of rarefied sympathetic vibrations, needed a human being whose mind was of a particularly complex yet stolid nature – one not given to the various excitements that cause the erratic brain vibrations in most other human beings and render them unsuitable as the necessary adjunct to the governing mechanism. So he searched out and married your mother, a woman – and I mean no disrespect to her memory, now – a woman of singular unresponsiveness. Against all difficulties, he managed to get her with child – you, Dower. Upon her death, you – a mere infant – were sent off to be raised by your aunt, primarily to keep your cerebral vibrations from close proximity to the devices upon which your father was working; it would have been disastrous if the conjunction had been made too soon."

For a moment, I felt as if I were inside the carriage, and yet at the same time far away, listening to someone else's life being narrated. A dream; this person with my face was describing mysteries – long-suffering puzzles of abandonment and a child's exile – and the answers to them that were as cold and intermeshed as the sharp-edged gears inside a watch. I brooded in my silence until the other spoke again.

"You see," said the Paganinicon, "the governing mechanism, once installed in the device it is to control, must be brought within a few miles of the adjunct brain – yours – for it to pick up the subtle vibrations and begin its operations. However, once it has been activated, distance between the device and the brain is no longer a matter of concern; the medium in which the vibrations travel is not bounded by space. Its nature is of another dimension entirely." He peered closely at me. "Do you understand that?"

"I– I believe so." My trembling hand passed over my brow. "Somewhat...It's all so strange..."

He nodded, moved by another form of sympathy. "I suppose it is. But the proof is before your eyes. Before he died, your father moulded my features" – he touched his face with one finger – "from a portrait your aunt had sent him. But then he died before he could send for you and bring you near enough for the vibrations of your brain to set me into life; I was but inert machinery, gears frozen, waiting. And, as you know, your father's estate was left in much confusion; though much of his work remained at the shop you inherited, the contents of other laboratories – he had several throughout the city – were dispersed. Such was my fate, though I was of course unconscious of it." He pulled at his lower lip, falling into sombre thought.

I felt a twinge of compassion for him, this device in my image. So we were moved, from place to place, all unknowing, like blindfolded chessmen upon an unlit board.

The Paganinicon roused himself from his reverie, and continued: "I am grateful to our mutual acquaintance Scape for this account of this

history we share; he is something of a self-taught
authority on the subject. And a leading character
in the drama himself, at least in the latter stages.
It was he who, in partnership with his charming
colleague Miss McThane, came into possession of
my inactive form; he had been circulating a few
gambling enterprises – so-called games of chance;
the odds were lamentably fixed in his favour – in
the North; an eccentric industrialist and collector
of curiosities squared a debt from the whist tables
by giving Scape a number of odd mechanical devices that had come into his possession through a
circuitous route, as these things do. Scape, ever a
tinkerer, gladly took the lot; chief among them was
myself. Being no more than a lifeless mannikin –
however complex internally – I was of little value
to him. A person in his business had many sources
of information, though; he knew that members of
the Royal Anti-Society were interested in con-
structs from the workshops of the senior Dower.
They brought me south and attempted to sell me
to Sir Charles, claiming that they would be able to
activate me; that was the motive for their visit to
your shop in London – they were looking for the
necessary governing device. A pointless quest, actually; if Scape had had a bit more theoretical
knowledge, he would have been able to determine
that a smaller version of that rather cumbersome
device – a second Aetheric Regulator, refined in
size from the original in the mahogany cabinet –

was already incorporated in my workings. Failing in his attempt to steal what he mistakenly thought was necessary to his enterprise, Scape was forced to the expedient this night of attempting to pass you off as me; a rather interesting notion of flesh and blood masquerading as clockwork, rather than vice versa."

"I discovered the fraud," interjected Mrs Wroth.

"So you did, my dear." The Paganinicon patted her hand. "And I'm very grateful for your keen perception. And your powers of persuasion." He turned back to me. "You see, Dower, in the general confusion engendered by the Godly Army's attack on Bendray Hall, the esteemed lady here discovered our good friends Scape and Miss McThane in the act of slipping out of the Hall through the scullery window. She made a rather forceful protest about the deception to Scape–"

"That loathsome little bugger," she muttered darkly.

"–and prevailed upon them to produce the real Paganinicon. Fortunately, it was close to hand: they had hidden it in a small hunting lodge on Lord Bendray's estate. Going thither, they were surprised to find the Paganinicon – myself, that is – activated, walking about and capable of conversing. Scape, in his previous attentions to my person, had left my main and various auxiliary springs fully wound; he was unaware that all that was then necessary to set me into motion was to bring the adjunct brain –

that's you, my dear Dower – within a few miles of the Aetheric Regulator contained within me. If Scape had been at my side, rather than riding in the carriage with you as it approached Bendray Hall, he would have seen this culmination of all the care he had lavished upon my poor, neglected workings – he really is very clever about mechanical matters; in a rough, untutored way, of course. It being a matter… shall we say… close to my heart, I, of course, was able to enlighten everyone in the party – Scape, Miss McThane, and the good Mrs Wroth" – he patted her hand, and exchanged smiles with her again "about a good deal of the mysteries surrounding this sudden animation of what had been silent and unstirring metal. There was little time for explanations, however, before we were joined by another bearing quite distressing news about your predicament, Dower." The Paganinicon looked at me, raising his eyebrows as if expecting me to supply the next word. "You know? Your friend – the swarthy fellow–"

I was still struggling with the revelations made so far. "You mean – the Brown Leather Man?"

"Is that what you call him?" the Paganinicon shrugged. "Suits him well enough, I suppose. I rather fancy he calls himself something else; unfortunately, the urgency of the situation precluded lengthy introductions. No matter; it seems the fellow had surreptitiously witnessed many of this night's events; I imagine that rather dusky hue of his is rather convenient for skulking about and spying on people. He informed us that you were in danger of being captured and killed by one or more of the various factions whose ire you seem to have aroused. This prospect was viewed with alarm, especially by me: I have more than a brotherly fondness for you, my dear Dower. Your death – more particularly the death of your brain, which serves as my own, may I remind you – would naturally put an end to my functioning as well. Thus plans were hastily drawn up, to ensure your continuing safety. By that time, the siege of Bendray Hall by the Godly Army had metamorphosed into the general pursuit of your person; the way was clear for Mrs Wroth and myself to return to the Hall, there to commandeer a carriage and driver, and set out for the *rendez-vous* which your friend, the Brown Leather Man, had appointed. Scape and Miss McThane have meanwhile gone ahead to the nearest seaport in order to arrange passage for you – just to some place where you'll be safe until things settle down a bit." The Paganinicon sat back, spreading his hands in a gesture of satisfaction. "There – you see? All perfectly simple; everything is made comprehensible, given enough time."

I nearly retorted that the explanations he had given were neither simple nor comprehensible, but held my tongue instead. Having recovered somewhat from the exertions of my flight across the fens, I could appreciate that I was out of danger, at least for the time being. And whatever motivations my rescuers had for their actions, they did not seem to be intent upon my immediate death. The results of my own efforts at negotiating a course across the world's perilous chessboard had met with more disaster than success; I was content to be the pawn of others for a while, as long as it appeared I was being shuffled to some obscure file far from the furious checks at the board's centre.

(Thus, having failed our trust in ourselves, we abandon that trust to others – to our cost!)

I looked at the two smiling faces across from me, the one so uncannily like my own. "I take it, then," I said, "that you are coming along with me… to whatever destination Scape has arranged?"

"'Coming along?' My dear Dower." The Paganinicon shook his head. "I see no need for that. After all, it's your skin for which all these people are out. I have no fear of them; I may look like you, but my accomplishments and ability will soon prove that I am another person entire." He gestured dramatically. "I have a great career ahead of me – one too long delayed."

Mrs Wroth levelled a more intent gaze at him. "That's not all that's been delayed too long."

"Yes, well – that, too." He shrugged. "Pity about that Guarnerius you smashed up back at Bendray Hall, Dower. Soon after I arrive in London, the first order of business will be to scout up a worthy-enough instrument; a decent Strad or some such, I think."

Her eyes narrowed to slits as she looked at him. "I'll get you such a Stradivarius," she whispered huskily. "You wait and see."

A thought struck me. "But if I'm sailing about somewhere, or lodged in some distant place… and you're in London – some considerable distance away – won't that rather interfere with your functioning? Being at such a remove from my brain, and all?"

"No, no; your concern for me is really very touching, but it's no matter for concern. The medium – the aether – in which the fine vibrations of your brain are conducted to me, thereby providing a base for my own actions and reactions to be modified, is a medium completely non-spatial in nature; it exists in another dimension entirely. Rather a difficult notion to grasp at first, but I assure you it's true. Your proximity to me was only necessary to set my workings into motion; but as long as you remain alive and no catastrophe upsets the remarkably placid operations of your brain – and I honestly can't imagine what could, given your rather stolid nature; all this fright and chasing about has produced no more than a passing ripple on the surface of a deep pond, as my own undisturbed operation demonstrates – then you could be on the other side of the moon, for all the difference it makes."

A salt breeze filtered into the carriage, signalling our arrival at the seacoast. Looking from the window, I could see the first light of dawn outlining the ocean's dull iron. A few boats, insignificant fishing craft, bobbed alongside a sagging wharf. A sailing ship of considerable bulk, incongruous among these sprats, was stationed in the deep water at the wharf's end; from its deck, a silhouetted figure had spotted the carriage and beckoned us to approach.

The Paganinicon instructed the driver to halt. "This is where we part company, my dear Dower. Do take care of yourself, for your sake as well as mine. When at last things settle down and you get back to London – a few months from now, a year; who knows? The public's moods are so capricious – at any rate, do look me up. If I'm not touring the Continent, that is."

He pushed open the door, and I stepped out. "Au revoir," he called as the driver whipped the horses into motion. The carriage wheeled about and headed back the way it had come. Behind me, I heard someone calling my name…

"Ahoy, Dower!" On the ship's gangway, Scape raised his arms in an exuberant greeting. Even from the landbound end of the wharf, I could clearly see how pleased he was with himself.

The blue lenses fastened on me as I came up the slanted plank. "Hey, catch this." Leaning over the rail, he gestured at the rest of the ship. "Pretty great, huh?"

Miss McThane was with him. Standing on the gently rocking deck, I looked from the two of them to the expanse of furled sail and crossing lines above our heads. "What ship is this?"

"Belongs to Sir Charles – just one of the little advantages of being rich, you know. Got a full crew aboard, supplies, the whole shot – we're just about ready to hoist anchor and go cruising."

"All right." Miss McThane sang and swayed against him, bumping him with one hip: "Won'tcha let me take you on a sea cruise."

Disconcerted as I was by the woman's eccentric behaviour, I was nevertheless pleasantly surprised by the sound of another voice calling my name. "Mr Dower, sir! You are alive!"

I turned and saw my faithful assistant Creff. He grasped my arm in both his hands and gazed at me, his face bright with glad tears. About our feet the terrier Abel gambolled, barking from an excess of joy. "They told me you was alive, sir. But I didn't know as to whether I should believe them, when they promised you'd be joining us on this ship, them being such blackguards and all–"

"Hey!" Scape, his arm around Miss McThane's shoulders, bristled at this comment. "What kinda talk is that?"

"–but as they said you might be needing me on the long voyage you're undertaking, I thought it only my duty to come and find out for meself. And here you are, safe and sound, after all those horrible commotions! I count it rather a miracle, I do."

I nodded wearily. "I confess I agree with you on that point. It is good to see you here, though."

Creff stood on tip-toe to reach my ear. "I'll do my best for you, Mr Dower, but I fear as to just how much good that'll be. I've never been any sort of seagoing man, and just in the little bit of time I've been swaying around on this thing, I feel as if me lights are all up in me throat. If we were to be out at sea, and any sort of storm should fall upon us, I couldn't warrant as to being able to keep my feet under me."

In truth, he did appear a bit green about the gills, with a desperate roll to his eyes mimicking the slight pitch of the tethered ship. "I think," said I, "that you'll do me more of a service if you go back to London, and keep an eye on the shop in my absence. No mob is going after your blood there, and you'll be able to keep the premises and contents safe from any who might bear a grudge against me."

"Right enough, sir," he said, with evident gratitude. He leaned over and with an upraised finger instructed the dog: "It's your job to keep an eye out for Mr Dower." Abel, ears pricked, looked up at him with no apparent sign of comprehension, but nevertheless stayed by my feet as Creff shook my hand in farewell and hastened for the gangway.

A sailor, one of several I had perceived going about their mysterious tasks in the growing dawn light, approached us. "There are cabins below," he said, respectfully taking off his knitted cap, "if you'd care to rest up a bit before we set sail."

I accepted this invitation readily, the realization of just how exhausted I was coming over me in a sudden wave. The sailor led me down to a small, sparsely furnished but clean room. All that mattered to me was that it contained a bed. No sooner had I laid my head upon its pillow than all the words and voices circling behind my brow rose into the darkness above my closed eyes, and I fell into dreamless sleep.

Some time later – how long I had no way of knowing I was awakened by someone roughly shaking my shoulder. I opened my eyes and looked up into the face of the sailor who had shown me the way to the cabin; around me I could feel the ship's rolling motion, and hear the creak of its hull and the slap of waves against it.

"On your feet," ordered the sailor. His earlier courtesy had gone. "You're wanted up on deck." I rolled over on to my side. "Please convey my regrets," I said. "I'm somewhat indisposed–"

He pulled me bodily from the bed and pushed me towards the cabin's door. "Step lively! Before I lose my patience with you."

I stumbled out on the deck and saw Scape and Miss McThane, sombre now, their hilarity diminished by the sight of a grim-faced row of sailors standing at attention. The ship was still within hailing distance of the small harbour from which we had sailed.

The sailor pushed me towards Scape and Miss McThane, then joined his fellows. "What's happening here?" I said, baffled by this sudden change in attitude. "What's the matter?"

Scape turned a sour grimace towards me. "I think," he said, "that we've been screwed."

A cloaked figure emerged from one of the forward hatches and strode down the line of sailors towards us; each of the men stiffened ramrod-straight as what was evidently some chief among them passed by. He at last, stood in front of us, and surveyed us each in turn, the raised edge of his cloak concealing his own face. "Good morning, gentlemen and lady," he said softly; my heart sank within me at the words.

The cloak and the voice together sparked my memory; this figure had looked at me once before, and rendered a harsh judgment. This was the man who had ordered the ruffians already guilty of the murder of the hapless forger Fexton, to cast my fettered body into the Thames.

He dropped his cloak, and I found myself staring into the eyes of Sir Charles Wroth.

My surprise, and that of Scape and Miss McThane, evoked some amusement in his features; a bloodless smile greeted us.

"Somehow," said Scape with a hollow laugh, "I get the feeling that I'm not working for you any more."

"Be quiet," ordered Sir Charles. "There's no time for your foolishness now. You would be better occupied setting your souls at peace with the Lord. I must inform you that you are in the hands of the Godly Army." He gestured towards the line of sailors. "These men, righteous Christians all, are under my command. Consider that the day of reckoning for your sins is at hand; there is no escape now."

"You're shittin' me." Scape shook his head in disbelief. "Aren't you?"

Sir Charles' glare silenced him. "Doubtless my previous masquerade had confused you; it was successful, then. In truth, I am not the effete music-lover and godless scientist for which you took me. Though the Royal Anti-Society – that heathen aggregate! – be but a fraction of what it once was, still they are sworn to secrecy among themselves, the better to guard their devilish knowledge. Through great pains, I infiltrated their number, posing as one given to such pursuits of vain arts; even my wife did not suspect my devotion to the good Puritan cause. At last, I thought the time to strike had come; it was I who gave the signal from inside Bendray Hall for the siege to begin; I also betrayed the various defences that fool Lord Bendray had organized, so that my men could enter. Unfortunately, the object of our sortie" – his eyes narrowed as he stared in my direction– "escaped in the confusion. But God makes all things right; no sooner were you lost to us, than Scape's request for my assistance in arranging a safe passage for you placed you again in our hands. So justice is accomplished."

"I– I think you've made some sort of mistake," I stammered. "I don't know what you think my… connection with all of this is, but–"

"Silence!" Sir Charles stepped back from the three of us. "All such prevarications are useless. We know God's truth; you shall soon know what fate has been deemed appropriate for your kind. I bid you farewell."

Two of the sailors assisted him down to a small boat that had been tethered at the ship's side. As they rowed him towards the harbour, the sails billowed over our heads. I gazed hopelessly at the edge of land sliding under the sea's horizon.

PART THREE

*A Description of a Voyage
to the Hebrides*

12
Glimpses of the Future

It has been my experience that being under a sentence of death produces in one's self a beneficial calm, both physical and spiritual. Time and the petty cares of the world recede, taking on their proper insignificance against notions of Eternity. These ennobling concepts are perhaps more easily entertained on board a ship, where the ceaseless rolling of the ocean and the featureless grey horizon provide no cheap distraction from one's meditations. But even here, in my refuge at a great city's edge, a fragment of that peace returns to me; the dog, my companion through so many arduous adventures, drowses before the fire, and I scribble on, heedless of the harsh costermongers' cries in the street below. I realise now that it was but a clearer vision achieved while under sail, of the condition to which we all, man and beast alike, are sentenced. Though at most times we are ignorant and forgetful of the fact, we all are on a Voyage of short duration, making towards the Landfall of our Death. Fortunate is that mariner who scans the horizon and spies a brighter cloud somewhere beyond.

The ship on which Scape, Miss McThane, and I found ourselves unwilling passengers was named the *Virtuous Persistence*, though the faded evidence of an earlier incarnation as the *Miss Clementina Peckover* was still visible on its prow. The crew – more of a Godly Navy than Army, though they clung to the military forms handed down from Cromwell's time – was captained by one Lieutenant Brattle; he it was who took upon himself the duty of informing his cargo of their ultimate destination.

"In time of war, cruel measures are often necessary." The lieutenant, a junior version of his superior Sir Charles, paced sombrely before us. Our party of three, four, counting the dog stationed at my feet, following the words spoken with keen expression if perhaps not full comprehension – had been assembled on deck a few hours after the ship had set sail. "And the war against Satan," pronounced the lieutenant, "is unceasing."

"Shit," muttered Scape beside me.

The lieutenant gave him a sharp glance, but pressed on. "This vessel is on a course bound for the Outer Hebrides. Very nearly the farthest from the coast of Scotland is the islet known as Groughay; it is the ancestral seat of the infamous Bendrays. What little population the island supported abandoned it some years ago. Its barren rocks will be the witnesses of the sentence passed upon you by the compassionate wisdom of God Almighty, through the persons of His appointed defenders–"

"What a load of crap."

Scape's louder comment brought an even sterner glare. "I would caution you to silence; you can only bring greater misfortune upon yourself through this show of disrespect."

"Hah!" The blue lenses swung to myself and Miss McThane. "Get him." He turned back to the lieutenant, having divined what the speech's import would be. "How much worse can you make it, huh?"

The lieutenant set his disdainful expression even more rigid. "Upon the island of Groughay, you will, each and all, be executed in a proper and merciful manner. It is the duty of myself and the men in my command, as soldiers in the service of Christ, to enforce this judgment upon you, for those heinous crimes committed against God and nation."

"You sonsabitches," said Miss McThane. For a moment, I thought I saw her lower lip tremble; then she stepped forward and kicked the lieutenant in the shin. One of the men guarding us interposed himself; before he could lay hand on her, she had flounced back between Scape and myself.

"Um... begging your pardon, Lieutenant." As much as I had expected his pronouncement, the words had still brought my heart surging into my throat. "Is it possible... do you think perhaps – you're being a bit... well, harsh?"

He nodded once, gravely. "Only upon the erring flesh, Mr Dower; upon the transient envelope of your immortal spirit. And upon that we confer a great boon: it will be a considerable period of time before we reach Groughay, and our fervent prayers for your souls will assist you in commending yourselves to your Maker."

"Thanks a bunch." Scape grimaced at the lieutenant's back as he and his men marched away. For a few moments he was silent, his head lowered in his brooding. Then he glanced over his shoulder at me, the corner of his smile flicking below the dark spectacles. "Well... that's the breaks."

Miss McThane leaned back against the ship's rail, looked up at the grey-clouded sky, then back to the two of us. "Now what the hell are we supposed to do? Play shuffleboard?"

I picked Abel up into my arms and stroked his head. The London streets down which he had come running after me, now seemed far away. "As the lieutenant said," I murmured, "perhaps we should make those certain preparations."

After the fury of my recent adventures, the life on board the *Virtuous Persistence* was not altogether disagreeable. Unlike poor Creff, betrayed by a poorly moored digestive system, I found myself to be one of those fortunates who find the sway and roll of a seagoing vessel to be comparatively relaxing. Even in the few bouts we had of blustery gale, I experienced little discomfort; so at ease was I that it occasioned some regret, not having discovered my mariner's ability until so late a date.

The prisoners were given the freedom of the ship, there being possibly no more effective gaol than the billowing waves on all sides, and too few of us to pose any threat of commandeering the vessel by force. Food was coarse, but ample; the Godly Army-men, in their roles as sailors and captors, treated us with some measure of respect, due perhaps to the enormity of the crimes that had brought this justice upon us. An inquiry on my part, as to the fate of the dog, evoked a considerable debate among the crew, some arguing as to the poor beast's innocence, others (the more primitive in their beliefs) maintaining that it might be a witch's familiar and thus liable to the same sentence as its master.

In such conditions of enforced leisure, and once a philosophical attitude towards one's imminent death had been adopted – that being the only possible attitude to take under the circumstances – I found the opportunity to reflect upon the singular experiences I had undergone. As a drowning man's life is said to flash before his eyes, so did the events since Creff announced an Ethiope in the shop pass, rather more slowly, through my thoughts.

My fellow passenger Scape came across me as I was deep in just such a reflective mood. I sat against the frame of an open hatchway, idly scratching behind the ears of Abel, panting from his labours of chasing gulls from the deck. "Yo, Dower," Scape greeted me, before sitting down. He rested his arms on his raised knees, studying the smoke from a cigarette he had cobbled together from tobacco cadged from one of the Godly Army, rolled in a Bible page from the same source.

"That's what you get," he said, nodding towards a group of the men engaged in some close-order military drill, "when you give people Bibles and guns. You should give 'em either one or the other, but not both. It just messes up their brains." The stub of his cigarette had a few words of Scripture still visible, before he flicked it over the rail and into the sea.

I shrugged noncommittally. "They seem pleasant enough sorts. Doing their duty, and all that. And they are letting us live all this time, instead of dispatching us immediately, as they could have done."

That brought a disgusted snort from him. "Get real. They've got their reasons for what they're doing. They want to pop us off, leave the bodies on that stupid island, and make it look like ol' Bendray had a hand in it. Groughay's his island, remember? These people just wanna stir up a ruckus on the old boy's head. So they can't very well kill us now – they want us to be fairly fresh meat when somebody else finds us."

As usual, Scape had a base explanation for anyone else's actions. Unfortunately, I could find no flaw in his reasoning. As the practical results were the same whether he were right or wrong, I let the matter drop as being of no importance. After a moment's reflection, I spoke again: "There are many things that still puzzle me–"

"Yeah, I bet."

"–such as how a person of your character came to be involved in these matters–"

"My character?" He gave me a glare of mock severity: "Hey, watch it!"

I pressed on: "–or the reasons for so many apparently nonsensical actions. Say, for instance, back in London, at the church that night–"

"Oh, that." He shrugged. "I could give you a reasonable explanation for all sorts of things."

"Such as?"

"Yeah, well, sure; why not? Got plenty of time now, I suppose." Scape flexed his spine against the edge of the hatchway, making himself comfortable.

The discourse that followed so impressed itself upon my memory that I may safely warrant the accuracy of its transcription here. A good deal of Scape's speech various words, different cant phrases – had puzzled me since the blackguard's initial appearance in my Clerkenwell shop. The mystery had been continuously reinforced by the certain strangeness (for lack of a more precise word) in his general aspect; alien, yet at the same time familiar, as though I were seeing him in a clouded, distorted glass, one that magnifies certain aspects while diminishing others. We view such a wavering reflection, and say that we recognize the figure contained therein, but cannot say from where. So with the enigmatic Scape his divergence from myself, or any Englishman, was made more unnerving by the similarity that still remained.

As to the veracity of the history he related to me, on board the *Virtuous Persistence*, I can give no avowal. At the time, *tête-à-tête* in our mutual captivity, the vision be spun from the empty air, of fabulous machinery and the Future revealed by it, weighted my soul with an oppressive certitude. At this remove, safe by my sanctuary's fire, I entertain neither Belief nor Unbelief; in this one matter, at least, I have fallen into that dismal position, below that of the most wretched atheist, of not knowing what I believe. The reader must determine his own stance with no assistance from me.

"The thing is," said Scape after a moment's thought, "I wasn't always this – what d'ya call it, 'person of your character'. I mean, I didn't talk like this, f'r instance. Maybe you've noticed I sound a little bit different from you?"

"It had struck my attention."

Scape nodded. "You see, I used to talk pretty much like you do; that kind of stodgy way. Maybe a little hipper, because I was – how d'ya say it – in the business. The life. You know what I mean?"

I hazarded a guess: "Criminal activity?"

His brow furrowed from the wince behind the blue lenses. "Christ, Dower; you don't have to make it sound that bad. Let's just say I was out there, doing a little... hustling. Just sorta getting by, no great shakes. Me and Miss McThane, she's still down below, sleeping; she had a late night, trying to put the moves on one of these Godly Army guys, before she gave it up as a lost cause anyway, the two of us had a little travelling-show sort of thing, what we called "An Assemblage of Curiosities". You see quite a few of 'em out in the towns and villages; those yokels really go for that sort of thing. We didn't have anything too impressive – a stuffed seal with a wig on it that we tried to pass off as a mermaid, a wind-up mannikin that could raise a horn to its mouth and go toot-toot except that it usually stuck it in its eye; just junk. Because, you see, the whole thing was really just an excuse to go travelling around from place to place, kinda give you a reason for pulling into some of these burgs." He nodded again, this time relishing some memory. "You'd be surprised, man, at the amount of money some of these old country squires have got stashed away. Or some pillar of the community in one of these grimy-ass manufacturing towns – fat city. Ab-so-lutely ready for the plucking. Because they got nothing else to spend it on, right –

the old guy and maybe his hot-blooded eldest son – they're *grateful* for a little excitement in their lives. Plus they all think they're too friggin' clever to get taken, because they've had nothing to compare their brains to except a bunch of dumb dirt-farmers out in the field." He smiled to himself, deep in his reminiscence. "I tell ya, it was great. Shoulda stuck with it – me and her could've retired by now, instead of being stuck out here with the glum bunch."

The recital disturbed me a bit. "What part did Miss McThane play in your enterprise?"

"Oh, she was in on the hustle, too. She pulled her weight."

"Are you saying…"

He caught my meaning straightaway. "Naww – she didn't have to put out, or anything. Well… not often, at any rate. Didn't have to. She'd just give the marks the eye while they were at the table, and they'd jack up their bets just to try and impress her. By the time they figured out they'd been fleeced, we'd already have split, down the road to the next town." His voice took on a more philosophical tone. "It's a living. But then one time, this old dude – I think it was up around Birmingham – he got into us for more than he could pay off. Said he had a couple of interesting clockwork devices, valuable collector's items; made by that renowned inventor George Dower, Senior. I've always been a sucker for that kind of stuff, so I took 'em instead–"

I interrupted him: "And one of the devices was the Paganinicon."

"Yeah, right. They filled you in on that, didn't they? Helluva thing, ain't it? Musta really knocked you on your ass when you saw it – I just about shit when I went back to Bendray's hunting lodge and there it was, walking around and talking."

"It was indeed... marvellous," I agreed.

He leaned closer to me. "Well, get this; the other device I got off the old guy, it was even wilder."

"Indeed? What was it?"

"To look at it," said Scape, "you wouldn't have thought it was much, of anything. I mean, compared to a whole clockwork violinist, for Christ's sake. What it was, was a box about yay big" – he held his hands a little over a foot apart – "like one of those slide projector-type things... what d'ya call 'em... magic lantern, right. With a little compartment for a paraffin lamp inside, and a lens on the front. But no place to put in slides or anything like that; most of the device was just filled up with your father's weird gears and stuff. It took me a while, but I got the thing working. And it was wild."

"What did it do?"

Scape gazed at me with smug complacency. "It flashed," he said simply.

For not the first time, I was mystified. "'Flashed'?"

"You looked into the lens, see, and it flashed at you. The clockwork controlled a shutter opening and closing in front of the light. Real fast, and with a certain rhythmic pattern." He nodded, pursing his lips for a moment. "Damnedest thing I ever did see."

"What was so wonderful about it?" Perhaps my earlier impressions of him were correct, and he was simply demented.

"You looked into it while it was flashing, and you'd see things." His voice lowered, imparting the secret. "You'd see... the Future."

The fervour in his voice, almost religious in nature, traced a shiver tip my spine. "The Future, you say."

He nodded. "Yeah – I thought I was going crazy when it started to happen. But it all just went on unreeling inside my head, and I knew it was the real thing. Really the Future; a hundred years or more ahead. Seeing everything that was going to happen, through the eyes of my children and grandchildren, and great-grandchildren. Wild, huh?"

"Indeed," I murmured.

"You see, Dower," he said excitedly, "your old man – what a genius that sonuvabitch was! – he figured out a way to alter, like, brain waves and stuff – all the things that go on inside your head – through this goddamn flashing light. And he wasn't even the first, man! Ol' Bendray showed me some stuff from the Royal Anti-Society archives; Catherine de Medici, back in the sixteenth century, had a tower built for her pet prognosticator Nostradamus, and that was how he worked it. He'd sit up there looking at the sun, and fanning his fingers in front of his eyes – real quick, like flickering – and then he'd see stuff! The Future! That's how he made all those predictions; more of 'em are gonna come true, too; you just wait and see. But anyway, what ol' Nostradamus just bashed away at, your father worked out scientific how to do it right. The Paganinicon – did he tell you a buncha stuff about a sort of medium, that certain fine vibrations from the human brain travel through?"

I nodded.

"Okay; what the deal is – that medium's not limited by spatial dimensions, like he told you. But it's not limited by Time, either. It extends through Past, Present, Future, all together. No difference, everything simultaneous. And the flashing light – if you get the speed and the pattern just exactly right – it can alter what section of that medium you perceive. Instead of this little piece that you normally see, you can just go sliding off into the Future. It's like genetic time-travel. What you get are the perceptions what they see, what they think and know – of your own descendants, laid on top of your own. Dig it: you see the world to come through your own children's eyes."

I hadn't understood some of the words he used, but I gathered the general import of his explanation. "So this is what you did? Used my father's device for this... Future perception?"

"Sure did. Me and Miss McThane both. We spent so much time staring into the lens on that box, while it went flickity-flick into our eyeballs – Christ, I'm telling ya." He shook his head. "I've spent so much time in the Future… I don't really belong back in this time any more. That's why I talk like this, you know? This is the way some grandkid of mine is gonna talk some day. And I got the personality, too – a Future personality. I mean, I was pretty much of a crook before; but since I've taken on the characteristics of the way people are gonna be in the next century – jeez, I'm a real sharp dealer. I guess it's just the way everybody's gonna be some day."

That was a daunting prospect. A world of Scapes – perhaps it was best that I was not meant to see anymore of such a dismal vista's approach.

"Actually," continued Scape, "I think I might've looked into it a little too much. All that flashing kinda screwed up my eyes – can't take anything too bright. That's why I wear the shades all the time. I guess it's a good thing that the device finally wore out and flew to pieces; otherwise I would've gone on staring into it until I was blind."

The subject worked a horrible fascination upon me. "What… what is the Future going to be like, then?"

"Hey, it's gonna be a gas," Scape assured me. "If you're into machines and stuff – like I am – you'd go for it. People are gonna have all kinds of shit.

Do whatever they want with it. That's why it didn't faze me when ol' Bendray first told me about wanting to blow up the world. Hey – in the Future, everybody will want to!"

He had satisfied my curiosity; I wished to hear no further of these dreadful days to come. "This device, then, is no more?"

"Yeah – when it went, it went like a bomb. I couldn't even begin to put it back together. So me and Miss McThane – with our new improved brains – figured maybe we could sell the other thing – the violinist we couldn't get started up – for a lotta money. We heard that sonuvabitch Sir Charles Wroth was interested in stuff like that, so we trekked down south with it to show him. To make the sale, we had to give him that line about being able to get the Paganinicon working if we went into London and got the Aetheric Regulator from you. He assumed we knew what we were talking about; actually, if I'd known that there was a regulator already inside the Paganinicon, and all it needed was to be brought close to you in order to start it ticking, I could've saved myself a lotta trouble. As it was, I only had an idea of what I was looking for when I broke into your shop because Sir Charles had recommended me to his Royal Anti-Society buddy Lord Bendray, and he told me what the Regulator he wanted for his earth-smashing machine looked like. Then when Miss McThane and I were staking out your place, we saw that dark-skinned guy bring around just the thing we needed, so we tried to get it off you. That's all."

"So you were employed by both Sir Charles and Lord Bendray?"

He nodded. "Yeah. I was trying to build up kind of a clientele among all those old farts in the Royal Anti-Society. You know, as sort of a consultant on the stuff that your father built for them; except I had to be careful not to let on that some of it was just a bunch of fakes, like that big contraption your old man unloaded on Bendray. No sense spoiling their fun."

I was still puzzled. "But what about the church back in London – with all that fishing tackle? What were you doing there?"

He laughed and shook his head. "You know – I'm still wondering about that, myself. I think it just goes to show that ol' Bendray's gone round the bend. We were there in London, me and Miss Mc-Thane, trying to get that Regulator off of you, and he shows up with that crackbrained scheme of going around to that old church and stuffing it with all that Izaak Walton stuff, and fishing rods and things. Weird. Just a weird business. Something to do with those ugly-looking people that hang out there. I didn't know there were any like that living in London until that night they showed up at the church; I had seen ones like 'em in Dampford, that village next to his estate, so I assume they're related in some way. Country and City cousins, I suppose.

But what Bendray wanted to accomplish by show-ing 'em a church with fish-hooks and lines all over it – beats the hell out of me."

We lapsed into silence together. I was about to put another question to him, when I heard the sound of him snoring. Lulled by the motion of the ship, and warmed by a momentary parting of the clouds, he had fallen asleep with his head tilted back against the hatchway.

I pushed Abel's head from my own lap, and stood up. With Scape's wild expositions – what part dementia, and what part truth, I still could not determine – whirling in my head, I made my way towards my cabin below the deck.

An ambush was sprung upon me before I reached my destination. In the dark passageway, a pair of arms encircled my neck and pulled me off my feet.

Miss McThane's breath was warm against my face. "I heard you talking," she whispered in my ear. "I was down in the hatchway, and I could hear you two."

"Please–" I endeavoured to free myself. The white expanse of her throat, and the soft shapes below, seemed almost luminous in the dark. "Please restrain yourself–"

"Hey–" Something wet touched the inside of my ear, startling me further; I was just able to discern the tip of her tongue withdrawing behind her sala-cious smile. "Everything Scape told you – it's all true. Everything."

"That – that may be–" The fervour of her embrace had expelled most of the air from my lungs. "But–"

She threw her head back, the sharp points of her small teeth glinting fiercely. "I got a brain out of the Future inside my head. This is the way it's gonna be some day – no more of that ladylike crap. In the Future, women are just gonna take what they want." Her mouth swooped down upon me again, an eagle on its prey.

"God help us." I broke free of her grasp, but was within seconds pinned against the door of my cabin.

Her voracious gaze locked into my eyes. "Not just women," she breathed. "Women – men – everybody. It's all they'll think about – all the time." Her panting breath became even more rapid. "Not like you – you drive me crazy. You're so goddamn cold – unexcited – like a goddamn machine. You're the one that's clockwork." Her eyes narrowed to slits. "Well, all that's gonna change, right now. I can't stand it – get ready, sucker–"

The door sprang open behind me, and I fell backwards, tearing free of Miss McThane's embrace. This sudden event so took her by surprise, that there was time for me to scramble to my knees, slam the door shut, and brace my shoulder against it to prevent her entry.

She went away, after several minutes of repeated entreaties. I sat wearily on my bed, my head in my hands, appalled at this vision of the Future – a foreign country far from this one, where a person such as I would be as out of place as though lost in the Mongolian wastes. If what Scape had told me was true, then they would be different people, those residents of the Time to Come; different, and crueller, rending the flesh of their pleasures in their shining teeth.

So unnerving was this vision, that for a moment I thought I had at last become deranged. I looked up at a sound of grinding wood, and saw a stalk of glistening metal rising from the floor of my cabin. A brass flower blossomed at its end, and swivelled towards me.

A voice – familiar, unforgettable – spoke. "Dower you are there?" The Brown Leather Man's words echoed hollow, as though coming through the tube from a great distance below.

13
A Lesson in Natural History

It was no apparition, engendered by the collapse of my reason; I had undergone enough extraordinary experiences by this time, to have some confidence in determining what was actually happening.

A dark stain of sea-water oozed around the hole the brass stalk had bored through the cabin floor; the metal apparatus glistened damply as the flower-like terminus rotated about. "Dower–" The voice came through it again. "You are there? Approach this device, and answer me."

It had risen to a height of a couple of feet from the floor. I knelt down and brought my mouth close to the brass flower. "Here I am."

The device ceased its rotation, the terminus pointing towards me. "You know who is this?"

"Yes," I whispered in reply.

"Good." The Brown Leather Man's voice, coming through the stalk, shaded darker. "Listen most closely. I can help you. These persons – your captors –

from them you can escape. You can evade their fateful intentions."

My heart sped when I heard these words. I had resigned myself to the – seemingly unavoidable – prospect of my own death. This was, perhaps, no more than the stoicism of the lamb being readied for slaughter, seeing no point in dashing itself against the unyielding limits of its pen. But had not this enigmatic figure, appearing when least expected, helped me to escape a grisly fate twice already? Though I could not imagine how it would be possible again, given the overwhelming numbers of the Godly Army surrounding us, yet I allowed a tremor of hope to quicken my pulse.

"Not now, but later," continued the Brown Leather Man's voice. "When dark it is, and these men are asleep. You must then meet me." He described a point on the ship's deck, unlit and out of the sight of any sentries.

"But – but how can it be possible?" I asked, my lips nearly touching the cold, shining metal. "How can–"

"Now, quiet," ordered the voice. "Explanations later. When we meet. Tell no one." The brass flower folded in on itself, and the stalk drew back through the floor. The only evidence remaining of its singular apparition was the round hole, no bigger than a finger's width, and a trickle of sea-water. I pulled a small rag rug that had been near the bed over the spot to conceal it.

• • • •

At the, appointed hour, when all the ship was asleep save for the single watch stationed at the prow, I slipped from my cabin and made my stealthy way to the deck. My passage went undetected in the night's darkness, and soon enough I was crouched down among the coils of rope and other nautical gear, hidden from all but the most thorough search.

I waited in nervous anticipation for the Brown Leather Man's arrival, The slap of waves and the answering creak of the ship's timbers were all that I could hear; the cloudless heavens scattered points of lights upon the troughs and crests of the ocean's expanse.

His journey to the spot was even more surreptitious than my own, though it included – as I was shortly to learn – his clambering up the side of the ship and over the rail, I was unaware of his presence until a hand touched my shoulder from behind and his voice whispered my name. Thus startled, I whirled about; his hand clapped over my mouth before any outcry could reveal our meeting. "Yet be quiet," he commanded softly.

"Where – where have you been hiding?" I asked when his stifling hand had been drawn away. "You've been aboard all this time?"

He gestured for me to lower my voice further. The moon and stars glinted from his dark face and shoulders, still wet from the sea. "To me listen," he said. "There is little time, and much to tell."

Thereupon followed, as I knelt close to his soft voice, the exposition I herewith summarize. Even if I succeeded in reproducing his exact words (minus my own exclamations of surprise, which rather lengthened the discourse), I would still fail to convey the eerie wonderment evoked by his narration.

He told me his real name, but the human voice lacks the facility to properly pronounce so strange a cognomen; I continued to identify him in my mind as I had done when he had first entered my London shop. He claimed and it was soon enough proven to me, banishing any residual scepticism I might have harboured – to be the last surviving member of an amphibious race, at home in the depths of the seas rather more than upon dry land. His people were the basis for the various tales and legends of "selkies" common to the Scottish islands. In support of this point, he demonstrated to me that what I had taken to be his brownish skin, was in fact a thin, pliable covering – a species of leather indeed, though marine in origin constructed to hold a layer of salt-water, essential to his survival, around his body; the marks that I had taken to be scars in the manner of African tribesmen were the finely worked stitches holding this garment together.

The Brown Leather Man continued from the singular to the general, his discourse forming a natural history of his race. Never very numerous and always secretive, the selkies – to use the most

convenient term – maintained through the long
years a few friendly contacts with human beings;
the various sailors' yarns of miraculous rescues
from ships lost at sea had this basis in reality. As
befit their piscine physiology, the selkies' repro-
ductive processes were external, fertilization and
growth of the resultant embryos taking place in
large beds of seaweed; these sites, the only ones
suitable, were located in the waters off the island
of Groughay. Unfortunately, the activities of
mankind had a disastrous effect upon the situation. Readers of sufficient age may recall that,
towards the end of the previous century, a lucra-
tive boom in the trade of seaweed occurred. It was
gathered in large quantities from the shores of the
distant Scottish islands, charred into a soft black
substance, and distributed throughout Britain for
use as a fertilizer. (Readers familiar with contemporary agricultural practices will be aware that
other, more productive substances have sup-
planted the seaweed for this purpose; there is
virtually no trade in it at the present time.) One of
those who had profited from the market for seaweed had been the young head of the clan based
upon Groughay, Lord Bendray. He had sought to
accelerate the process of turning seaweed into
money by commissioning a device from a clever
London inventor – my own father. The device that
resulted from this commission was a set of wooden
booms that, once installed under my father's

personal supervision on Groughay, extended into the ocean, and were kept submerged by heavy chains. When directed underneath the offshore seaweed beds, the booms would be released from the chains, thus rising to the surface and tangling into the marine vegetation. The seaweed could then be drawn towards the shore by winches, at a rate many times greater than the tides previously had brought it, and thus harvested. My father's device worked well, securely establishing the Bendray family fortune before the collapse in the seaweed market came.

(This history related by the Brown Leather Man brought back to mind Lord Bendray's rambling words in his cellar laboratory beneath Bendray Hall. I had then dismissed his talks of seaweed as nothing more than the wild ravings of a disordered mind; but I did recall that he had made passing reference to his first commission to my father having something to do with the substance.)

It was while on Groughay (so the Brown Leather Man's exposition continued), while my father was installing this seaweed gathering device, that he came into contact with the aquatic race of selkies. Perhaps there was some attraction between minds of similar brilliance: the selkies, being of a philosophical and inquiring breed, possessed much advanced theoretical knowledge pertaining to matters little investigated by human scientists. It was from them that my father learned those arcane principles of sympathetic vibrations in rarefied media, that he subsequently employed in his later inventions such as the Paganinicon. The Brown Leather Man related that my father made several journeys to the island of Groughay, long after the price of seaweed fertilizer had plummeted in 1811, the gathering device been abandoned, and the island depopulated, for the express purpose of consulting with the learned selkie elders on scientific issues.

Or, at least, my father had done so while the selkies still survived as a race. He had, all unwittingly, unleashed the machinery of their doom upon them. The seaweed gathering device so disrupted the cycles of their lives and breeding, that the race began to die out. This fatal process accelerated at a geometric progression, the lifespan of those already born being shortened as well, perhaps through a collective grief. No rancour had ever entered into the relationship with my father; even now, only forgiveness existed in the heart of the Brown Leather Man, the last of his people. Their gentle wisdom had seen that such an outcome had never been intended.

The Brown Leather Man, however, had determined that there was yet some hope. The seaweed beds of the coast of Groughay, unmolested for so long a time, had re-established themselves to their original extent. Even more heartening was his discovery that a number of selkie embryos, in a

spore-like state, had survived the process of con-
verting the seaweed to fertilizer. In one spot where
the fertilizer had been used, the fens around the
village of Dampford, the embryos had matured,
come of age, and even managed to mate with the
inbred and somewhat devolved natives of that
sorry region. The Brown Leather Man was not the
first to discover this: Lord Bendray himself had
made his decision to buy up the district and estab-
lish his residence there, prompted by his
recognition of the Dampford villagers for what they
were – a cross between humans and the selkies he
had been aware of from his youth on the island of
Groughay. Being remarkably dull-witted, the cross-
bred Dampford villagers were easily victimised by
another of Lord Bendray's moneymaking schemes,
in which the village girls – their unlovely visages
matched by corresponding alterations to their
anatomies (I did not press him for elaboration on
the subject) were lured into Mollie Maud's service
in London to satisfy the jaded passions of her
wealthy and bored clientele. So successful had this
trade been – as trades dealing in the seemingly endless lusts of men usually are – that eventually a
whole subculture of Dampford villagers, male and
female, had been established in London, forming
the amorphous borough of Wetwick that I had
stumbled upon. To increase these innocents' isola-
tion and thus reduce the chance of their escaping
from Lord Bendray's and Mollie Maud's domination,

Lord Bendray had created a mock religion for them, centred upon the fictional Saint Monkfish. To avoid detection, the Church of Saint Monkfish has no set place of worship, but rather floats from place to place in the city. The denizens of Wetwick – for so their supposed benefactors Lord Bendray, had named them – are summoned to services by a bell that Lord Bendray had especially cast for the purpose, with a note pitched too high for ordinary humans to hear; the selkie crossbreeds, with their seaborne origins, have a range of hearing different from that of ordinary human beings. The elderly of the tribe (as with humans long in tooth), having lost the highest-pitched portion of their hearing, have dogs trained to listen for the striking of their church bell and to guide them to the location of the services. Just such a "bell-dog" was the eponymous Abel, sleeping below-deck in my cabin. The dogs served another, even more sinister purpose: they were useful for various cabbies catering to depraved tastes, in order to deliver their passengers to the district where their pleasures could be catered to by the wretched employees of Mollie Maud. The coiner Fexton, as a convert to the worship of Saint Monkfish, had need of such an animal as well. Lord Bendray, with his thorough scientific mind, had even created an alternative economy for the Wetwick residents; its coinage, with the portrait of the mythical Saint Monkfish upon it, also served as an identifying emblem for those humans who had been initiated into the secrets of the borough's clandestine existence.

However, even as dull-witted as the Wetwick crossbreeds were, they had come to suspect that things were not as their patron Lord Bendray had told them. In addition to creating their own religion for them, he had blasphemously told them that the Christianity practised by the ordinary population surrounding them, was a faith all the sacraments of which dealt with fishing, a practice that the piscine Wetwick denizens would naturally view with horror. The bedecking of the church of Saint Mary Alderhythe in London with fishing tackle and copies of Izaak Walton was a scheme concocted by Lord Bendray to confirm in the minds of his deluded parishioners the belief in the basic hostility of the human race towards them.

All this, the Brown Leather Man had learned from his own investigations. Some call in his blood had motivated his leaving his sea home by Groughay, and finding these lost cousins of his tribe. Thus, he had found how cruelly they had been exploited to service the lusts and greed of land-bound man. Another reason prompted this pilgrimage: he had wished to determine what knowledge of the potentially dangerous principles of sympathetic vibrations taught to Dower's father still remained in the possession of the land-dwellers. This had been the reason for his visit to my shop, bearing one of my father's Regulators

that had been left by him on the island of
Groughay. In his haste caused by the broken
watch-spring tearing his leather "skin", the Brown
Leather Man had mistakenly given me the Saint
Monkfish crown, collected by him on a visit to the
borough of Wetwick.

His overriding goal, however, was the re-estab-
lishment of his own race. Having discovered the
fate of the spores that had been carried in the seaweed fertilizer, he first had gone to London in
hopes of obtaining ova to be quickened with his
own seed; these he had hoped to carry back to the
ancestral seaweed beds near Groughay, and thus
breed back to the original line. His normally for-
giving nature had been outraged by the servile and
deluded state of the Wetwick denizens; he had
tracked down the coin forger Fexton in order to
determine precisely who was behind the cruel deception. Fexton, the Brown Leather Man had
discovered, by reason of the general deterioration
of his reason, had come to believe that the religion
concocted by his employer Lord Bendray was in
fact true; he had joined in the observances of the
blasphemy that his criminal talents had helped
sustain. While the Brown Leather Man had been
speaking to Fexton, members of the Godly Army –
ever vigilant against blasphemy, they had learned
of the Saint Monkfish religion through their spying
on Lord Bendray – broke into the room and at-
tacked them. In the ensuing scuffle, Fexton was

killed and the Brown Leather Man received a wound that triggered a state of reduced respiration and heartbeat, a normal process in his amphibian race. I was taken to be one of their fellow blasphemers when the two soldiers of the Godly Army returned to Fexton's rooms and discovered me there. Fortunately, being dumped into the chill waters of the Thames revived the Brown Leather Man, and he had overturned the boat, then bore me to the safety of the riverbank.

Our paths parted then, only to be entwined again in the village of Dampford. His efforts to obtain the necessary ova from the female Wetwick crossbreeds had been a failure, so he had gone to their native village. There – just prior to witnessing the contretemps into which I had managed to land myself, and extricating me from it – he had met with more success.

The first glimmer of dawn was tracing the sea's horizon by this time; the hours of the night had flown while I listened near-mesmerised by the strange account. Little time was left before this mysterious yet familiar figure would have to return to the ocean to avoid detection by my captors. He grasped my arm as he spoke: "Dower you must take from me something. And safely hide it." He reached behind himself, then handed me an object, a cylinder of brass glinting in the faint light. As I turned it about in my grasp, I saw that a section of thick glass was set into it; clear water sloshed inside, slightly clouded by a heavier milky liquid.

"This," said the Brown Leather Man, tapping the cylinder in my hands, "is what I journeyed for. This is the seed of my blood, and that of those lost descendants of my blood. All the children of my race – you hold them now."

It was the ova collected from the Dampford villagers, fertilized with his own seed. My hands trembled as I gazed at the contents. "What am I supposed to do with it?"

"Just hide it. That is all. The children – they are so tiny now that you cannot see them. They are delicate; in the seabeds near Groughay they should be sleeping; not in these turbulent waters of open sea. Hide them, where they will be safe. For me, do this."

I looked up into the narrow slits concealing his eyes, then nodded and tucked the cylinder inside my jacket. "But what about the Godly Army? Here on the ship? What are you going to do about–?"

"Shh. " He raised a cautioning finger, and glanced behind at the reddening horizon. "Do not worry of these things. From these murderous people I will save you. There is nothing to fear." Crouching down, he started to edge towards the ship's rail.

"But – when…"

He looked back at me before clambering down the side. "Soon. You will see."

No sound came of him entering the water. I was alone again. The brass cylinder, cold from the sea, weighed against my breast; avoiding the posted watch, I scurried below deck to my cabin.

Throughout the balance of the *Virtuous Persistence's* voyage, I had a single focus to my attention. Not a day passed but that I withdrew to my cabin and took the brass cylinder from beneath the clothing in my trunk. This was the tangible evidence of the fantastic narration that had been related to me; somewhere below me, submerged but attached to the ship, was the man-like figure who had entrusted me with this, his progeny. For some time, I hoped that the brass flower, by which he had communicated to me, would reappear, rising through the floor of the cabin. It did not; the aperture it had bored in the ship's hull remained sealed from beneath.

Over the next few days, my constant: study of the cylinder was rewarded. Straining at the limit of my vision, I first spied small specks swimming in the fluid. They developed rapidly, each day growing in size, until I could discern them as minute sprats, wiggling shapes with paired black dots evidently serving as eyes. These signs of animation spurred me to even greater care with the cylinder; I bedded it as carefully as a newborn infant.

Growing apace with these developments was my own anxiety. The Brown Leather Man's promise of rescue had renewed my attachment to the world of the living the complacency with which I had viewed the prospect of my own demise was now evaporated. While yet there is a chance, the slightest spark is enough to warm our blood.

From the railing of the ship, I viewed with dismay our approach towards the southernmost of the Scottish islands, rounded shapes on the horizon, labelled on the charts with coarse monosyllables such as Muck and Rhum and Eigg. The end of the voyage – and my life – was fast nearing, with yet no sign of the Brown Leather Man's intervention.

At last, the dreaded time came. A knock sounded on the door of my cabin; I hastily shoved the brass cylinder, with its minute living cargo inside, under the covers of my bed, as one of the Godly Army pushed open the door and informed me that my presence was required on deck.

I was greeted by Lieutenant Brattle when I emerged from the hatchway. "Mr Dower," he said with a formal nod. "I hope you have used your time wisely, and commended your soul to the Lord."

Scape and Miss McThane stood together at the rail. Beyond them, I could see the rocky coast of a small island. "Hey – we're here!" said Scape with a mock gaiety. As I was led to my position beside them, the dog Abel sat himself at my feet, gazing up at me with trusting eyes.

"We have indeed arrived at our destination," said the lieutenant solemnly. "That is Groughay you see before you. Soon, a landing party will make for its shore. You and your companions – will be numbered in that party. But not, however, among the living."

I scanned the ocean's rolling surface for any sign of the Brown Leather Man. I saw nothing but the empty expanse of water; my heart might just as well have been sinking beneath. Perhaps the Brown Leather Man's schemes, whatever they had been, had come to naught; perhaps he had been washed free of his attachment to the ship, and lost in the dark night sea, or lost his own life to the teeth of some fearsome creature. Hopes are raised most often, only to be cruelly dashed.

"You would have been wise, Dower, to have used your time in prayer, and not found your soul unprepared for the moment of its parting from the mortal shell." Lieutenant Brattle shook his head. "But I sadly fear you have not done so."

His words brought my attention back from studying the ocean. "I don't know what you mean."

He signalled to one of the crew, who stepped forward and – with evident distaste on his part, and dismay on mine – handed him the brass cylinder that I had left in my cabin. The lieutenant looked from the object to me. "What is this thing, Dower?"

"It would be – rather difficult to explain."

The lieutenant tapped the thick glass set into its side. "No explanation is necessary. It's obviously the evidence of further deviltry on your part. Even at the moment of your death, when your immortal soul stands in full peril of eternal damnation, your degradation is such that you dabble in these filthy practices. What demons these are inside this flask, and to what purposes you intended to put them, we thank the Lord we shall remain ignorant." He handed the cylinder back to the crew member. "Dispose of this."

I heard the weight of metal splash into the ocean; the crew member rejoined the rest of the Godly Army lined up on the deck before us. All had their rifles; there was a rustle of activity as they loaded and raised their weapons. From the rail, Miss McThane glared fiercely at them, as if daring them to shoot; Scape leaned across her and shook my hand.

"It's been a gas," said Scape. "See ya in the funny pages."

Even though a product of dementia, his brashness under the circumstances provoked my admiration. "Maybe sometime in the future," I answered, biting my lower lip to suppress its trembling.

The soldiers of the Godly Army raised their weapons at Lieutenant Brattle's command. The salt tang of the ocean filled my nostrils, and a gull cried overhead; all I could see were the dark holes of the rifle barrels trained upon us. The argument about poor Abel's complicity in the evil acts of which we stood accused, had been apparently resolved against him: a pair of the soldiers lowered their sights towards the dog. He thought it a game, and barked cheerfully at them.

Before Lieutenant Brattle could order them to fire, however, the line of soldiers was knocked askew by a sudden lurch of the ship beneath their feet. Scape, Miss McThane, and myself were likewise thrown, forced to grab the rail behind ourselves to maintain our balance.

With a grinding howl, the ship rocked again, seeming to rise nearly out of the water. Several of the Godly Army panicked, shouting and breaking ranks; they ran to the opposite rail and peered over. From where I stood, I could see great shapes moving beneath the waves, tangled with dark wreaths of seaweed.

"Demons!" shouted one of the soldiers, pointing a quavering finger at us. "They've called 'em – come to rescue 'em!"

This hypothesis met with a hurried acceptance among their number, as the ship wallowed about, the grating noises sounding even louder through the hull. They had convinced themselves of our being in league with satanic forces; the consequence of this was the sudden upsurge of unreasoning fear in their own breasts. Even their commanding officer, Lieutenant Brattle, lost his self-control; he joined his men in their flight towards the pair of small boats on the ship's deck.

They were soon launched, some of the men being forced to leap from the railing into the churning ocean; they swam to the side of the boats and fought their way aboard. In their panic, no thought – other than the brief accusation – had been given to the three of us. Gripping the rail, I watched as the boats' oars splashed and drove our captors as quickly away as was possible.

"Jesus jumping Christ," said Scape. The ship lurched again, knocking him heavily into me. "Now what?"

He was answered by a furious volley of barking from Abel. He had stood up with his paws on the opposite rail, and was yapping at the island of Groughay as though it were some particularly noxious pest.

"Good God," I said. I could see what had captured the dog's attention; the island's coast was clearly discernible, the sound of the waves battering it even louder. "We're going into the rocks."

Scape and Miss McThane scrabbled across the sloping deck to where I stood. "Hey – you're right." The ship gave another lurch, and was drawn several yards closer to the shore; whatever was grating against the hull was also responsible for our motion landwards.

"This doesn't look too good," said Miss McThane. "Maybe we'd better abandon ship."

"With what?" Scape pointed over his shoulder to the receding figures of the Godly Army. "Those chicken-shits took the boats."

We could only watch helplessly as the jagged rocks loomed nearer. Our approach accelerated, a crest of water surging up the hull towards the rail. The grating noise of the objects below the surface was drowned by the sharper noise of the timbers splintering into pieces.

Billowing canvas and slack lines came tangling about us as the masts swayed and toppled. The deck split open, casting Scape and Miss McThane away from me. I grabbed for Abel, but missed as my own feet were yanked out from under me by the buckling wood. For a moment, I heard the clog's barking somewhere above me as my back struck the rail; it splintered in two, and I was falling towards the white lace dashing against the rocks. The great bulk of the *Virtuous Persistence* lifted into the sky, the hull gouged and broken by the rocks. Then I struck the furious water.

All was dark; as my mouth filled with salt, I thought I saw the even darker shapes of giant chains strung through the depths. A wave lifted me into air; a shattered timber crashed against my brow, and I saw no more.

14
The Hopes of a Race

I dreamt my face was being washed with a soft, damp flannel; I opened my eyes and found Abel standing on my chest, licking my chin. He barked at this sign of my resurrection; I pushed him away and groggily sat up, my palms digging into sand as I did so. The smell of the ocean was strong in my nostrils, owing perhaps to the quantity of seaweed tangled about my limbs.

A jagged piece of flotsam nudged my foot, impelled by the lapping waves. Other debris, splintered fragments of the ill-fated *Virtuous Persistence*, were strewn about the small, rock-bordered cove.

"Dower," said a voice behind me. I turned around and saw the impassive countenance of the Brown Leather Man gazing down at me. His dark hand reached down and helped me to my feet. "Good it is to see you awake. I had seen no injuries upon your person, but of these matters one cannot be sure."

I shook my head, both to clear my thoughts and to disperse the water lodged inside my ear. "What place is this?" I asked, looking about at the high cliffs that lined the shore.

"You're safe on the island of Groughay." He gestured at the surrounding rocks. "You will forgive, I trust, for the necessary violence of the means employed to bring you here. But you are free from the Godly Army, at least."

"That was all your doing? But how?"

"Your father enabled me thus. The device he created, for the purpose of gathering seaweed, exists still in working order. In the sea, the chains and wooden booms are yet in place – I had only to activate the device to create such havoc as you saw, and to draw you and your companions to safety here."

"My companions? You mean, Scape and Miss McThane? Where are they?"

"No fear," said the Brown Leather Man. "They are but a small distance from here, on another point of the shore. But of you I must ask – where is that which I gave you? The wreckage of the ship I have searched, and not found it in that which was your cabin. You had hidden the object elsewhere, I trust?"

It was the brass cylinder, with his minute progeny inside, of which he spoke. With a heavy heart, I informed him of how Lieutenant Brattle had thrown it overboard. He staggered backwards on learning this, as though struck above the heart. His gaze turned from me towards the ocean, as though contemplating the enormity of searching its depths for the precious item.

The currents of fortune saved him from this impossible task. I heard Abel barking several yards away from us; a gleam of bright metal rolled in the seaweed at the water's edge; some movement inside had caught the dog's attention. "Look there." I grabbed the Brown Leather Man's arm and pointed.

He saw it, ran and gathered it up, cradling the brass cylinder as tenderly as a newborn infant. I could see the dark-eyed sprats swimming about inside.

"I must leave you," he said. "They have reached the age that into their proper bed they must be placed." He turned from me and waded into the sea.

"But what about us?" I shouted after him. "What's to become of us?"

The waves lapped up to his chest, and over the cylinder held there. "Do not worry. You shall see me again soon. All will be taken care of."

I stood gazing at the spot where he had disappeared. With Abel at my heels, I headed in the direction where he had indicated I might find my fellow castaways.

They were alive, and evidently unharmed. I spotted them from the top of the outcropping of rock that separated another small cove from that where I had been washed ashore. Scape was sorting out various bits of debris from the wreck – nothing of any value was arranged on the sand – while Miss McThane watched his labours from her

seat on a rounded stone. Her shoulders and arms
were bare to the sun, while her tattered dress dried
itself on the rocks next to her. They looked up at
my shout, and Scape gestured for me to descend
and join them.

"Good to see ya, man." He jovially slapped my
back, One of the blue lenses had a slight chip on
its edge, but he showed no other sign of damage.
"We all made it safe and sound."

Miss McThane laughed scornfully. "Yeah, we're
doing fine, all right." Her words were heavy with
sarcasm. "Stuck on some goddamn pile of rocks
in the middle of nowhere. Now what are we
gonna do?"

Scape's mood was considerably more buoyant.
"Not just any pile of rocks, sweetheart – I think we
might find some interesting stuff here. And be-
sides – at least we're not gonna starve." He pointed
up to a section of cliffs above our heads.

I followed the direction of his finger and saw the
vacuous faces of several sheep gazing down at us.
"I wonder how many there are here."

"Who knows? Place has been abandoned for
quite a while. They've had nothing else to do except breed. There's probably enough to last us until
we figure a way of getting off here."

"Yeah?" Miss McThane remained sceptical. "What
do you know about butchering a sheep? They're not
just a bunch of cutlets running around in a woolly
jacket, you know."

He shrugged. "Can't be too hard. You get a knife, rub a coupla sticks together – we'll all be singing around the ol' campfire tonight. You wait and see."

I looked towards the grey clouds mounting over the ocean. "I suggest our first concern should be finding some sort of shelter. The weather in these parts is reputedly severe."

"Good thinking. See, baby – ol' Dower here's getting into the swing of things. Cheer up a bit; think Boy Scouts."

"Screw the Boy Scouts." Grumbling, she stood up and wrapped her dress over her shoulders like a shawl. "What this place needs is a goddamn en-chilada stand."

We climbed up through a cleft in the rocks, the loose stones sliding under our feet. As Scape led the way, Miss McThane stopped and laid her hand on my arm. "Actually," she said, smiling, "there are some advantages to being, like, shipwrecked. Out here where there's nobody around, and it's all kinda... wild and primitive. You know?" She brought her face closer to mine. "Sometimes people get... inspired..."

"I assure you," I said, drawing as far away is possible on the narrow path, "my feelings remain unaltered."

"We'll see about that." She turned and resumed climbing after Scape.

Having gained the top of the cliffs, Scape reached down and assisted the rest of the party up beside him. "What'd I tell ya?" He waved his hand about at the rugged, sparsely grassed landscape. Sheep, numerous if thin-shanked from their scanty fare, gazed at us with placid equanimity. "Groceries on the hoof." Abel ran barking at them; they turned their mild faces at his furious noise before shambling slowly away in search of their next meagre mouthful.

I directed Scape's attention to what appeared to be crumbling walls some distance away. "Perhaps we can find shelter there."

"Must be old Bendray's place," he said. "I don't think he'll mind, under the circumstances."

The stones turned out to be the remains of a castle, its rude structure indicating considerable antiquity. Portions of one hallway were still roofed over; the rest had fallen into hollow decay. A crumbling table and chairs were soon reduced to firewood; flint and steel found by a towering chimney brought a welcome blaze, by which Miss McThane and I huddled while a hungry Scape went back into the surrounding fields.

He returned a few hours later, a spectre of spattered blood and exhaustion, with an excited Abel yapping behind him. "Damn things are more complicated than I thought," he announced, wiping his pocket knife on his trousers leg. The ragged lumps he had carried back were forthwith skewered and held over the fire until sufficiently blackened to hide their grisly origin.

So passed our first day upon the island of Groughay, in no great discomfort, considering how recently we all had been resigned to surrendering our lives. A more cheering discovery was made when a cache of whisky was found underneath a section of rotting floorboards. The skies opened during the night; I awakened to the sound of a storm lashing the stone walls against which we huddled. Close by me, Miss McThane hopefully whispered my name. I feigned sleep, and she gave up for the time being.

Following a breakfast of cold mutton, Scape made further explorations of the ruins. His triumphant shout announced the fruit of his labours. "Get a loada this." He stood in the middle of what had once been a room of considerable size, truncated at one end by the collapse of one of the walls. Around him were various metal constructions, all now sadly lapsing into rust. "It's your father's old workshop – when he was here years ago!"

I came down beside him and gazed about at the scene. The kaleidoscopic variety of my father's genius was rendered even more confusing by the decrepit state of the devices. Some towered above our heads as though they were the skeletons of some species of metal giant; others were mere handfuls of gears and wheels, rusted into lumps. The workbenches had rotted away, spilling the discarded tools and partial assemblages into the puddles on the stone floor.

Scape, undismayed by the decrepitude of the machinery, set about rummaging through the tangled remnants. "Hey, this one's in pretty good shape," he said, tugging at an iron strut. "Gimme a hand."

Between the two of us, we pulled free the device in question. To me it seemed the fleshless carcass of a bat, though on a considerably magnified scale. The thin struts formed umbrella-like ribs, arching out when unfolded to a distance of several yards. They were connected by a system of chains to the gears of a central clockwork apparatus; shreds of rotten canvas hung about the figure.

One of the wings – if such they were – grated harshly through its layers of rust as Scape waggled it back and forth. "Far out," he said admiringly. "What a find."

I surveyed the thing dubiously. The fragility of its construction, in combination with the disrepair into which it had fallen, gave the impression of imminent collapse. "What is it?"

He patted in tenderly, flakes of rust drifting from under his hand. "Remember how ol' Bendray told you that line about how he came to believe that there were people – I mean, like aliens – zooming around in outer space? From other planets? Did he say he'd seen them himself, zipping around in the sky out here at Groughay?"

I cast my mind back to Lord Bendray's monologue in his cellar laboratory at his Hall. "Um... yes. He did, as a matter of fact."

"Figured he did. He goes rabbiting on about that crap to everybody he meets, given half a chance. Well, the funny thing is, he really did see 'em zooming around." He worked the metal strut harder, so that the entire device squeaked and groaned, wobbling where it stood. "This is it, man – visitors from outer space. This is what ol' Bendray saw."

My gaze went from him to the device. "This… whatever it is? He saw this?"

Scape nodded. "It's a flying machine. Great, huh? I told you your old man was running a few numbers on Bendray. The way I figure it, your father had to convince him that there were guys from other planets, flying around checking out things here on earth, so Bendray would go for that bullshit pile-driver he's got in his basement. You know, the one he thinks he can blow up the whole planet with. Your father already had a workshop out here, from the work he'd already done for Bendray; all he had to do was come out here, build this contraption, then let Bendray see it flying around and tell him it's aliens from outer space. He'd probably already got a pretty good idea by then of how much guff he could get Bendray to swallow."

I let these aspersions on my father's moral character pass by, finding it preferable to believe that he had engaged in a fraudulent manipulation of Lord Bendray, rather than actually having built a machine capable of destroying the earth. "I find it difficult to credit that this... device could actually go up in the air."

"Well, when it was in better condition, it could. All these spaces here were covered with some kind of fabric, so it was like real wings." The rotting canvas fell apart at the slightest pressure from his exploring finger. "Then the gears and stuff ran off the master-spring there, and off it'd go, flapping away."

"Hm." I was still not convinced, though I could envision no other purpose the ungainly contraption could have served. "Interesting enough, I suppose. I don't see any great cause for excitement in it, though."

"Don't you get it, man?" Scape's voice rose with excitement. "This is how we can get off this flippin' island. We can fix this sucker up, and just fly off."

"What! With this? Don't be absurd. The thing's nothing more than a... a mechanical kite."

"Your ass." He pointed into the device's spindly framework. "Right there – look. See? Those are the steering controls; those lines run out to the wings. And right there's where you sit. Christ, maybe your own father flew this thing around."

The notion brought a scoffing laugh from me. "Really... how gullible do you think I am? A flying machine! Capable of bearing a person's weight aloft – the idea is patently ridiculous. Completely beyond the realm of possibility."

"A lot you know," said Scape with some irritation. "Hey, I've been there – in the Future. All the flying machines you could want. The sky's gonna be just full of 'em some day. Huge goddamn things – carry hundreds of people. Believe me, I know what I'm talking about."

I didn't care to dispute the point with him; his visions of the Future – I retained a healthy scepticism about their origin – were a matter of some conviction with him. "Yes, well," I said in an attempt to mollify. "It might be diverting to… muck about with it a bit."

"Muck about, my ass. We gotta get this thing working. Up, up, and away, and off this stupid island. And fast."

"Why such urgency?" His eyebrows arched above the rims of his spectacles. "Hey – have you forgotten about those Godly Army characters? It's not gonna take 'em long to get their courage back up, and come around here to hand our butts to us. Those kinda guys – they're fanatics – they don't give up. And they wanted to kill us before – what kinda mood do you think they're gonna be in, the next time?"

In truth, I had forgotten about our former captors, so great had been my relief at finding myself still alive and in one piece on this island.

Aroused from slumber by our voices, Miss McThane picked her way through the rubble to join us. "What's all the shouting about?"

Scape's thumb indicated the device. "We're gonna fly off the island. In this."

"Neat-o." With no sign of trepidation, she grasped one of the struts and waggled it through its groaning motions.

"But surely," I protested, "there must be some other means of leaving this place."

"Like what? You can't swim to the mainland – it's too far. And the currents around here are murder; I looked at the captain's charts back when we were on the ship. And there's no wood on this flippin' rock, so we can't build a boat. No, man; this is the only way." Scape patted the rusty metal. "Up into the wild blue yonder."

The more confident he sounded, the more my heart filled with dread. "But – the wings... the fabric has all rotted away. What do you propose covering them with?"

Scape dismissed my objections with a wave of his hand. "No problem. We're surrounded by the woolly bastards, aren't we? Sheepskin, man; we just skin 'em and pop it on to the frame here."

Miss McThane laughed. "This oughta be good. You're really hot with a knife and a sheep."

He glared at her for a moment, then turned back to me. "Nothing to worry about," he said reassuringly. "You'll see."

The awful premonition mounted in my breast that I would indeed.

I left Scape to his work upon the supposed flying device my fear of it having reached the point where I could not bear to lay a hand upon it – and wandered down to the shoreline where I had awoken after the wreck of the *Virtuous Persistence*. Perhaps some article of value, a portion of the ship's stores undamaged by the salt-water, had washed up on the rocks and could be used to supplement our bleak diet of mutton.

A few scraps of wood lay on the sands – the bulk of the ship, holed by the violent action of the seaweed gathering apparatus, had apparently gone to the bottom, beyond our reach. I poked among these until I heard a familiar voice call my name.

The Brown Leather Man stepped out from behind a sheltering line of stones. He grasped my arm in both his hands, this gesture of good will transcending any gulf of nature between our races. "Much gratitude I owe you," he said. His voice thickened with emotion, though the stitched covering over his face remained impassive.

"For what?" I said, puzzled. After all, it had been he who had saved me, and the others, from execution at the hands of the Godly Army.

"The children. Of my blood. Safe they are, and growing." He stretched his arm out towards the ocean, where the beds of seaweed lay.

"Oh. Yes, indeed. Yes, I imagine you must find that most gratifying." He seemed to overestimate any responsibility I might have had for this happy event; I could see no reason to correct him on the point. "Um... a, uh, certain concern has sprung up among my companions and myself. I was wondering if… perhaps… you could be of some assistance regarding the matter."

"Hm?" He made a slight noise, more from courtesy than any attention to me. His gaze remained focussed on the sea, his thoughts obviously far away.

"Yes, we were concerned about the wisdom of staying for very long here on this island. After all, there are some people about who seem to bear a marked hostility towards us, and we thought–"

"Do not with thoughts of those others disturb yourself." His chin sank on to his chest. "It is my undertaking – in gratitude – to protect you from them."

"Oh. Well; very good of you, I'm sure." I mulled over how best to broach my suggestions. "Perhaps – it struck me, you understand – perhaps that might best be accomplished if we were to… find a way off the island. Over to the mainland, that is. Perhaps if you could bring us a boat, or alert someone on the mainland as to our presence here, and they could come for us–"

He was deep in his contemplations, barely conscious of me standing beside him. "All in good time," he said abstractedly. "These things will be done."

Our brief conversation at an end, he returned to the sea.

The next few weeks settled into a pattern. Our island captivity continued; I scanned the horizons from the highest Groughay cliffs, anxiously

awaiting the return of the Godly Army to finish
their interrupted task; Scape, with Miss McThane
as his assistant, laboured on the purported flying
machine. He had unearthed a cache of tools and
auxiliary parts, wrapped in oil-soaked cloth to
protect them from the weather, which greatly fa-
cilitated the project: chains worked around the
teeth of what were determined to be the appropriate gears, and the metal armatures no longer
grated through the years' accumulations of rust.
The taste of mutton became sickeningly familiar
to all of us, but there was at least a plenitude of
it. A growing section of the castle ruins began to
resemble a charnel house, with the bloody skins
of sheep draped about on the stones. Only the
chillness of the northern air prevented rapid de-
composition; Scape's methods of preparing the
hides were marked by a crude haste and a complete lack of any appropriate knowledge; many of
the poor animals' heads lolled, still attached to
their skins, the dumb eyes seeming to wonder
how such indignities had been visited upon them.
The living sheep divined Scape's cruel attentions
towards them, and became increasingly difficult
to catch; the dog Abel, with his terrier cleverness,
soon became expert at turning back the fleeing
herds and driving them into Scape's clutches.

My vigil upon the cliffs was ended the morning
after a particularly severe storm. All night long, the
stone walls of the castle ruins were lashed by driving

rain; a section of the remaining roof was torn away
by the gale. As Scape inspected the machine to see
what damage had been done to it, I went to see if
the storm had brought anything of value to land.

From my vantage point, I could see the waves
rolling in, thick with tangled seaweed; the tempest
had raged through the offshore beds. As I looked
over the churning rocks, an unearthly cry of despair sounded up to me, the wail inarticulate in its
anguish. I knew whose voice it was, though I had
never heard it torn by any such emotion. The loose
stones grated under my boots as I scrambled down
the path to the point from which it had come.

I found the Brown Leather Man upon his knees
at the edge of the lapping water. The sand was covered with the thick drapings of seaweed. His hands
were thrust deep Into the dark foliage, lifting it to
his gaze, the salt-water running from his arms.

He made no response as I touched his shoulder
stepped closer to him, to see what spectacle bound
him in such fierce regard.

Dead things twined in the seaweed.

A sob broke from the Brown Leather Man's
throat as he tilted his head back to face the blank
sky. I could see the tiny forms, monstrously misshapen, idiot piscine skulls, innards everted and
exposed. The storm had not killed them, but only
brought their twisted corpses to view. The blood
with which he had mixed his own had degener-
ated too far; the seed he bore could father only

such abortions as these, when mated with the crossbreeds' wretched line.

I could think of nothing to say; a race's final progeny was mired in the dark mass, the infants' miserable flesh pallid with decay. "I'm sorry." That was all that was possible.

His fearsome gaze turned slowly around towards me. One hand pulled from the mass of seaweed; from where he knelt, his arm swept into my chest, knocking me backwards.

He towered above me, where I lay gasping to regain my breath. His finger jabbed towards me as though it were some dark lightning-stroke of judgment. "You–" His voice was tortured into a choking rasp. "Your kind see what you have done. While yet there was hope – hope that again my blood could live – then I could forgive you. I could all of your kind forgive. But now... now that your folly has murdered my blood, and hope is no more–" His hand raised above his head, gathering its force for a blow.

I shrank back into the sand, unable to flee. For a moment he remained, his arm trembling in air. Then, with another wordless cry, he turned and plunged back into the ocean's depths.

When I had managed to regain my feet, I looked out across the empty sea. There was no sign of him. With a piece of driftwood, I dug a shallow trench in the sand, and buried as much of the seaweed, and its rotting burden, as I could gather.

Scape greeted me cheerfully when I returned to the castle ruins. His shirt was spattered with sheep's blood as he announced, "Just about ready, Dower! Maybe give it the first test flight tomorrow." He returned to his work, rubbing his hands with anticipation.

I was still somewhat dazed from the events out on the shore. It took a few moments before I realised a hand was caressing the back of my neck. I turned and looked into Miss McThane's smiling face.

"He's going to be busy for a long time," she said. "And I get so bored…"

"No–" I shook my head; a violent tremor seized my limbs. I backed away from her, then turned and ran towards the empty fields.

15
Mr Dower Sees it Through

A hand shook me awake; I opened my eyes to a silhouetted figure, dark, against the stars, bending over me. At first I took it to be Miss McThane; then the voice spoke, and I knew what entity had stealthily entered the castle ruins.

"Come with me, Dower," the Brown Leather Man said softly. "I have much with you to discuss."

I had shrunk back against the stone wall upon recognising him, but there was no trace in his voice of the rage he had displayed earlier; only an urgency that compelled my hasty obedience to his request. Scape and Miss McThane were still asleep some distance away; the Brown Leather Man gestured for my silence. We picked our way together over the rubble until we were well outside.

"You must forgive me," he said, grasping my arm. The night's darkness seemed to be absorbed and condensed into his form beside me. "My anger today – you will understand. Great had been my hopes. But always I have meant you no harm."

"Yes, of course." I could think of no other words to reassure him. "A very sad occasion." That sounded even more inadequate.

"That is of the past. Other things are to be thought of. You must leave this island. At once."

I breathed a sigh of relief. My earlier entreaties, it seemed, had had the desired effect. "I'm glad you feel that way. Soon as morning comes, I'll tell the others. I imagine a boat would be the most practical–"

He shook his head. "No time is there. You must leave now. You alone – the others are unimportant."

"But why? Surely–"

His grip on my arm tightened. "Things of great urgency – great dangers that only you can avert. You must leave now, and back to England go. To Bendray Hall – when you are there, all will be explained."

A petty annoyance welled up in me. "I cannot calculate the number of times that has been said to me. "Everything will be explained." And every time I do what's asked of me, based on that promise, I end up being chased by packs of bloodthirsty maniacs. I find it tiresome in the extreme."

"My word I give," said the Brown Leather Man. "As we speak further, the precious moments flee. Only this one thing more, this one task, and all mysteries will be dispelled. But if what I bid you is not done – if to Bendray Hall you do not go – then great misfortune to all of us will come. Any harm to you will be the least of the consequences."

The fervour of his speech dispelled my objections. "Very well, then – how do you propose I should leave this island?"

"Come – to the water's edge we must go."

He led me down the rocky path to the shore. The ocean, faintly luminous under the moon's glow, splashed against the rounded stones. "You I will carry," said the Brown Leather Man. "In my arms, through the waves. My native element is the sea; you will be safe."

I looked dubiously at the ocean, the chill spray dampening my face. "Isn't it quite a ways? And... somewhat cold?"

"Have no fear. In the sea, I have no need of this–" His hands traced the scar-like stitching across his chest. "The outer covering which on the land enables me to walk about. You I will wrap in it; such it is that it will protect you from the harshness of the sea."

"Hmm…"

"No other way is there. Your very life, and much else, on doing this depends."

The life of which he spoke had been in his hands more than once; what trust was possible, if not in one who had already preserved me from death? "Very well," I said, steeling my nerve. "Proceed."

Certain of the stitching eased and opened under his fingers. After a few minutes, the leathery covering wrinkled away from whatever nature of flesh lay beneath. As a snake sheds its

skin, only in this instance standing upright, the
Brown Leather Man slid the artificial epidermis
from his frame.

His own, more pallid skin shone wetly in the
moonlight. A slit-like mouth, and eyes of perfect
circularity, only marginally comparable to the fish-
like denizens of Wetwick and Dampford, were
revealed when his head was bared. Released from
the confines of the covering, a pinkish frill swelled
about his throat. "Hurry," he said. "In the air, as
this I may stay only a little while."

I let myself be draped with the garment he had
discarded. As I was of considerably smaller stature,
the thin "leather" hung loosely about me, with no
need to exert any force to slide my limbs into the
appropriate places. It hung in overlapping folds
over my legs, as though I were a child appropriat-
ing his father's trousers for play.

The Brown Leather Man – brown no longer, but
rather shining in the manner of a sea creature
catching the faint light – gathered the loose cloak
tighter about my chest, fastening it into this position by a twisted knot at my shoulder. He led me
into the waves; when the water came surging up
to my chin, he reached down and easily lifted me
from the sea floor, my weight distributed between
his own inordinate strength and the buoyancy imparted by the salt ocean.

The assurances made as to my comfort turned
out to be well founded: the garment kept me

reasonably dry, only my face catching the salt spray as the Brown Leather Man bore me above the waves, and provided sufficient insulation to retain the warmth of my own body. After my initial apprehensions had passed, I endeavoured to relax as much as possible, as though I were lying on the bottom of a secure boat instead of being lifted across the surging water by the other's arm clasped tightly about my waist. His powerful strokes with his free arm, and the easeful motions of his lower body, cleaved through the waves with a rhythmic grace, proving his natural adaptation to the element.

Against the splash of water, I suddenly heard a distant cry. I tilted my head back to look. The morning sun was just breaking across the cliffs; a figure stood at their crest, having spotted us in the waves below. It was Scape; from this distance I could not see the expression on his face, but his fist shaking in air was clearly visible.

"You sonuvabitch!" came his howl. "Running out on us – you'll see! You bet your sweet ass..." The sound of his voice faded as I was carried farther away from the island.

The singular voyage lasted more than an hour, despite the Brown Leather Man's speed of progress through the water. Only once, when a particularly high wave washed over us, had I experienced any degree of discomfort, and then only a mouthful of salt water that left me sputtering for breath. When we waded ashore on the Scottish mainland, the sun was well lifted above the horizon. Its rays brought an additional urgency to my companion's request for the return of his garment. I hastily stripped the dark skin off; finding my own clothes somewhat damp underneath.

"Extraordinary," I said, brushing my sodden hair away from my face. The island of Groughay was visible only as the smallest speck on the horizon. I turned to look at the heather-covered hills at my back. As I did so, a rifle-shot rang out, sending up a puff of sand at my feet.

"Quickly!" The Brown Leather Man pushed me towards the shelter of an outcropping of rocks. "Run!" He was unable to follow me, the skin-like covering that would have protected him on the land still wadded up in his arms. He dived back into the sea and disappeared.

Another shot sounded before I reached the outcropping's safety. The marksman was evidently some distance away, by the faint sound of the report; no doubt I had been spotted from some high vantage point in the surrounding hills. With my heart pounding in my chest, I circled around the rocks and began climbing up the slope on the opposite side, screened from view by the brushy foliage…

I soon gained the top of the small hill. As I crouched down, the shore was down below at my left hand. In front of me, across the valley at the hill's foot, was the confirmation of my first guess as to what person might have directed the shot at me. I could recognize, even at this distance, the figure of Sir Charles Wroth, dressed in hunting tweed, his rifle cradled in the crook of his arm. He commanded a party of considerable size, tramping through the countryside's thick heather: on either side of him, more men, undoubtedly of the Godly Army, were arrayed in line, each similarly armed. Before them, several score of the local men, unarmed save for their keen knowledge of the terrain, swept ahead in the nature of grouse-beaters in search of game to flush for the hunting party's pleasure. It was easy enough to conjecture how they had been enlisted in this cause: the Highlanders' lack of education and sternly Calvinist religion would make them enthusiastic pursuers of anyone accused of deviltry and various other blasphemous acts. I could expect much the same fate from their bare hands as from the bullets of the Godly Army.

No doubt, this force had been assembling here, the nearest point of land to Groughay, waiting for the eventual arrival of myself and the others. With the numbers of men available for the purpose here, it had very likely seemed a strategy preferable to chancing a further expedition to Groughay itself.

As I watched, Sir Charles listened to the news of my having been sighted and shot at, brought to him by one of his men come running from the end of the line closest to the sea. He quickly gave out his orders, dispatching the line of beaters around the base of the hill at the top of which I knelt.

Few avenues of escape were left to me. Directly facing me were the guns of the Godly Army, working their way across the valley; I was cut off as well to my left by the shoreline, on the sands of which I would be an easy target for my pursuers. The beaters would soon have me encircled, trapped on top of the hill, if I did not hasten away. I scrambled over the ridge and through the brush on the other side.

I was soon halted by the edge of a sheer cliff-face dropping down to a river below. No handholds were visible by which to climb down; the rocks churning the rushing water to lace: assured death if any foolhardy leap were to be attempted. Behind me, I could already hear the rude accents of the native men as they shouted to one another. Crouching low to avoid detection as long as possible, I ran along the cliff's edge, hoping to gain the bottom of the hill's slope before the beaters completed their movement around its base.

Too late; as soon as I reached a point where I could see the cliffside crumbling into a loose scree of rocks into the river's bank, the far edge of the line of beaters reached the water, cutting me off from that final angle as well. Worse, I had been spotted. One of the men shouted and pointed, alerting the others. Hurling various imprecations and threats at me, they began scrambling up the hillside, their hands digging into the heather for leverage. I turned and, caution abandoned, ran back towards the hill's crest.

Gasping for breath, I mounted the hill with no more thought of strategy in my head than has a winded fox turned on every side by the baying hounds. The shout went up from the other side; Sir Charles and the rest of the Godly Army had spotted me. They mounted towards me, sure enough of their prey to wait until they had a clear shot.

Spinning about on my heel, I could see the barring jaws of nature, the sea and the cliff, on two sides; the men intent on blood forming the rest of the box. I watched in dread anticipation, frozen to the spot, as the line of men ascending from the valley halted halfway up the slope. The rifles rose to the shoulders of the Godly Army, their stern faces sighting over the barrels.

A roaring, beating noise came suddenly from above my head. For a moment, I thought my racing pulse had burst through the limits of my temples. Then I heard cries – not of triumph and excitement as before, but of astonishment and fear – and saw the hunters raising their round-eyed gaze from me to the skies. Amazingly, from the heavens, someone shouted my name.

I looked up as a great shadow swept over me. Something like a bird, but many times – larger, shot past, its ragged-edged wings beating against the air. It swooped low through the valley, flattening the men on the hillside as they scurried for cover into the heather. As it tilted and swung back in my direction, I could see the figures upon the thing: a man, a woman, and a barking dog.

Scape stood upright, holding the lines controlling the machine's gyrations in his hands in the manner of a Roman charioteer; his face, I saw as the beating wings bore him close again, was lit with a wild excitement. Kneeling beside him, Miss McThane held on to the thin struts, her head tilted back, laughing as the rush of wind sent her unbound hair streaming behind. A cord secured Abel from falling; his barking seemed to hold more enthusiasm than fear.

The flying machine came low enough over my head that I felt the force of its wings keeping it aloft. Drops of blood spattered across my brow as I ducked from its path; the sheepskins covering the armatures of the wings were little more than raw carcasses with the meat and bones hacked away; the matted fleece was still thick on most of them, and blank-eyed heads dangled and swayed with the device's motions. Scape's haste to get the machine up into the air had yielded this grotesque result.

"I told you, sucker! I told you!" His triumphant cry edged on sheer mania; he had broken through to his own true element. The dark spray from the sheep carcasses coursed across his chest and face, as though spelling an emblem of the Future on his form. The machine mounted into the sky again as Miss McThane's laughter mingled with his. "Eat shit, turkeys!" came her mocking shout.

Another voice came from behind me. One of the beaters, an aged Scot with a beard like an Old Testament prophet's, lifted a trembling finger towards the apparition in the sky. "The Beast!" he cried. "Frae th' Book o Revelation! D'ye ken the heads, and th' Whore 'pon its back?" His eyes wild, the old man exhorted the others. "Laughing; she was – th' whore o' Babylon! The last days have come 'pon us!" This hypothesis was rapidly taken up by the other men, their voices rising into a panicky babble. Over the valley, the flying machine turned around, its. wings bending almost vertical, and headed back towards the hill.

"The Beast!" Voices from the hillside in front of me took up the cry; the recognition had swept through all of the religiously minded. It was no respecter of persons; several of the Godly Army had thrown away their rifles, the better to clasp their hands in fervent prayer.

Another cry went up from around the hillside: "Its fiery breath!" Smoke and flames billowing along the device's wings had been spotted by several of the aghast onlookers. I could see sparks shooting from the metal joints; the results of Scape's hurried assemblage of the machine were now becoming apparent. The sheepskins covering the wings had begun to smoulder, sending greasy smoke trailing behind.

The machine started to disintegrate, from the inadequacy of its construction and the violence of its manoeuvres through the air. Flaming carcasses peeled away from the wings; sheep's heads, smelling of singed meat, rained upon the men circled about the hill. This last sent them into complete terror, as well it might; with inarticulate shouts, they turned, Godly Army and native Scot alike, and sprinted in all directions, fleeing the burning wrath of Satan visited upon them.

Above me, I saw the flying machine wheel about, the controlling lines in Scape's hands no longer functioning. Miss McThane screamed as the device turned upside down; she grasped desperately for one of the metal struts to keep from falling. Poor Abel howled as the cord tethering him to the disintegrating machine tangled into the gears and chains. Struck dumb, I watched in horror as it spun about, glided for a moment with flames and smoke billowing, then plummeted into the range of hills on the other side of the valley.

For a moment I was rooted to the spot. Then remembered my own plight; however tragic the consequences, the sudden appearance of the flying machine had afforded me a chance of escape. The beaters and the Godly Army had taken to their heels, pursued by the Biblical demons of their own

imaginations. I hurried to the cliff's edge behind
me and headed down the slope to where I could
cross the river below.

"Dower!" the voice froze me in my tracks. I
nearly fell forward as I halted, the small stones sliding out from beneath my boots. At the bottom of
the slope, by the river's bank, Sir Charles stood
waiting for me.

Our eyes met across the distance. He then lifted
his rifle to his shoulder, his narrowed gaze squinting into my chest. The hillside afforded no place to
hide;. I was trapped against its heathery flank.
With no hope, no thought, I turned and ran, my
feet scrabbling at the stony trail.

I heard the shot, sounding as if from miles
away. For a moment I thought he had missed
me, and I might yet reach the top of the hill and
be able to scramble down the other side towards
the sea. Then something seemed to hit my
shoulder, and it felt unaccountably warm. The
cliff's edge slipped out from under my boots, and
I was falling even as the darkness welled up to
swallow me.

The sound of water splashing against rocks came
first to me. I opened my eyes and saw a dark mass
of soil, tangled with roots, above my face. Daylight
sparkled against the river, setting its reflections
dancing across me where I lay beneath an over-
hang carved from the bank.

A dark face moved between me and the light. I focussed and saw the Brown Leather Man – as I had first seen him so long ago, the stitched covering masking his true features – peering at me. "Dower," he said. "You can hear me? How do you feel?"

I raised myself, my palms pushing against the wet gravel. The space was a hollow cleft only a few feet high; the top of my head brushed the roof of the space. "I feel... terrible," I announced. Every part of my body ached as though flogged, and when I moved my left arm I felt something binding it. I looked around and saw a bandage, fashioned from my shirt torn into strips, crossed over my shoulder blade. The centre of the cloth showed a faint red from beneath.

"Of that do not worry," said the Brown Leather Man. "You were already falling when the bullet struck you; the flesh was but grazed. Your fortune it was to land in the deepest part of the river; some bruises you have, but no bones are broken." He nodded reassuringly. "A fortunate man you are."

"Hm." I rubbed my throbbing brow. "I wish I could share your opinion." An anxious thought struck me. "Where is Sir Charles now? He must still be hunting for me."

"Of that have no fear. I was concealed nearby when upon you he fired; I saw him look down from the cliff for your body. One of his men, having his panic overcome, returned. I could hear them speak;, the conclusion was made that into the sea your body was washed and there lost."

I felt a certain relief at this assumption regarding my own death. "That is fortunate," I said. "I think – I'll just rest here for a while."

"No; no, you must not." He prodded my arm. "No time is there to lose. You must go to England, as quickly as is possible."

Again I noted the overriding urgency in his voice. "But why?" He shook his head. "No explanations can there be, so great is the crisis. Go to Bendray Hall; when there you will know all."

With his assistance, I crawled out from under the bank, and stood up. He bade me follow the river, which led away from the spot where Sir Charles and his followers were encamped, and towards a small village.

"Aren't you coming with me?" I asked.

"I cannot. Much else must I do. But you will see me again." He turned and headed in the opposite direction. When I was quite alone again, I struck out, limping, for my own destination.

I made surprisingly rapid progress southward to England, given my somewhat battered state. Certainly Fortune, which had so often knocked me askew in recent days, now seemed propitiously disposed towards me.

The initiation of my travel was particularly well-omened. When I reached the small village a few miles along the river's course, I found it deserted. All had fled, leaving their valuables behind, and even their rough meals still in the trenchers upon the tables. Only one sour crone, tottering back from the well in the village square, remained behind; she waspishly informed me that the entire population had scattered to the hills upon hearing a report of Satan drawing nigh, leading a cavalry of a thousand flying dragons. She herself had a withering contempt for her neighbours' intellects.

From the inn I appropriated the sturdiest-appearing horse, a change of clothes from an upstairs room, and since all that was left in my pockets was the Saint Monkfish sovereign – a small quantity of money I found in a cupboard. I left a promissory note for these things pinned to the door, with my London address appended. On the road outside, I overtook the crone hobbling homeward, and she curtly directed me to the crossing that led to the border.

By stages, my strength renewing with every day of travel, and with every meal bought at a wayside inn – I only ordered beef, and never mutton – I made my way south to England. Reaching Carlisle, I had another stroke of fortune. A client, for whom I had restored several chiming watches built by my father, lived in the city. He recognised me from his visits to my shop in London, though he marvelled at how etched my features had become. Equally astonished was he to see me this

far from my home. The most amazing reports had
reached his ear from London, which he imparted
to me, much to my distress. Great scandal (so he
informed me) had become attached to my name.
I had reputedly embarked upon a new career as a
violinist – the Paganinicon had apparently found
it more convenient to appropriate my identity and
residence. My musical abilities were reportedly
such as to have conquered the concert halls of Europe, while certain other talents generated a
rapidly growing flock of female admirers. These
certain attributes were apparently much whispered about in the most fashionable of salons;
more than one hair-pulling duel had occurred in
public, with myself gazing with wry amusement
at the scene.

My chagrin was complete at hearing of these
things. My informant had the charity to advance
me a sum of money – bonded against my future
work for him – sufficient to pay for the rest of my
journey by carriage. I thus travelled the rest of
the way in relative comfort. Ever gnawing at my
mind, though – beyond the humiliation of the
scandals being conducted in my name by my
clockwork double was the urgency that the
Brown Leather Man had imparted to me, to
reach Bendray Hall as soon as possible. All possibility of rest was precluded by the speculations
churning in my mind, as to what the emergency
could be.

I abandoned the notion of first going to London, considering my own affairs to be the lesser priority. Heeding the Brown Leather Man's orders, I made direct for Bendray Hall. Once near the district in which Dampford lay, I hired a single horse and waited until the fall of night, the better to pass through the village unnoticed; I had no idea what memory the Dampford villagers might have retained of me.

In darkness, I passed through the gates of Bendray Hall, and rode up to the great building itself. A few signs of the siege by the Godly Army remained: a new door to replace the one that had been battered down, some scorch marks around the lower windows. I dismounted, climbed the stone steps, and brought my fist against the door's timbers.

A hobbling step, as of a man using a crutch, was audible from inside, coming to answer my knock. The door swung open, and the grand hallway's light poured over me, its brightness momentarily blinding me after my ride through the night. Then I heard the person's voice.

"Jesus H. Christ," said Scape. "If it isn't ol' Dower."

I blinked, and discerned his figure. He did indeed bear a crutch under one arm; he tilted noticeably towards that side. "My God," I said. "I thought you were dead."

His manic grin returned. "Can't keep a good man down. Come on in." He shouted to someone descending the staircase, as I stepped inside. "Hey – look who showed up."

It was Miss McThane, her hair considerably shorter and sections of it somewhat crimped in appearance, as if singed sections had been cut off. She smiled delightedly at me. "For Christ's sake. And we all thought you'd been snuffed."

"You – you both survived?" I said in amazement.

"Looks like it," said Scape. "We both kinda bailed out before that damned thing hit the ground." He nodded sadly. "The dog bit it, though. Never did find the little sucker."

"But what are you doing here?"

He shrugged. "Where else was there to go? We figured we might as well head back here and get our old jobs back. Hey, lemme go get ol' Bendray; he'll get a kick out of seeing you again." There proved to be no need for him to fetch Lord Bendray; one of his servants had already informed him of my arrival. He tottered into the hallway. "How good of you to come, Dower." Smiling broadly, he grasped my hand in both of his. "I thought I would never see you again. But now you have returned; and all that I hoped to achieve is made possible."

"Your Lordship–" I began, but he waved me off.

"No time to talk now. Waited quite enough time already." He turned and walked away, one elbow supported by his servant.

Scape studied me quizzically. "Why did you come back here, anyway?"

"I thought... I was informed... that there was... some sort of crisis here." I looked about in confusion; all was quiet in the house. "And that I was needed here."

"Crisis? I don't know about no crisis." Scape looked round at Miss McThane. "You know anything about a crisis?"

She smiled at me. "Just the usual one."

Another knock came at the door; a different servant hastened towards it. I looked round at the person stepping in, and was staggered backwards by the sight.

"You!" cried Sir Charles Wroth, sighting me.

"What's going on?" said Scape as I cast desperately about for some means of escape. He turned and saw the man who some weeks past had ordered his execution. "Shit!" he said in evident consternation.

Sir Charles staggered into the hallway, his face ashen, his features contorted with an inarticulate horror. His devastated aspect rooted me to the spot. His voice dwindled to a stricken gasp: "I thought... you were... dead." He looked as if he himself were about to collapse.

Scape assisted him in standing upright, fear dispelled by the sight of the Godly Army leader thus disarmed. "Hey, are you all right?" asked Miss McThane, bending close to him.

At that moment, a tremor ran through the structure of the great house. It seemed to come from below, a pulsing vibration that shimmered across the walls and ceiling. The sound, at the very bottom limit of human hearing, brought a groan of anguish from Sir Charles.

My innards suddenly felt hollow, as a grim thought seized me. I remembered words spoken to me, in a carriage racing through the dark countryside. A face that was my own, but another's words: the governing mechanism, once installed in the device it is to control, must be brought within a few miles of the adjunct brain – yours, my dear Dower – for it to pick up the subtle vibrations and begin its operations. My own face was frozen with the realisation, as I gazed at Sir Charles.

He nodded sadly at me. "I would never have willingly done you harm, my boy. But I thought it was necessary, the only way to ensure against this dread event occurring."

"What dread event?" demanded an impatient Scape.

Sir Charles looked round at all of us. "The destruction of the very earth we stand upon."

Scape looked at him incredulously. "You mean that bullshit contraption ol' Bendray's got in the basement?"

"That very device. It is no fraud; it can – and will – do all that is claimed for it." He turned to me. "Your father was of that nature, that cares not for whatever consequences may ensue from its genius; he valued only the achievement of whatever task he was commissioned to perform. I have seen the working models he constructed, and the theoretical calculations on which he based his work. I am a servant of Her Majesty's government, and a member of a special committee of that august scientific body, the Royal Society; our function has long been to observe, and intervene in when necessary, the activities of those who style themselves as the Anti-Society. These men know much of a sinister value, and hold no creed that prevents the unscrupled use of such knowledge. I am no latter-day Puritan, though you have seen me pose as one; the Godly Army, already well familiar with the Anti-Society, served as a useful blind by which to make my own observations; for that purpose I inveigled myself into their ranks, and rose to a commanding position."

His speech, much of it murmured almost to himself, seemed to exhaust him. He swayed against Scape's arm before continuing.

"I knew," he said, "that once the regulating device had been given to Lord Bendray, he would set about placing it in the machine below. And that you, Dower – innocent of evil intent as you may be – your presence would be all that was necessary to set the earth-destroying machinery into motion. I knew that, if I had had the time to inform you of the dilemma, you would have gladly made the appropriate sacrifice, and laid down your own life.

Thus, with a clear conscience, I ordered the siege upon this house, with your death the object. You escaped, alas, but were delivered into my hands again; your long voyage, under sentence of execution, was but to remove all possibility of your returning here. But an evil fate has frustrated all my labours; you have made your way here, back from the watery grave into which I believed I had laid you." His chin fell upon his chest; he seemed an old and broken man. "And now the earth, and all upon it, must die instead."

"Yes!" cried another voice from the top of the staircase. We turned as one at the note of hideous triumph contained in the single word. The Brown Leather Man stood there, gazing down upon us, his arms lifted above his head.

He had gained entrance through secret ways, and now gloated at our despairing situation. "See!" His voice was a wild howl, all resemblance to humanity removed. "Your folly is this! This you brought upon yourselves – your blood cares not for others' blood! Their death you bring about, your stupidity and greed kills, and you care not! Now has come your death!" He turned, and with one blow of his arm, shattered the window behind him. The glass shards rained about him as he leapt out into the darkness.

The vibration emanating from beneath the Hall had mounted in pitch and volume. Scape seized one of the servants standing by the door. "Where's

Bendray?" he demanded, lifting the man by his shirt-front. "Where is he?"

With placid loyalty, the servant replied, "Lord Bendray has retired to his laboratory. He sends his regrets that he will not be able to join you for the evening's entertainment."

Scape pitched the man away. "Let's go bust in there!" he shouted to the rest of us. "Throw a wrench in the works, or something."

Sir Charles wearily shook his head. "I am familiar with the preparations Lord Bendray has made for this occasion. The entrance to the laboratory is well fortified; we could never gain entry in time to stop this process."

"That sonuvabitch," muttered Scape as Miss McThane, pale and wide-eyed, took his arm. A painting fell from the quaking wall and crashed to the floor. In the next room, a suit of armour toppled and clattered into bits. "He's probably down there in that goddamn hermetic chamber of his, having champagne served to him by one of his butlers. That asshole."

Hooked about the Hall, every inch of its walls seeming to shimmer with this destructive animation. The vibrations from the device below us – the device that my own father had created – seemed to resound dizzyingly inside my skull. Was it for this that I had struggled through so many desperate hours? I whirled upon Sir Charles.

"Then kill me now," I said. "If this device is operating off the vibrations of my brain – then put a stop to it. Here." I struck my chest with the flat of my hand. "Silence my brain, and thus silence the machine."

He gazed at me with regretful admiration. "It is too late for that. The regulator has already employed the fine vibrations to determine the rate of pulsations necessary to shatter the earth. It is not like the Paganinicon, which must continually vary its actions according to the various situations in which it finds itself. The earthdestroying device will continue at that same rate now, whether you are alive or dead. Those pulsations will ripple outward from this spot, until the whole world is vibrating in synchronization with them, and shakes itself to its component atoms."

The foundations of the building groaned, as if already being torn apart. The servants cast frightened glances at each other, the nature of the peril having at last made itself clear even to them. Panicking, they ran from the room.

Scape stepped closer to Sir Charles and myself. He gazed at me, his mouth parted, before speaking. "But what if–" His hand raised to point at me. "What if something happened to his brain? Your brain, Dower. I mean, isn't it because he's got such a… what's it… stolid nature, right?" His speech became even more rapid. "His brain just goes ticking along like clockwork – that's why the regulating device can use the vibrations he gives off, to control the device it's hooked up to – right?"

Sir Charles nodded. "That is correct."

"So, if something happened to his brain – something to make it un-stolid... you know, like excited, right down to the spine – then the vibrations would be off! Outta whack! That machine down there would read them, but they'd be all wrong – it'd screw up the pulsations it's beating out, and they wouldn't work. It wouldn't be able to blow up the world, because it would be picking up new vibrations that were all haywire and resetting itself to them. The goddamn thing would screw itself up! All we gotta do is – *change the vibrations from Dower's brain.*"

Miss McThane was the first to realise his meaning. Slowly, I turned towards her. Our eyes met; then I saw the corner of her mouth twitch into a smile.

I watched, speechless, as she grasped the neck-line of her gown in both hands. She tore the bodice open, the fabric bunched into her fists. "All right, sucker!" she shouted. "England expects every man to do his duty!"

A strange, previously unknown feeling came over me. Perhaps by then I had gone mad, driven from my senses by the many travails through which I had passed, or the imminent destruction of the earth served to put all into a new perspective. The very walls of the house seemed to recede far from me, as I gazed upon the roseate satin of her skin. I let her take my hand and lead me up the trembling staircase. The chandelier swayed loose from the ceiling as we mounted the steps, the crystal shattering upon the floor below.

EPILOGUE

"With a sigh to the departed, let us resume the dull business of life, in the certainty that we also shall have our repose."

LORD BYRON
in correspondence to R. C. Dallas,
12 August 1811

The rain has ceased, for a period. It will recommence presently, wrapping in its grey shroud the brief interval of sunlight. Through the dark hours I have written, the dog guarding my labours even as it sleeps in front of the grate's last embers; with the dawn I will append the last stop to this History.

No great discernment is required to note that the earth was not destroyed; we stand upon its dull surface yet. Whether the failure of the attempt to render it asunder was due to Miss McThane achieving her long-desired satisfaction of me, or from a flaw in the device that my father had created, I know not. Suffice it to say that the walls of Bendray Hall still stood after the shuddering vibrations emanating from its cellar had ground to a halt.

Lord Bendray's grasp upon his own sanity proved rather more tenuous. He emerged from his Hermetic Carriage completely mad, obsessed with the notion that the earth had been destroyed, and that he had been taken to another planet by those beings whose acquaintance he had so desired to make. Though silence has been purchased by the proceeds from the Bendray estate, the receivership of which has passed into the hands of distant cousins, rumours still circulate about the pitiable crackbrained Lord, in the hospital wherein he is restrained. He is said to believe that the attendants are in fact those wise creatures from other worlds, and is only quieted by their fabricating absurd details about life on Mars or Venus.

No rumours, whispered or otherwise, have ever reached my ear concerning the Brown Leather Man. In my heart, I believe that dark figure to have returned to his ancestral home off the island of Groughay, there to brood and pass away with the others of his race. The brothel-keeper Mollie Maud is reported to be living in France, her carnal trade in this country having been abandoned due to the loss of most of her bullies in a pitched battle with the Dampford villagers. The simultaneous disappearance of Mrs Trabble, the noted morality crusader, remains a matter of speculation in genteel circles.

Upon making my return to London, I found my reputation to be irreparably blackened. The Paganinicon, passing itself off as me, had gone berserk during a concert attended by all of English society's loftiest members. This breakdown, unexplainable by those who witnessed it, I believe to have been caused by those same actions on the part of myself and Miss McThane, that overrode the earth-destroying device's regulatory mechanism. The Paganinicon's basic nature, already inclined to romantic conquests, was thus further stimulated by the temporary alteration to its adjunct brain. I must leave vague the details of the ensuing events – they are too indelicate to transcribe; I could scarce credit them when they were told to me – but it should be noted that Mrs Wroth and several other ladies of quality retired after the fateful concert to the seclusion of a convent. They are still there.

Due to the harassment of the crowds attracted by the scandals generated by the Paganinicon, I was unable to resume life and business in my shop as before. Fortunately, Sir Charles Wroth, perhaps to make amends for his earlier attempt to take my life (albeit in a good cause), arranged for the august scientific body of the Royal Society to purchase all the other devices left by my father in his workshop. The resultant sum of money was enough for me to go into seclusion in this little-

trafficked district of London, accompanied by the
loyal Creff, who had so patiently and faithfully
awaited my return.

Another touching example of faith presented itself as Creff and I were loading my baggage into a
carriage. Limping down the street came a bedrag-
gled figure, its ribs protruding from the rigours of
its journey, still scarred from the crash of the flying
machine, scarcely recognisable. It was the dog
Abel, who – as animals have been reported to do –
had made his way over all England's hills and
rivers, to return to that home where he was first
kindly treated. The warm fire, by which he sleeps
even now, and the fattening dish will be his re-
wards to the end of his days.

My own reward will be to lay down this pen,
and pick it up no more. My apologia is finished,
for all the good it will do.

Reports have reached my ears, of a lame man
with tinted spectacles, in company with a woman,
travelling from village to village in the North of
England and Scotland. They are said to exhibit a
few crude music playing automata, but are soon
chased away by the town constables when various
gambling and confidence games come to light.

Though I myself have come to this safe harbour – if safety can be found in this life – yet I
mourn my former simple days. I have lost my Innocence, in more ways than one. I have seen the
gears and furious machinery of the world that lies

unreckoned beneath our feet. No longer can I note, as other men do, the passing hours upon the heavens' gilded face, without a vision of a hidden master-spring uncoiling to its final silence. I await the day when all clocks shall stop, including the one that ticks within my breast. Do thou the same, Reader, and profit from my example.

ABOUT THE AUTHOR

K. W. Jeter attended college at California State University, Fullerton where he became friends with James P. Blaylock and Tim Powers, and through them, Philip K. Dick.

Jeter wrote an early Cyberpunk novel, *Dr. Adder*, which was enthusiastically recommended by Philip K. Dick. Jeter was also the first to coin the term "steampunk," in a letter to *Locus* magazine in April 1987, to describe the retro-technology, alternate-history works that he published along with his friends, Blaylock and Powers.

As well as his own original novels, K. W. Jeter has written a number of authorized *Blade Runner* sequels.

He currently lives in San Francisco with his wife, Geri.

www.kwjeter.com

INFERNAL INVESTIGATIONS, CLOCKWORK PROPAGATION

By Jeff VanderMeer

It's rare indeed for any writer to coin a term that results in hundreds of thousands of people over a quarter century participating in a multi-media entertainment experiment centered around outdated technology. Yet that's exactly what K. W. Jeter accomplished when he, half-jokingly, offered up the term "Steampunk" in a letter to the editor in *Locus Magazine*, the *Variety* of the genre fiction world: "Personally, I think Victorian fantasies are going to be the next big thing, as long as we can come up with a fitting collective term... Something based on the appropriate technology of the era; like 'steampunks', perhaps." Jeter was attempting to identify, with no little amount of satire, the kind of alt-history, Industrial Age Victoriana being written not just by him but his fellow writers Tim Powers and James Blaylock. Powers' major contribution to the subgenre would be *The Anubis Gates*, while Blaylock would write a short story, "Lord Kelvin's Machine", that he later turned into a Steampunk novel. All three were to some extent influenced by Henry Mayhew's book, *London Labour and the London Poor*.

What is Steampunk? Modern steampunk fiction derives at least in part from the influence of novels by Jules Verne and H. G. Wells in the 1800s and early 1900s that featured wildly imaginative steam-powered inventions, or even just inventions based on technology from the time that no one uses anymore. Even when wildly romantic, the work of Verne and Wells tended to also be somewhat cautionary in nature, with a healthy unwillingness to accept "progress" as always inevitable and good. The American Edisonades of the 1800s, meanwhile, used steam inventions as a way of visualizing Manifest Destiny through simplistic wild west adventures. These adventures, as might be expected, have not dated well and have not.

The general gist of proto-Steampunk fictions and even later full-on Steampunk like *Infernal Devices* or William Gibson and Bruce Sterling's *The Difference Engine* (1990) can be boiled down to a general equation: *Mad inventor + invention (steam x airship or metal person/robot) x [pseudo] Victorian setting) + progressive, reactionary, or neutral politics x adventure plot.* (The supernatural also plays a part in many such adventures.)

Since then, Steampunk has by fits and starts entered the mainstream. Kit Stolen created the first Steampunk looks in the 1990s which led to a thriving fashion/cultural scene. In parallel, Steampunk-related pseudo-Victorian settings infiltrated movies and comics, including anime and manga, along with a parallel rise in the art and tinker/maker involvement.

The result? A slow burn leading to an explosion of interest. Since about 2008, Steampunk has been *hot*. Steampunk's popularity – its incredible, almost viral rate of growth – has been widely documented in, and fed by, national and international media, from newspapers like the *The New York Times* to such high-profile publications as *Newsweek*, *Wired*, *Popular Science*, and the journal *Nature*. Each of these media outlets has chosen to highlight different aspects of the Steampunk community, typically those that relate most closely to the publication's or journalist's specialty. *The New York Times Style Section*, for instance, focused primarily on the fashion aspects of Steampunk. Technology oriented publications have focused on the efforts to remake and modify technology in the Victorian mode, while the journal *Nature* related Steampunk to science and education.

All of this attention has sparked new energy and diversity in a sprawling community that ranges from the involvement of neo-Victorians to sites like Beyond Victoriana and a burgeoning scene in places like Brazil, from the anarchist/DIY *Steam-Punk Magazine* to those who casually dress up and have tea parties at conventions. Many Steampunks seek to reject the conformity of the modern, soul-less, featureless design of technology – and all that implies. They also seek DIY solutions to the damage caused by industrialisation. This isn't simply an impulse to whitewash the bad parts of the Victorian era – it is instead a progressive impulse to reclaim the dead past in a positive and affirmative way.

Gradually, too, Steampunk has circled back to the literature, even though many of those who participate in the subculture may not know the original fiction, beyond those pre-Steampunk influences of Verne and Wells. But even when Jake von Slatt of the Steampunk Workshop creates some elegant machine with cogs and wheels and tubes, he is in a sense not just emulating the crafts-people of the Victorian era – he's also pulling from the zeitgeist of images and approaches found in the fiction. Mike Libby's clockwork beetles have at least as much in common with the automata in *Infernal Devices* as with anything actually produced during the Victorian era. Reality and fiction, imagination and making feed off of each other.

Within that context, it's not surprising that Jeter says that a good deal of his initial inspiration for *Infernal Devices* "came from a visit to London and discovering a shop [near Covent Garden] that specialised in old scientific gear.... You knew that real people living in a real time had created them, and that they weren't just stamped out of plastic in some hellhole factory in China."

Inspiration also came from closer to home: "The advantage of growing up in Southern California in the fifties and early sixties was that there was still some evidence of that sort of machine-age hand-craftsmanship, such as the now-vanished Angels Flight tram in Los Angeles, the old steamship modern Pan Pacific Auditorium (now gone as well), the Craftsman bungalows in the old neighborhoods of Pasadena and Glendale, etc. So to some degree the whole Victorian craftsperson period seemed like a glorious tide that had once washed over the world, and left a few shining bits behind in odd places."

However, *Infernal Devices* is not so much a love song to London by an American as it is an ironical tribute, permeated by elements of dark humor and social critique. A Ladies Union for Suppression of Carnal Vice is both hilarious and all too true to the spirit of the age. A Royal Anti-Society almost enters Monty Python territory. From the first pages, too, Jeter deploys the drunkard Creff not just for comedy but to pointed effect, juxtaposing him with the "Ethiope" who comes to George Dower's shop. While Creff claims the Ethiope is "maddened with some heathen liquor, and prepared for murder," Dower knows that "Intoxication was indeed a possibility" – on Creff's part.

The Victorian era overlapped the rise and fall of the Decadents, who had a fascination with pushing limits, including views on drugs, sex, and disease.

So it's perhaps no surprise that the humor and absurdity veer into the, well, decadent, with much verbiage devoted to depraved habits and even more depraved acts. Readers easily turned off by such things may find solace in placing certain passages in the context of the stylised outrages of Oscar Wilde, Rimbaud, and the like.

But wherever it originates, this healthy sense of humor – Scape: "You turkey!" – is perhaps best exemplified by the absurdism of a "Saint Monkfish" and the seamless way in which Jeter combines fish-men and brilliant descriptions of clockwork devices. Indeed, there's an entire subset of Steampunk fictions that indulge in a mecha-organic aesthetic, presaged by the gooey/clockwork back-and-forth of *Infernal Devices*. (The most notable example may be Paul Di Filippo in his 1990s *Steampunk Trilogy*.) Jeter seems as invested in weird biology as in clockwork contraptions, and this tends to humanise and soften what might otherwise be simply a gleaming recitation of the contents of the chest cavities of various automata.

In terms of authenticity, the clever insertion of what appears to be contemporary American vernacular through the speech of Scape and his assistant contributes, by way of contrast, to the believability of the English settings and characters, and helps to make the narrative more fluid, with very little period piece stiffness. Scape as rogue has both those elements of likeability and cruelty that make the reader question their enjoyment of him... even as you're enjoying him.

Jeter may be an American writing about London, but the quality of his descriptions does an excellent job of conveying action and place, as in the aftermath of a most chaotic encounter: "In the midst of the fishing tackle strewn about, and the copies of Izaak Walton that had been flung from the hands of the panicking Wetwick residents, the choristers lay tangled as though in the aftermath of some juvenile battlefield. Their shrill piping voices were silent now; the porcelain faces, those that were still intact, gazed with rosy-cheeked serenity at the ceiling."

Stories within stories also delight, as when the Paganinicon spins a yarn that includes "sympathetic vibrations" and decidedly eccentric methods of animation. The final revelations concerning the "Brown Leather Man" are appropriately bizarre and yet make sense. Even chapter and section titles are used to maximum effect, my favorite being "The Complete Destruction of the Earth."

There's a sense of playfulness in this narrative that works well even when events turn serious, and Jeter imbues his narrator with the kind of sardonic sincerity that both undercuts his account and supports it. You're left with the feeling you've been sold a bill of goods by novel's end, and yet you don't mind at all.

• • • •

Mostly because of the spark and inspiration provided by the existence of the subculture, more and more writers are once again writing steampunk fiction. However, it's very different from what came before. The books that form the core of the canon from the first wave of steampunk – Jeter, Powers, Sterling, Gibson – are generally a small part of the influence on this next wave of steampunk, except through secondary associations. (It's somewhat ironic that some of the newer steampunk fictioneers are going to read *Infernal Devices* for the first time in this edition.)

This next wave is also largely dominated by women, including Gail Carriger, Cherie Priest, Karin Lowachee, and Ekaterina Sedia, and has begun to move away from being purely Victorian or English in setting or culture. In another generation, the true energy behind steampunk may have moved away from Anglo settings and perspectives altogether.

But a term can also become a trap, and although there's a certain element of ghosts and séances in the way that Infernal Devices has been called back into print by the new-found popularity of modern-era Steampunk fiction, it's also a kind of irritation that I feel in having Jeter conjured up this way. Jeter wasn't a Steampunk before the publication of *Infernal Devices* (and *Morlock Night*) and he wasn't really a Steampunk afterwards. Instead, he was, and is, a subversive agent in the service of dark science fiction.

Jeter's fiction, throughout his career, has been intelligently idiosyncratic and literary, with similarities to writers like Richard Calder and Philip K. Dick (who named a character in his novel *Valis* after Jeter). In short, he's always given readers his dark take on the world. It's with great fondness that I remember reading novels like Jeter's cult classic *Dr. Adder*, *The Glass Hammer*, *Mantis*, *Farewell Horizontal*, and *Noir*. Hopefully, *Infernal Devices* will serve as a gateway drug for readers who want more of Jeter's unique vision.

As for Steampunk, it's in the process of re-investigating itself, as publication of *Infernal Devices* proves, but also of going beyond what's come before. The commercial success of Steampunk fiction is gradually opening up possibilities for lots of strange and interesting stuff to be published under that term. In addition, more and more international and multicultural steampunk is being written, and Steampunk may even eventually move out of the 1800s, exploring other periods while applying a similar aesthetic.

Will Steampunk eventually eat itself and die out? Perhaps, perhaps not. But at least we'll always have *Infernal Devices*.

Jeff VanderMeer, Tallahassee, Florida, January 2011

Quotes attributed to K. W. Jeter are excerpted from The Steampunk Bible, *Abrams Image, copyright 2011.*

ANGRY ROBOT

Prepare to welcome

Web **angryrobotbooks.com**